shadowland

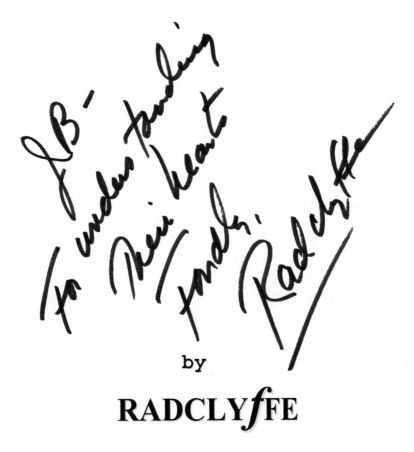

by

RADCLY*f*fE

shadowland
A BookEnds Press Publication
PO Box 14513
Gainesville, Florida 32604
1-800-881-3208

Cover design by Sheri

For distribution information:

StarCrossed Productions, Inc.
PO Box 357474
Gainesville, Florida 32635-7474
www.starcrossedproductions.com

By the Author

Safe Harbor

Beyond The Breakwater

Innocent Hearts

Love's Melody Lost

Love's Tender Warriors

Tomorrow's Promise

Passion's Bright Fury

Love's Masquerade

Honor Series

Above All, Honor

Honor Bound

Love & Honor

Justice Series

A Matter of Trust (prequel)

Shield of Justice

In Pursuit of Justice

Dedication

For Lee,
For the Adventure

Acknowledgments

This book exists solely because so many dedicated and persistent readers asked (perhaps insisted, begged, and bargained would be more truthful terms) that I expand the web version of *shadowland* for publication. The original story was conceived as a personal exploration of a subject that fascinated and intrigued me, and that, more importantly, challenged me to expand my vision of romantic love.

Contrary to first appearances, this *is* very much a love story as well as an exploration of a particular form of erotic expression. I was fond of the characters and their passion with the initial telling, but it wasn't until I delved more deeply into their lives during the revision process that I realized just how much this work means to me. Therefore, I must thank first and foremost those readers who believed in this work and who urged me to give it the attention it deserved.

Kathy Smith was one of those people who gently but relentlessly pushed me to publish this book. Her expertise and that of the great crews at BookEnds Press and StarCrossed Productions are deeply appreciated.

Stacia Seaman edited the manuscript with a sensitive understanding of how the story needed to be told, and my beta readers, Athos, Eva, Diane, Denise, JB, and Tomboy, provided me with constant encouragement, insight, and support. Their influence is evident on every page.

Sheri was another of those true believers who always loved the story, and the cover is inspirational, even when measured against her always brilliant visions. Thank you so much for capturing the heart of the work with such elegance and power.

Lee graciously accepted my absence, mentally and often physically, for almost six weeks while I revised the manuscript eight hours a day. There was supposed to be a vacation in there somewhere, but I think I might have missed it. Thank you, love, for always understanding what it is I need to do.

CHAPTER ONE

The setting sun pulsed red where ocean and sky bled into one as the rider slowed the big bike and turned off the narrow, winding highway onto the overlook. She brought the motorcycle to a halt along the shoulder, well away from the few cars whose occupants had stopped to watch night eclipse day. With a long leg planted on either side of the heavy machine for support, she cut the engine, pulled off her helmet, and absently ran a hand through her dark, wavy hair as she stared out over the water. The rocky coastline far below, battered by plumes of angry surf, lay cast in half-shadows as the dying sun slipped away, leaving darkness in its wake. The steady rhythm of the waves breaking against the base of the cliff was unexpectedly soothing in a wild, untamed way. *Odd, how something so violent can be so calming.*

She loved to ride this stretch of coastal highway, even though it was often crowded with sightseeing tourists who slowed the Harley's progress. The road was demanding, and she could lose herself for miles in the steady drone of the engine and the hypnotic ribbon of macadam sliding beneath her headlights. While her conscious mind was occupied with the mechanics of driving, her unconscious thoughts came to the forefront, and often the solution emerged to some problem that she hadn't even been aware was bothering her. When she'd described the phenomenon once to a friend, she'd been told it was a form of meditation. Maybe it was. She didn't question the process; she rarely questioned the workings of her own mind, allowing instinct to guide her instead.

Tonight had been different. She hadn't lost herself in the challenge of maneuvering the twenty-mile ride filled with tight, tortuous turns, nor had she discovered the source of the simmering unrest that had plagued her for weeks. Always most comfortable with action, she found her present introspection unsatisfying and frustrating. Sighing softly, she reached into the left inside pocket of her leather jacket for her cigarettes. She fingered one out of the pack and held it lightly between her lips while she fished the black and gold lighter from the right front pocket of her tight black leather pants. The tiny flare of flame lit her features for an instant as she touched it to the tip of the cigarette. A chiseled profile, square chin, and straight, slightly high nose were highlighted briefly by the flickering orange glow. As the lighter snapped shut, the image disappeared, and her figure became a long, lean silhouette against the deepening sky.

Kyle Kirk hunched her shoulders slightly against the cold wind blowing in from the sea and focused her gaze on the shifting shoreline where land and sea struggled endlessly for dominance in a war never won. With the roar of the surf so constant it verged on silence, all she could hear were her own questioning thoughts.

What the hell am I doing out here tonight? And where am I going?

It had been many weeks since she'd last made a Friday night journey into the city, seeking company in one club or another. She went for the comfort of women, for the irresistible sight and sound of them. For the mystery and wonder of them. More often than not, she returned home alone in the still, dark hours before dawn, her soul inexplicably soothed by the memories that clung to her during the long ride home. Sometimes, when she needed more than memories, she unlocked the second helmet she always carried on the side of her Harley and brought a woman home to fill the emptiness in both her body and her spirit for a few hours on either side of morning.

Tonight, she hadn't intended to go out at all, but as soon as she went into the house from her workshop, she had set about getting ready to go out again. Without considering her destination, she'd showered and donned a crisply ironed white shirt and black leather pants that encased her muscled thighs like soft, warm flesh. She tucked a slim leather wallet, contoured to her form from years of use, into her right rear pocket with her license and enough cash to last the weekend. A fresh pack of cigarettes went into the left inside pocket of her favorite leather jacket and the lighter into her pants. She pulled on the jacket and zipped it partway up as she headed through the kitchen. It was as she switched on the floodlights subtly tucked under the eaves of the house and carport that she realized she was setting out for the city. Still, she had driven twenty miles before she had allowed herself to think about why.

For the last few days she'd been unsettled and short-tempered, and as she thought about it, she admitted that she hadn't been herself for weeks. It wasn't the solitude of her life that disturbed her—she'd grown used to that in the five years since her last serious relationship had ended. She had several good friends, which was more than most people could say, and work that she enjoyed. Her sex life was as fulfilling as she needed it to be. Not constant, perhaps, but she could have had more if she'd cared to. She didn't. Recently, though, she'd become aware of an uneasy sense of dissatisfaction, as much emotional as physical, that threatened to disrupt the comfortable routine of her life. And what made it so frustrating was that she couldn't define just what she wanted, or needed, or lacked.

Kyle took a last drag from her cigarette and dropped the butt near the toe of her boot. Carefully she dug a little hole in the gravel of the turnoff and pushed the bit of trash into it. With her heavy black boot, she meticulously covered it with a small mound of stones and tamped it down flat again. Satisfied that no trace remained, she pulled her left leg up onto the curved tank of her black bike and rested her chin on her knee.

As she sat, darkness slowly lowered a veil between her and the cars steadily streaming along behind on the highway. She slid her hand into her jacket pocket and removed a small folded square of paper. There wasn't enough moonlight yet to read by, and she didn't bother opening it. She already knew what it said.

Leathers - Where women hold the power
719 S. Van Nye

The chain of events, so un-noteworthy at the time, that brought her to this place on this night had begun with a magazine she'd picked up as an afterthought in a women's bookstore where she'd gone in search of the newest novel from her favorite author. Disappointed to discover that the book was still on order, she'd grabbed a few magazines at random rather than return home empty-handed. Once at home, stretched out in front of the fireplace with a brandy, she'd looked through her purchases. The cover of the second magazine immediately caught her attention.

A woman, her bare back boldly scripted with a black Celtic tattoo between her shoulder blades, knelt with her forehead pressed to the thigh of another woman, who stood above her with legs spread wide and arms akimbo. A black leather vest, all the standing woman wore above tight leather pants, barely covered small, firm breasts. The faint swell of a phallus nestled in the curve of her thigh just millimeters from the supplicant's cheek brought Kyle up short. As she stared at the image, her blood had raced hot, and a knot of arousal had fisted in her stomach. She'd imagined the feel of smooth leather, softened by the heat of flesh, sliding against her face, had seen herself press her lips to the subtle bulge restrained against a muscled thigh, had heard the distant groan of approval and need. Stunned by the unexpected beat of desire between her thighs and the first sweet rush of lust, wet and hard, she'd opened the cover with shaking hands to the first article. Quickly she discovered that the short stories, essays, and poems contained some of the most graphic erotica she had ever read. All of it, in one way or another, explored issues involving sexual power, and she'd been instantly captivated. She was no stranger to the allure of love between women. But those glimpses of the dark edges of desire had left her aroused and almost insatiably curious, as if she'd caught a glint of long-lost treasure only to have it quickly disappear. She'd read the magazine cover to cover and a few days later had gone back to the bookstore to pick up the two previous issues.

And then she'd found the story that wouldn't let her go.

The Edge of Trust. She'd read it enough times that she knew every word.

"Keep your eyes on me."

Silently, she swallowed and stared straight ahead at her lover, who was seated in the large leather chair ten feet in front of her. She had to look down slightly, not only because of her height, but because she was standing on a raised platform. She was also completely naked.

Her lover, on the other hand, looked totally at ease in a turquoise silk shirt that was almost the same lustrous color as her eyes. The fact that it was unbuttoned its entire length and she was wearing nothing else appeared not to faze her. She reclined slightly in the depths of the soft cushions, her arms outstretched along the curved arms of the chair, her legs parted only enough to reveal a faint hint of dusty gold.

Her lover waited until she met her gaze, until she was in her power, before she spoke again.

"Restrain her."

Not knowing what to expect, she tried to keep breathing, to concentrate on the reassurance in her lover's face, as another woman she couldn't quite see moved quickly around her in the semidarkness. In a moment she found herself spread-eagled, arms and legs held out by wide, soft leather shackles attached to short chains which ran somewhere beyond her vision. A padded pole was at her back. Her lover was all she could see. When she shifted slightly, the chains grew taut. She was exposed, helpless. Her lover's eyes were hot. She shivered almost imperceptibly with a combination of fear and the beginnings of arousal.

"She has a beautiful body, doesn't she?" her lover remarked almost clinically. "Run your hands over her—see for yourself."

Just as the stranger smoothed a hand over her torso and belly, she watched her lover flick the shirt off her chest and slide her fingers lovingly over her own breasts. Seeing her lover's nipples stiffen, her stomach muscles twitched, first in surprise, then with quick jerks of excitement.

She didn't look at the stranger who touched her; only her lover mattered. She knew what that long taut body—that smooth, hot skin—felt like beneath her hands, and her clitoris stiffened at the sight of her lover sensuously circling her breasts, then stroking slowly down to her navel, hips lifting slightly to greet the touch. The bound woman leaned forward, unconsciously offering herself, all the while imagining *her* hands claiming her lover.

Then her lover smiled, eyes dreamy but voice commanding. "Now her nipples."

"Oh!" she cried softly as fingers grasped, then twisted—first one, then the other. Her hips convulsed as the sensation shot ruthlessly between her legs. Moisture began to seep between her thighs. "Lover?" she questioned uncertainly, voice unsteady, as her body responded to the stranger's manipulations. *I can't help it. It's making me wet.*

"Squeeze harder," her lover instructed huskily, both hands palming her breasts, pushing them together, fingers tugging the reddened nubs.

The captive groaned, fire curling in the pit of her stomach, streaking along her spine.

"Kneel in front of her," her lover ordered, dropping one hand between her legs and trailing her fingers up and down the sensitive skin of her inner thighs. "Work on her legs, but don't go near her clit."

Moaning steadily now as hands kneaded the muscles in her buttocks and thighs, the bound woman arched her back, unable to contain the pleasure. Her clitoris throbbed painfully, sharply demanding attention. Quivering, mesmerized by the sight of her lover slipping slick folds of swollen flesh lazily between her fingers, she thrust mindlessly against the chains that held her prisoner. She heard her lover cry out softly, saw trembling fingers brush against the base of the exposed clitoris, and felt her own body clench deep inside. *Stroke yourself, lover. Do it, you know you want to, do it, do it—*

She sobbed, hips jerking in the air, desperate for her lover's touch. The tantalizing whisper of approaching orgasm fluttered through her belly when a finger explored lightly between her legs, sending showers of fire bursting from her clitoris into her pelvis. If she pushed forward just a little that finger would touch her hard enough to make her come. She didn't know she was whimpering as she fought against the leather and steel.

"Please," she begged, her clitoris twitching ceaselessly and the promise of relief so near. She twisted impotently in the restraints, watching through heavy lids as her lover spread her legs further, resting her knees over the wide leather arms to expose her desire. "Please."

"Stroke her," her lover demanded hoarsely, doing the same to herself. "Be careful with her. She'll come if you stay on it too long. And I *don't* want her to come!"

Helplessly, she struggled to focus on her lover, but she was rapidly losing all control. She didn't care who was touching her any longer, as long as the touch didn't stop. If she didn't come soon she was going to implode. "No more," she begged. "I can't stand it—oh, yes—touch me there—harder—"

"You are not to come without permission," her lover gasped, her fingers a blur as they slid rapidly up and down her clitoris.

Too late—I'm gonna come. Gotta come. The captive merely grunted, jerking desperately against the fingers that tormented her.

"Work her faster, squeeze her," her lover managed, breathing unevenly through clenched teeth, twisting on the chair, legs outstretched and rigid. "She loves that."

"Lover, oh...she's making me come." She panted, stomach hard, ready to explode. "Oh, can I—"

"Lick her!"

She wailed as the warm, soft tongue ran the length of her, ending with one long, firm caress along her clitoris. With the last ounce of strength she possessed, she sought her lover's face through eyes nearly blind with need. "Please...oh please...is it all right?"

"Yes, baby—yess—" her lover screamed, tugging her clitoris frantically. "Oh, baby, I'm coming."

As her mind went white, the stranger reached up, grasped her hips, and sucked her all the way into her mouth. With hands clenched into fists beyond the restraining cuffs, the bound woman jammed herself against the stranger's face. Head thrown back, the tendons in her neck standing out in tight cords, she shouted as the wrenching spasms tore her apart.

For an instant, the only sounds were those of their joint release reverberating throughout the room. Then, there was but the whisper of soft sobbing.

"Get her down," her lover gasped weakly.

When the captive collapsed to her knees, shattered by more than pleasure, her lover was there to shelter her in waiting arms.

Kyle drew a long, shaky breath and contemplated another cigarette. She laughed softly and jammed her hands into the pockets of her motorcycle jacket. *Not even my orgasm and I want a cigarette. Lousy time to be trying to quit.*

The story had gotten to her. Still got to her. It wasn't just the sex, which had blistered her mind and still made her want to come just remembering. It was the unexpected fusion of love and dominance, trust and submission, that had twisted and tantalized her previously unquestioned vision of emotional connection. It confused and excited her. She wasn't even sure which called to her more, the control or the relinquishing of it. Sometimes when she came, she imagined herself the bound woman. Other times, she climaxed as she saw herself in that leather chair, ordering a stranger to pleasure her lover while she masturbated.

Christ, if I keep this up, I'll never be able to ride this bike. I'm out here so I won't have to keep thinking about it.

Carefully, with hands that shook as much as when she'd turned the first page of that first magazine, Kyle unfolded the small rectangle of paper and peered at it. The sky above was obsidian, punctured by stars and streaked with moonlight. She held up the paper and turned it in the silvery light, but she couldn't see the words. Just as carefully, she refolded it and stowed it in her jacket again. As she kick started the powerful engine and muscled the bike around to face the highway, she repeated the address from memory one more time.

CHAPTER TWO

Kyle rode through a light rain, noting that the city seemed eerily deserted—unusual for a Friday night. Even now, years after she had moved north to where the air was cleaner and the stars could still be seen at night, she was at ease negotiating the steep avenues and narrow alleys. Although she was sure that the advertisement had specified women, she found the street she was looking for in the Tenderloin, an area frequented mostly by gay men. Whatever the case, it was too late now to turn back. She was more than ready.

Coasting in the mist, she surveyed the unadorned buildings, many of which appeared empty or abandoned, until finally she saw the sign she had been seeking. The name flickered in the uneven glow of a pale blue neon sign: Leathers. Kyle pulled her bike into line with a half-dozen others already angled along the curb and switched off the ignition. She sat for a second watching the fitful light cast shadows on the trash-strewn sidewalk, then took a deep breath and swung her leg over the tank to the ground and stood. She could ride away, but if she did, she knew she'd be back. Perhaps there were answers on the other side of that windowless black door. Maybe there weren't. She had to know.

Her boot heels echoed hollowly on the empty pavement as she approached the door. She glanced up and down the street, looking in vain for the sight of a familiar face, but she was alone. The door to the club stood slightly ajar, and the music that wafted out on a breeze of booze and smoke was a song she recognized. That small bit of familiarity settled her and served as a reminder that this was no different than any other strange club she'd chanced to enter, and there'd been quite a few of those over the years.

Well, not that *much different, at any rate.*

She took a quick breath and shouldered through the door into the darkness beyond. A bouncer in black T-shirt and black leather chaps stretched tightly over denim jeans sat just inside the entrance behind a waist-high divider that blocked access to the room beyond. The bouncer pretended to check Kyle's ID as she collected the ten-dollar cover charge. Heavyset, her dark eyes opaque, she looked Kyle over wordlessly, took the offered bill, and jutted her chin toward the bar.

"Have fun."

"Thanks."

The room was long and narrow, with a bar down the right side. To the left, round pedestal tables were scattered along the edge of a small dance floor made smaller by people standing about and chairs pushed askew. The ceiling was open-beamed with exposed heating conduits and unevenly spaced spots casting irregular circles of light over the room and its occupants. Somewhere a DJ played music with a heavy bass beat that reverberated through the rough wood floor. Kyle was not a stranger to new surroundings, and she moved through the small crowd near the door with practiced ease. She walked directly but unhurriedly toward the bar and found a free space between two lone drinkers who eyed her for a moment before looking away. Women two-deep leaned or sat along the scarred but clean surface of the bar and moved about in the shadows opposite her. At first glance, it looked much like any other lesbian club on a Friday night.

It wasn't until she caught the bartender's eye and ordered a beer that she looked around more carefully. Casually leaning with an elbow against the bar and her legs stretched out in front of her, she allowed her eyes to travel as she lifted the bottle to her mouth. Her vision had adjusted to the darkness of the room, and as she looked out across the dance floor through the softly wafting curls of cigarette smoke, she focused on the figures before her. What she had first taken as a strange sameness about the women turned out to be the fact that they were all clothed in some form of leather or denim. Leather chaps and pants, leather vests, and tight denim jeans abounded. She smiled inwardly, aware that she had unconsciously chosen exactly the right thing to wear. Knowing that outwardly she appeared to be like everyone else made her more comfortable, although she felt anything but confident of her role in this new theater. Nevertheless, the sight of women standing about in groups, talking or simply watching each other as she was doing, elicited the anticipated surge of excitement she always associated with being in the company of others like herself. This was the stage upon which anything might happen and where anyone could become a player.

After finishing her first beer at a leisurely pace, she started on her second and began to relax. Out of habit, she picked out, in a detached, almost objective way, the women who were attractive to her. One in particular, leaning with a shoulder against a pole on the opposite side of the room, stood out from the rest. About Kyle's age but slightly taller than Kyle's five feet seven inches, she was slender, with an athletic body accentuated by tight blue jeans and a denim shirt open far enough to show the inner curve of her breasts. Thick blond hair fell in casual layers to her collar in the back. Her sleeves were rolled halfway up, exposing a thin leather band encircling her left wrist. As she talked to several women nearby, she lifted a bottle to her lips, and Kyle caught a glimpse of the strength in her well-muscled forearms. The stranger's gaze swept the room at intervals, but she seemed to take little note of those around her. Her eyes skimmed over Kyle's face without stopping.

Under other circumstances, Kyle would not have hesitated to introduce herself to someone she found attractive, but tonight she was uneasy about making the first move. Ordinarily, her approach to a woman was dictated by the signals offered and returned—a smile that lingered, the slow perusal of her body by an appreciative glance, a touch that lasted too long to be merely friendly. Sometimes she offered a drink, other times she struck up a conversation or asked for a dance. On rare occasions, she simply suggested to a woman that they find a private place to consummate their obvious mutual attraction.

In this arena, however, she sensed there were rules she didn't understand and that left her feeling unaccustomedly inhibited. When one woman approached another, a polarity was evident: it appeared initially as if one woman was the aggressor and the other passive. Yet Kyle soon appreciated that there *was* interplay, that the move was not completely one-sided; often the apparent aggressor would walk away, her overtures seemingly rejected. Obviously, some dynamic—understood to both women—was at work, and after Kyle had been in the club for an hour, she had her first experience with the ritual.

A woman materialized from the shadows and stepped close to Kyle's side. There was an almost imperceptible pressure against her left thigh as the woman spoke softly, her lips close to Kyle's ear.

"Are you just looking tonight, or are you playing?"

Although startled, Kyle kept her voice even and her gaze fixed straight ahead. She didn't move away from the leg that pressed just a bit harder against hers. Considering her reply, she decided she couldn't play a game whose rules she didn't know. "I'm not sure I know what the game is."

The woman laughed in surprise. "You'd never guess from looking at you."

"Actually, this is the first time I've been here," Kyle said, turning slightly amidst the crowd of bodies to study her companion more carefully. She was an inch shorter than Kyle, with curly dark hair and warm, dark eyes. She wore a leather vest over a white T-shirt and jeans.

"I'm Chris." She extended her right hand while casually giving Kyle an obvious once-over.

"Kyle."

Chris shook Kyle's hand, leaned her back to the bar, and faced the dance floor. The slight pressure against Kyle's leg disappeared.

"You picked a good night to drop in. The crowd's better than I would have expected this early."

"I'm not sure what I expected."

"You here by yourself?" Chris gave Kyle a questioning look.

"Yep."

"Well, probably not for long."

Kyle laughed. "I think for tonight I'm just watching."

Chris shrugged. "Will you have another beer?" When Kyle nodded her assent, Chris ordered two, waited silently for the bartender to pass them to her, and then took a long pull on hers before speaking again. "I'm not much on initiations, but I'll tell you anything I can."

"Well, I think I get the general idea," Kyle said slowly as she sipped her beer. "But I'm not real sure what the ground rules are."

"It's not much different than any other club," Chris replied. "It's just that most of the women here share a certain kind of interest, if you know what I mean."

"A certain sexual interest." Kyle's tone was matter-of-fact. "That I *do* understand."

"Well, because of that, if someone is interested in you, they're not likely to come up and ask you to dance. More likely than not, they're going to ask you if you're available to play—like I did. Or not say anything at all—waiting for *you* to ask."

"Why not just ask outright?"

"She might want to find out how much you know about what's going on before she makes a move." Chris tried again when Kyle frowned. "Some of the women here will feel most comfortable if they take the lead and you follow. Others prefer it if they are told exactly what to do—at least during the scene. Either way, you'll need to negotiate those terms for the length of the scene."

"How do you know who wants to do what, then?" Kyle asked, genuinely puzzled as to what Chris was trying to tell her.

"Good question. I've been fooled myself, and I've been in the community for a long time." Chris chuckled. "*Most* of the time, it's easy to tell what people are interested in just by looking."

"You mean like the way it used to be when the butches always asked the femmes to dance, and even if the femmes *did* turn out to be the aggressive ones in bed, they never let on in public?" Kyle smiled, thinking that there was a certain security in knowing what was expected of her. "And of course, two butches never got it on together?"

"Uh-huh," Chris said with a grin. "At least none *admitted* it. But yeah, like that."

"But times have changed," Kyle pointed out. "Those old roles aren't so clear, or necessary, anymore."

"Not socially, maybe, although things never change that much," Chris replied. "Even though the dynamics in the leather scene don't really have a lot to do with butch-femme roles, they *do* have a lot to do with what we want to express physically. And what we want sexually says a lot about who we are."

"So how do you let someone else know exactly what you're into?" *And what do you do if you don't know?*

Chris surveyed the crowd. "Look at that woman next to the jukebox over there."

Kyle followed Chris's direction and saw a woman dressed predominantly in leather—leather pants with a wide, studded belt, heavy black motorcycle boots, and a leather jacket covered with zippers. She appeared to be alone and yet she looked directly at no one. "Hot."

Chris smiled. "Well, what do you think she's looking for?"

"She looks like she'd be the one to call the shots."

"Ah, but I know her, and she isn't," Chris said. "If you look more carefully, there are a few signs that tell you just what she wants. For instance, she's wearing a leather bracelet on her right wrist. She's also not cruising—she's waiting."

When Kyle nodded in agreement, Chris explained, "She's a bottom, not a top. She wants someone to approach her, set the scene, and take control. She wants someone else to take charge."

"Does that mean she's passive, then?" Kyle asked, surprised. "Just going along with what someone else wants?"

"Not necessarily. It just means that she's willing to let someone else determine how things begin. You'd be surprised how often the bottom actually calls the entire scene."

"What if someone approaches her that she's not interested in?" Kyle asked. "What if she doesn't want to play?"

"She doesn't reply with the correct answers, or she just says no."

"So she *does* have something to say about it then?"

Chris appeared startled for a second. "Of course—if she doesn't agree, nothing can happen. Both partners must be willing."

"So what if I see someone I like, and I want to...get acquainted?"

"It depends on what you want." Chris shrugged, then eyed Kyle speculatively. "What *do* you want?"

Kyle held her gaze. "I don't know."

Chris said nothing.

"But I'm here," Kyle said softly.

"It's all in how you present yourself," Chris said just as softly. Her eyes slid once more over the length of Kyle's body. "And your presentation is just right. I don't usually bring people out, but..."

Kyle shook her head. "Thanks, but..."

"Not tonight?" Chris finished for her.

"Right."

Chris nodded, her eyes still warm. "It seems strange at first, but I think you'll find out it's just another way of communicating your desires." She finished her beer and regarded Kyle seriously. "I can't stay tonight, but I hope you do. Maybe you'll find what you're looking for."

Is that why I'm here? To find...something? Kyle returned her gaze intently. "I'll be staying."

Kyle noted with regret that it was almost closing time. She'd quit drinking right after Chris left, because riding the bike high was suicide. Now she was sober and restless. The atmosphere was charged with sex and had become more so as the night wore on. At one point she'd walked into the labyrinthine hallway looking for the bathrooms and had practically stumbled on two women in the midst of a tryst in the shadows. One woman leaned against the wall, head back and eyes closed—clearly about to come—as another rhythmically pumped an arm between her legs. At first glance, they looked like any two women having sex until Kyle noticed that the hands of the woman against the wall were handcuffed behind her back. Kyle couldn't look away, fascinated by the intermittent glint of dancing silver as the bound woman thrust her hips and jerked her restrained hands from side to side. Kyle couldn't remember having made a sound, but maybe she had, because the woman opened her eyes and stared into Kyle's as she started to come, crying out in a strangled voice. Kyle had held the woman's gaze, watching the orgasm rage across her face, until the woman sagged against the wall, head lolling, moaning softly. The other woman reached around, released the cuffs, and pushed them into her back pocket. Then she turned and saw Kyle.

Kyle met her cool, appraising look unflinchingly.

"She likes to come again right away," the stranger advised in a nonchalant tone. "Don't make any marks, and don't forget—she leaves with me."

And then the woman who had pocketed the cuffs walked away, leaving Kyle to stare into deep blue eyes, still glazed and unfocused.

"Please," came a soft whisper.

Kyle's belly had twisted with sudden lust, a fierce wanting that burned still. She lowered her eyes, saw the expanse of bare stomach tapering down to the vee of the open fly. She'd hungered to slide her fingers beneath the worn denim and slip through the slick heat that she knew awaited her. She longed to enter this stranger and feel the last tremors of the climax she had witnessed ripple around her fingers. She ached to hear that choked cry of pleasure again—for her.

She'd fisted her hands and swallowed her need and slowly shaken her head. "I'm sorry," she'd murmured and walked away.

But she'd wanted her. She didn't even know her, but she'd felt some connection as basic and simple as a shared need to touch and be touched. She could have taken her, would have reveled in her, would in all likelihood have come just from being inside her, but she hadn't. And she wasn't entirely sure why. She *still* wanted her or someone—something—so much that the arousal had turned to pain.

Lost in the memory of the scene, Kyle failed to notice a woman approaching until her vision was suddenly blocked and, at the same time, she became aware of a body so close she could feel its heat. With a sharp intake of breath, she recognized the blond she had seen earlier leaning against the pole. So near to her now, Kyle observed that her hair was indeed a rich gold and her eyes so blue they verged on indigo.

Kyle found she had to look up at the woman, who regarded her with an air of easy confidence, her hands thrust deep into the pockets of her jeans, her long legs straddling Kyle's. Her amused smile was nearly insolent, softened by the merest hint of a dimple adjacent to one corner. Her eyes, however, were not smiling. They were fiercely intense and searching.

Uncertain of what showed in her own eyes, Kyle was at once uneasy and intrigued, and, unaccountably, she dropped her gaze. In that second, she fully realized that she did not know what to expect next.

"How's the sightseeing going?" a cool voice questioned. "Got it all figured out yet?"

Kyle's head snapped up, heat rising to her face. "I'm not a tourist!"

"Oh my...touch a sore spot, did I?"

Kyle was pissed. *Who does she think she is, coming up uninvited and giving me a hard time?* Jaws clenched, she started to turn her back. She would have told her to fuck off, but she'd learned a little patience over the years and knew it wasn't worth a confrontation.

A hand closed firmly on her upper arm and held her in place.

"Wait a minute. We're still talking." There was just a hint of laughter in the voice, as if at a private joke that Kyle had missed.

"I don't think we have anything to say." Struggling to appear unaffected by the monumentally annoying stranger, Kyle reached for a cigarette. She felt a little cornered with her back to the bar, and she needed the familiar ritual to give herself time to think. As she pushed her hand into her pocket for her lighter, a match flared before her.

"Well, that's up to you, isn't it?" the woman asked softly, cupping the flame in her long, tapering fingers.

"Is it?" Kyle frowned slightly as she drew on her cigarette, pulling the smoke deeply into her chest. She exhaled slowly, searching the perfectly sculpted, perfectly remote face. She didn't know the right answer if there was one, but she knew what she felt, and she went with it. "Somehow I thought you were the one calling the shots."

The blond nodded, touching the match to her own cigarette. "Very good—but only if you *want* me to. Only if you *let* me—understand?"

Kyle sighed, looking directly into the blue eyes that still calmly searched her face. "I'm afraid that I'm going to disappoint you."

Suddenly the woman smiled, a flickering luminescence that dispelled the aura of aloofness that had surrounded her. Just as quickly, it was gone. "Oh, I don't think so."

Kyle felt foolish. This was a woman like her, a woman in a club filled with other women, all of them linked by a common bond. *Why did I think that these women would be so different from all the other lesbians I've known?*

She'd been so caught up in the mystique of the dress and the attitude of these leather-clad figures that she had failed to recognize the women beneath the costumes. Her body relaxed as her old confidence returned. She might not know all the signals, but she knew who she was.

"My name is Kyle."

"I know."

Kyle raised her eyebrows slightly.

"Chris informed me."

"I'm slow tonight," Kyle said, shaking her head.

The woman was only inches away from Kyle now, and her next words were spoken so softly that only Kyle could hear them. "I'm not rushing you."

The blond had not changed her stance but still stood boldly in Kyle's view, legs spread, her thighs just brushing the outside of Kyle's. Kyle realized that this stranger was presenting herself, a gesture at once arrogant and vulnerable. She took advantage of the moment to study her, having only gotten a sense of her lean build and sharply sculpted features from her earlier appraisal. This time, she slowly surveyed the slim torso beneath a faded denim shirt that molded to a solid waist and disappeared into well-worn denim jeans. A black leather belt rode low over narrow hips, and a few keys hung from a leather strap on her left hip. Kyle took note of the thin leather band buckled around her tanned left wrist. Her study was interrupted by the woman's voice.

"Like what you see?" Her voice was low, intense, intimate.

"Yes," Kyle answered honestly. She raised her eyes, met the deep blue ones unflinchingly.

"Come dance with me then." It was not a request.

The room came sharply into focus as Kyle became acutely aware of the heavy, pounding rhythm that reverberated through the air, through the floor, through the very walls. Insistent and unrelenting. It echoed the pulse that beat through her blood and her bones. *This is it. Do you really want to do this?*

Without a word, she nodded and followed the woman onto the dance floor. There were other couples there, but they quickly faded from Kyle's consciousness as the stranger turned and put both arms around Kyle's waist, pulling her near. As they pressed close together in the crowded space, Kyle felt for the first time the strength contained in her companion's deceptively lithe body. The arms that held her were sinewy and strong, the slender frame solidly muscled and hard. The soft swell of breasts was a startling counterpoint to that stark physicality, and the desire that had simmered for hours in Kyle's depths flared to life.

It seemed entirely natural to rest her head against the blond's shoulder where the sweet scent of soap and something more primal made Kyle's belly flutter. The hand in the curve of her back held her confidently, and when the woman insinuated one tight thigh securely between Kyle's, her hips lifted in silent welcome. As they danced with their breasts slowly melding, Kyle felt the blond's nipples harden beneath the fabric of her shirt. Her own stiffened in response, painfully taut and aching. When the hand on her spine guided Kyle's hips rhythmically against that slow-moving thigh, all the heat of their two bodies seemed to coalesce into one point between Kyle's legs. She moaned without meaning to and could almost feel those long fingers on her skin.

Never had she responded so quickly or so certainly to another's touch. The people around her, the soft hum of conversation, even the steady beat of the music faded as she lost awareness of everything but the firm muscles, demanding hands, and hot breath skimming her neck. The promise of those hands, that insistent pressure calling blood to her loins and urgency to her flesh, were all she knew. When Kyle slid her hands down to the woman's hips, striving to pull her closer, hoping to ease the aching pressure, the woman's deep voice penetrated the blur of arousal.

"You don't get it for free."

The denim-clad stranger's lips brushed Kyle's neck and a single arrow of excitement pierced her to the core. She wanted only that the exquisite torment not end. "Tell me the price, then."

"Later." The woman reached one hand up into the soft waves at the back of Kyle's neck and spread her fingers in her hair. Her mouth against Kyle's ear, she murmured, "Come home with me. Now."

For an instant, reason intruded, and Kyle hesitated. *Who are you?*

The blond slipped a hand between them and slowly, deliberately, squeezed Kyle's nipple. Kyle's knees buckled as her clitoris stiffened, and she leaned heavily against the unyielding stranger. *Oh, Jesus, God!*

"Say yes."

There was just enough urgency in the whispered demand to let Kyle know that it was not her need alone that brought them together.

"I..."

"Say yes."

Another brush of soft lips along the edge of her jaw, another roll of her nipple between thumb and fingers, and Kyle was forced to close her eyes against the sweet torture.

"Yes."

CHAPTER THREE

Kyle, her legs still shaking, allowed herself to be led from the club by the stranger's touch on her back. The cool steady drizzle slapped into her face, shocking her. She'd forgotten that there *was* a world outside the hot, dark shadows of her own desire.

"What about my bike?" Kyle asked hoarsely as they reached the street.

"We'll take it. I'll tell you where to go."

Kyle took a deep breath of the chilly night air, hoping to clear her head for the drive. She was uncomfortably swollen inside her tight leather pants. She unlocked both helmets and extended one.

"What's your name?" Kyle asked quietly.

The woman stared at her for an instant, and for a moment, Kyle thought she wouldn't answer. Then she reached for the second helmet and settled it over her head, drawing the opaque visor down. "Dane."

Wordlessly, Kyle straddled her motorcycle and, raising her right leg to kick start the engine, felt Dane climb on behind her.

"Do you know where Cole is?" Dane shouted above the roar of the powerful machine.

Kyle nodded in acknowledgment.

Dane reached around Kyle's waist, slid one hand beneath the leather jacket against Kyle's stomach, and with the other, cupped her crotch. "Drive."

Kyle maneuvered her bike as quickly as she dared over the rain-slicked streets, aware only of the engine throbbing rhythmically between her thighs and the steady pressure of Dane's hands. By the time they reached Cole and Dane signaled for her to pull over, she was trembling. Despite the chill of the night air, sweat dampened her hair and soaked her shirt. She was wild for the feel of Dane's hands against her naked flesh, unencumbered by the barriers of leather and denim.

Dane led the way up six stone stairs to a narrow building, unlocked the front door, and motioned Kyle into the vestibule. From there, Kyle followed her up another flight of stairs, through another door, and into a darkened apartment.

Once inside, Dane said, "Wait here."

Kyle was aware of lights being turned on in other rooms and the sound of soft music. She stood and waited, not thinking at all. When at last she heard Dane's sure footsteps approaching, her body stirred in anticipation. The effect this woman had on her was inexplicable, and, lost in the moment, she didn't try to understand. She responded purely with her senses, and she reveled in that feeling of abandon. She didn't want to think. She wanted to feel.

Dane took her hand. "This way."

Kyle found herself in a bedroom lit solely by soft blue lights in a recessed ceiling track. A small table stood next to a large rectangular bed that dominated the otherwise bare room. When Dane turned suddenly to face her, she stood absolutely still. In silence, Dane reached out and loosed the buttons on her shirt, being careful not to touch the skin laid bare as the shirt fell away. Once exposed, Kyle's nipples contracted almost painfully, an urgent plea for contact.

"Your boots."

Kyle hesitated only for a second, then unbuckled her heavy black boots and pulled them off. Naked except for her leather pants, she stood before Dane, still waiting. Dane reached out a slender hand and traced the muscles in Kyle's shoulders and arms with a finger. Then she placed both palms flat against Kyle's chest and pressed, softly massaging the muscles beneath the smooth skin. Her hands moved down to Kyle's abdomen, carefully avoiding her breasts, until she stood with her thumbs together in the middle of Kyle's firm body, her fingers splayed out against Kyle's sides.

The muscles in Kyle's stomach twitched beneath Dane's hands, and Kyle caught back a moan. The slow, wordless survey of her body had brought her blood to a boil again. She felt her clitoris swell and moisture flow in response to the stimulation. Her chest was covered with a thin film of perspiration, and she panted slightly in the still room.

"Lie down on the bed," Dane instructed, her voice perfectly controlled. "Face me."

Kyle complied, her eyes fixed on Dane, who came to stand at the foot of the bed. When Dane's eyes traveled from Kyle's leather-bound crotch slowly up to her face, Kyle felt as if a hand had caressed her naked flesh. Her stomach tensed and her thighs quivered. She knew the wanting must show in her face.

"You can say anything you want to me right now," Dane said, "but after this, no more. I won't hurt you, but I won't stop until I'm done."

Kyle looked back at her steadily, searching for a clue as to what was about to happen. *Who are you?* The face was edgy and strong. The eyes, even in the half-light, were piercing and clear. Although she saw no answers, inexplicably, she sensed not danger, but honesty.

"I'm all right."

Dane nodded once and then moved purposefully to the side of the bed, reached somewhere beneath the frame, and pulled out soft, padded leather restraints. Deftly, she bound Kyle's left hand, then moved to the other side and restrained her right hand, then her ankles, leaving Kyle securely but not painfully bound with her arms and legs spread wide.

Dane stood once again at the foot of the bed, slowly removing her own shirt, methodically baring her upper body. Small high breasts accentuated the finely muscled torso, and a pulse beat close to the surface of a pale throat. Silence enclosed them in the cone of blue light.

Kyle was bombarded with conflicting sensations. The feeling of being helplessly bound was at once frightening and exhilarating. She wanted this woman on top of her, she wanted her inside of her, she wanted more than she could put words to. Her inability to actually seek her own release made her even more acutely aware of her desires. Her clitoris strained against the seam of her pants, threatening to explode just from the constant contact as her hips rocked back and forth. She stifled a groan as she stared transfixed at Dane's body, so close to her and yet so completely untouchable.

After what seemed like hours to Kyle, who had lost all sense of time, Dane moved to the head of the bed. From that vantage, Kyle was totally exposed to her view but Kyle, in turn, could barely see Dane. Dane placed her hands firmly on either side of Kyle's face with her fingers curled around Kyle's lower jaw. She moved surprisingly gentle fingers over the flesh and bones of Kyle's face, as if imprinting a physical sense of Kyle in her mind. Then, with one hand under her chin, Dane tilted Kyle's head back, exposing her neck to its fullest.

"Close your eyes and keep them closed."

With one hand still firmly controlling Kyle's head, Dane traced the vulnerable structures of Kyle's throat, feeling breath flow in the fragile windpipe and blood ripple through the pulsating arteries just below the skin. With her fingers pressing into the muscles on either side of Kyle's neck, Dane leaned closer. She ran her tongue lightly from Kyle's collarbone to her ear. When she spoke, her voice was barely a whisper.

"I don't want you to move. Just keep remembering my hands on your throat while I'm making you come."

The words made Kyle's hips jerk, and she bit her lip to stifle a cry. She had never felt so physically vulnerable in her life. The restraints on her arms and legs were barely perceptible and yet she was totally immobilized. Now, with her throat exposed, locked in darkness, she felt as if she had lost control of her very life. Despite the helplessness of her position, she was powerfully excited. The merest touch was going to set her off.

Dimly, in the last part of her thinking mind, she knew she could break the spell of her own bondage with a word to Dane. But she didn't want to escape. She wanted to *feel*. She wanted to experience the sensations Dane aroused in her. She wanted to know how far into her physical self Dane could take her.

Much more than she wanted to come, she wanted to *know*.

A slight motion near her feet told her that Dane had moved onto the bed. She sensed that Dane was close to her, but she did not open her eyes. Suddenly a sharp sensation centered in each nipple as Dane's hands caught her breasts, squeezing the erect nipples sharply. Kyle gasped at the unexpected contact, her back arching, pressing more of herself into Dane's hands. The entire surface of her body was sensitized with need and her clitoris twitched urgently.

Kyle understood that she was not to speak, but the pressure in her depths begged for release. She moaned softly.

Dane continued to flick the tight nipples until she brought a choked cry from Kyle's parted lips. Only then did she trail her fingers ever so lightly down Kyle's abdomen, watching the tense muscles contract at her touch. Deftly she pulled the snap at Kyle's waist and slid the zipper down on her leather pants. Leaving Kyle for an instant, she released the buckles on the ankle restraints to free Kyle's legs and remove the last vestige of her clothing. Just as quickly, she re-secured her ankles. Now Kyle lay helplessly bound and completely naked. The dark triangle of soft hair between her legs glistened with the evidence of her desire. Dane could almost taste her.

Forcing herself to lie still, Kyle waited desperately for the next contact, burning inside and out. *Where is she? Oh God, let her touch me soon. I can't stand it. I can't. I can't.* She moaned again.

What Kyle could not discern through the heady mist of her own desire was the control that Dane now exercised on her own raging senses. The image of Kyle lying helpless before her, ripe with readiness, was powerfully erotic. She longed to press herself full-length against Kyle's naked body and feel skin against her skin. She was wet and hard, had been since they'd danced, but she ignored her insistent urge for relief to concentrate all her attention on bringing Kyle to the razor's edge of ecstasy. She held back her own need, knowing it was not yet time. *Soon.*

Kneeling upright between Kyle's spread legs, Dane slipped the leather belt from around her waist and placed it vertically down the length of Kyle's body, the buckle resting between her breasts. The soft tongue of leather was pressed into the triangle between Kyle's legs. The edges of the belt rode against her distended clitoris, and she knew that the roughness against the exposed nerves would push Kyle closer to orgasm. With the thin barrier of leather between them, Dane finally rested her body fully upon Kyle for the first time, her hands lifting Kyle's hips to meet her own as she sought Kyle's mouth.

Kyle fought against her restraints for the first time, wanting connection, needing to feel flesh against her own tormented flesh. Her mouth opened to pull Dane inside, and still she could not get enough. She wrenched her head away from Dane's seeking lips.

"Please, no more," Kyle groaned. "Please, please...I have to come."

"I'll decide." Dane's voice was harsh with barely restrained urgency as she thrust her denim-clad hips tantalizingly against Kyle.

Kyle sobbed deep in her chest and turned her face once again to Dane, claiming her lips. As their mouths found each other and their tongues met in a probing duel, Dane lifted her body slightly and slipped one hand between them. Her fingers slipped into Kyle's wetness, and Kyle moaned into her mouth. Then she was inside of her, and Kyle's muscles contracted around her hand. Slowly Dane pressed further, feeling the flesh open beneath her. With her thumb beneath the thin tongue of leather she beat an insistent rhythm against Kyle's clitoris. When Kyle cried out, Dane closed her eyes tightly and clenched her jaw, determined to resist her own rising need.

Kyle, however, would not be denied. Her body arched and bucked as she closed around the fullness of Dane's hand. Ripples of pleasure raced along her thighs and coiled through her belly. A strangled cry escaped her lips as the pounding in her head fused with that in her body, and her orgasm crested in one wave of unbound fury.

"Oh yesohyes..."

Dane gripped her firmly, riding out the raging storm.

Kyle had barely begun to relax from the paroxysms of pleasure when Dane reached up and released the restraints on her arms and then her ankles. Dimly, she was aware of Dane gently massaging her wrists and then rolling her over onto her stomach. Drifting on the edge of consciousness, she was jolted back to the moment when Dane stretched naked along her back and pressed urgently against her hips. Pushing upward to meet Dane's downward thrusts, Kyle curled an arm back to encircle Dane's neck, holding her closer. Dane's breath seared over her neck in ragged bursts as she worked herself toward orgasm against Kyle's body.

"Yes, yes," Kyle whispered, her heart pounding wildly as she felt Dane shudder. "Come on, baby. Let it go."

Kyle wanted nothing more than to bring Dane the same pleasure she had just experienced. Wanted it so much she hurt. When Dane gasped brokenly and jerked erratically, fingers clenched on Kyle's upper arms, Kyle thought her head would explode. There would be bruises. She didn't care; she welcomed them, exulted in the intensity of Dane's desire. When Dane stiffened and groaned, Kyle smiled triumphantly.

When Kyle opened her eyes, she had the impression that it was morning, just barely. There was no hint of sunshine through the shuttered windows and no noise in the building. She lay quietly in the thin gray light, adjusting to the unfamiliar surroundings and the even stranger sensation of awakening with a woman beside her. Dane, naked and pressed close against her back, slept deeply. The slow, steady rise and fall of her breasts was a quiet comfort against Kyle's skin. Even in sleep, Dane related possessively to Kyle's body. She held Kyle as if she always had, one arm curved around her middle and her fingers lightly clasping Kyle's breast. Oddly, Kyle was at ease with Dane's presence, even though she almost always slept alone and wasn't used to being held even when she did share her bed.

How did I get here? And who are you?

Carefully, she drew her hand up to cover the one holding her breast. She pressed Dane's fingers to her flesh. Warm. Pleasantly rough skinned. Real.

At the touch, her body stirred with memory.

Closing her eyes, she replayed the night's events. She remembered Dane collapsing as her climax ebbed, silent except for her uneven breaths, her body trembling like a thoroughbred after a hard run. Her cheek had been soft against the damp skin of Kyle's neck, her fingers gentle on Kyle's upper arms. The satisfaction Kyle found in Dane's pleasure had been exquisite. Knowing she had excited Dane that much was tremendously arousing. Just remembering the sensation of Dane driving against her, desperate to orgasm, made her hard again. She tensed her thighs, knowing she was wet and already ready.

She wanted it all again. She wanted Dane's touch; she wanted Dane to take her to that plane where every cell was alive with sensation, where it was impossible *not* to feel. And even more, she wanted the ultimate satisfaction of forcing Dane to lose control. She lusted to ignite Dane's passion, because Dane's orgasm was her power.

Tense with renewed excitement, Kyle unconsciously pushed her hips back against Dane's body. Murmuring faintly, Dane stirred and tightened her hold. Kyle wasn't certain Dane was awake until she felt the slight pressure against her breast become a gentle massaging motion and fingers tugging lightly at her nipple. Closing her eyes, Kyle focused on the aching point of pleasure. When the hand left her breast and moved to her abdomen, circling in slow, firm arcs, Kyle arched her back as pressure built between her thighs. She tried to steady her breathing, but every caress inflamed her more.

No words were spoken as Dane pressed her mouth to the back of Kyle's shoulder and bit gently, sliding her hand lower at the same time. Gasping softly, Kyle shifted to allow Dane to slip a hand between her thighs. When Dane found her clitoris and began gently circling, Kyle whimpered quietly. Each teasingly slow stroke brought her closer, but it wasn't enough. She wanted to ask—to *beg*—Dane to press harder, but knew instinctively that she would be denied. She would wait, as long as it took. She closed her fingers on Dane's wrist, but did not try to guide her. A trail of fire burned down the inside of her thighs, and her stomach clenched.

"Pleas—"

"Shh." Dane ran her tongue along the rim of Kyle's ear. "Feel me."

Dane leaned up on one elbow, her hand still between Kyle's legs as Kyle fell back. She eased one finger deep inside the waiting warmth and watched Kyle's eyes lose focus. A twist of desire so sharp it hurt slashed through her. *God, she's beautiful.* Gently, she stroked.

Kyle stared wordlessly into Dane's blue eyes, her breath catching when she saw her own desire reflected there. She held the hypnotic gaze as Dane filled her, one finger at a time. She'd come soon, was building to it, holding Dane fast. She still gripped Dane's wrist, her fingers digging into flesh and bone, feeling Dane take her.

Dane watched the orgasm rise in Kyle's face, and just before it broke, she slipped out and quickly slid onto Kyle, her thigh gliding easily between Kyle's legs.

"Oh," Kyle cried softly. Dane's smooth skin rubbed over her clitoris, triggering the first spasms of release. She tightened around Dane's leg and pushed hard against her.

"Don't," Dane warned, growing still.

Kyle struggled not to surrender, to hold the pleasure at bay, to wait until Dane gave her permission. She closed her eyes as Dane rocked her hips, then met her thrusts as the cadence of their passion became a force of its own. For moments beyond knowing, she trembled on the brink of completion, but finally, the pulse of blood and nerves grew too strong to contain, and she broke.

"I'm coming," she whispered, her face pressed to Dane's neck, hands clutching the straining back.

"Wait," Dane gasped, even as she felt Kyle arch with the first wave of release. Nearly blind with the pounding pressure threatening to explode her entire body, she thrust harder along Kyle's thigh. Then fire burst from her belly and burned along her spine. "Ah...God!"

Her cry carried Kyle beyond anything she'd experienced into a swirling chaos of sensation. The only reality was Dane, and she clung to her as their bodies stormed and their senses raged. At that instant, she was as close to anyone as she had ever been in her life.

41

CHAPTER FOUR

Kyle opened her eyes and blinked. This time sunshine streaked the room. She turned her head on the pillow and discovered Dane propped up beside her, smoking a cigarette, the covers resting across her naked thighs. It was the first time Kyle had seen her nude. Her body was lean and tanned, her breasts small and high. There was an old scar, white and thin, angled over her ribs and down the right side of her abdomen. Kyle wanted to draw her fingers over it but held back. Dane had not asked to be touched, she realized. Had not let Kyle touch her when they'd made love. *Made love...or had sex? No, whatever it was, it was something more than sex.*

"Good morning," Dane said softly. She looked for the questions she knew would be in Kyle's eyes. She looked for the regret, too. She wanted to run her fingers through the thick tousled hair, but she held back.

"Hi," Kyle said, stretching languorously. Her muscles were sore, the result, she thought idly, of coming so hard while restrained. *Restrained. Jesus.* Beneath the aching stiffness, she felt wonderful. "What time is it?"

"Uh." Dane faltered, confused by the unanticipated question and by the sudden light in Kyle's eyes. "About ten, I think."

Kyle laughed. "Indulgent, aren't we?"

"Do you mind?" Dane's tone was cautious.

"Not at all." Taking a chance, Kyle turned, resting her head against Dane's bare shoulder and her palm on Dane's stomach. "You?"

"No." Dane hesitated, then twined her fingers into Kyle's thick hair. Surprised at how true that was, and how unexpected, Dane stared at the large yet finely sculpted hand that gently stroked her abdomen. "Are you...hungry?"

"I think I might be, as soon as my body wakes up."

Kyle listened to Dane's heart beat and continued to caress her. She knew absolutely nothing about her, except that being with Dane physically had touched her in places she hadn't known existed. "Do you have to be anywhere this morning?"

"Unfortunately, yes." Dane sighed. "I usually make it a point never to work on Saturday, but today I have an appointment."

Kyle wasn't sure what to say or do next. In her experience, after a night of sex some women preferred to just say goodbye in the morning, careful never to dispel the mystery of a brief encounter by dealing with the ordinary demands of daily living. Kyle herself had often felt uncomfortable with a stranger in her house in the morning, finding that the woman she had desired in the late-night hours was not someone she wanted to face across the breakfast table. She didn't feel that way now. Still, she asked, "Would you rather I left?"

Dane regarded her curiously, but, out of long habit, kept her surprise at Kyle's straightforwardness concealed. "No. I'd rather you made some coffee."

Kyle's eyes narrowed speculatively as she studied Dane's face, unable to read anything in the strong, even features. *Is this another scene? Or a test?*

"All right."

"The kitchen—"

"I'll find it." Kyle slid out from under the covers and dug around in the pile of clothing on the floor for her shirt.

Dane smiled, admiring Kyle's naked backside as she left the room. Then she leaned back, closed her eyes, and listened to the sounds emanating from the kitchen. Soon she could smell coffee brewing. It surprised her to realize that she was enjoying herself, enjoying these first non-sexual moments with Kyle. Usually she found her bed partners disappointingly boring, and often discovered she hadn't a single thing to say to them. She tried not to bring women home for a scene, but when she did, she had gotten into the habit of finding some excuse to get them out of her apartment as quickly as possible. Her reluctance to become involved with anyone for more than a night had enhanced her reputation in the club as a loner. That suited her just fine, since it released her from the pressure of being sociable. No one expected it of her. She remained something of an enigma and accountable to no one.

That morning the situation had been very different than what she was used to. When she'd awakened next to Kyle, she hadn't experienced her typical compulsion to escape. She'd felt...good. Holding Kyle had seemed natural, and when the easy comfort had spiraled into hunger, the lovemaking had come naturally, too. Kyle had read Dane's body language well, which wasn't all that common, and just looking at her made Dane hot. More than hot...an aching want deep inside. Dane felt a twitch of arousal and smiled, leisurely drawing her hand down her stomach and between her legs. *Still hard.* The light touch made her shiver, and she moved her hand away.

It wasn't just the exceptionally fine sex that had been a surprise. *Kyle* wasn't what she'd expected, either. She must have had questions, but she hadn't asked. She must have *wanted* something, but she hadn't pushed. Her calm acceptance of what had happened between them and her relaxed approach to the morning put Dane at ease. For the first time in a long time, she wasn't sure of what was going to happen. Or what she *wanted* to happen. That was both exciting and disquieting.

Her thoughts were interrupted by Kyle's return with two steaming mugs of coffee. Dane took one cup and pulled the blankets back for Kyle to crawl under.

"So, how *are* you this morning?" Dane ventured. She sipped her coffee gratefully and stretched one leg out over Kyle's.

"Fine." Kyle considered what else to say. Dane was so hard to read. "I guess you know last night was new for me."

"You mean sleeping with a woman?"

"Of course not," Kyle flared. Looking quickly at Dane, she caught the twinkle in her eyes. "Very cute. No, I meant sleeping with a woman in quite that way."

"I knew. Did you...enjoy it?" Even as Dane spoke, she wondered why she'd asked. *What does it matter? She got off; she got what she was looking for. What else is there?*

"Yes, I did." Kyle almost smiled at that understatement. "It wasn't what I expected."

"What do you mean?" Dane couldn't remember any longer how she'd felt at the beginning. She had changed so much since then. Usually, she wasn't interested in how other women felt about their encounters with her. They all seemed to have their reasons for seeking her kind of company, and she rarely took the time to understand what those motivations might be. The women had chosen to have an encounter with her; she always made certain they understood what that would mean. Sometimes it was good and sometimes it wasn't. With Kyle, it had been better than good. And how she felt about it seemed to matter.

"In some ways it was more than I anticipated," Kyle began carefully. "It was more natural than I had thought it would be, for one thing."

"Oh?" Dane replied, raising an eyebrow, instantly on guard. "Did you expect it to be *un*natural?"

"No—I guess I thought it would be more contrived." Kyle had heard the challenge in Dane's voice but thought she understood the defensiveness. She wasn't naïve, only inexperienced, and she knew that a good many people would not approve of what the two of them had shared. "Somehow, I couldn't imagine just *feeling* when there were so many other things going on. The roles we both played—the separateness of our positions." *The fact that I couldn't touch you.* "I thought I would be too self-conscious to really get into it physically."

"For some women I think that happens. They can't...let go. They can't enjoy not knowing what will happen next." Dane had never talked about these things with anyone she'd had sex with. In fact, only a few friends knew how she felt. *How did I end up saying these things to you?* "They discover they don't like it, and that's fine."

Kyle met Dane's eyes. "*I* liked it."

Thank God she's not feeling guilty. Dane relaxed, somewhat assured by Kyle's frankness. "For me, creating the mood, setting the scene—it's part of what turns me on. I like the...control."

"I found out it turns me on, too," Kyle responded. *And I especially like it when* you're *in control.* She sighed and stretched, enjoying the contented way her body felt.

Dane reached over to the bedside table, picked up her watch, and grimaced. "Sorry. I'm going to have to get up soon."

Kyle groaned in mock distress.

Dane grinned and, before she could think about it, kissed Kyle lightly on the nose. "Work, remember? I'm self-employed, so I'm afraid I have to work when the work is there." And because she wanted to kiss her again, and not stop, she swung her legs over the side of the bed and stood.

"What do you do?" Kyle watched Dane move around the room, enjoying the long, strong body and trying to imprint each small detail in her mind.

"Dogs." Dane's voice was muffled since her head was in the closet while she searched for a shirt.

"What?" Kyle asked, not sure she had heard correctly.

"Dogs," Dane repeated, turning with a smile. "I breed dogs."

Kyle looked around her, perplexed. "Here?"

Dane laughed. "No—I own a kennel. I only keep one here, and he's been away at a show." She pulled clean jeans from a drawer and glanced over at Kyle. "I'm going to shower."

"Want company?"

Dane regarded her steadily. "Yes."

"If you turn around, I'll wash your hair," Kyle offered. What she wanted to do was smooth her hands over the wet planes of Dane's body, over the curve of her breasts and the line of her abdomen. But even though they stood together naked while warm water cascaded over them, there was a barrier she wasn't certain how to breach. She was reminded now more than at any time in the last twelve hours that she didn't know the woman, or the rules.

Dane hesitated, then nodded. "Thanks. That would be great."

47

Kyle took her time, enjoying the way Dane gradually leaned back against her as she worked the suds into a thick lather and circled her fingertips over Dane's scalp. When Dane didn't protest, she slid her palms over the sculpted shoulders and along the muscled back, massaging ever more firmly until Dane groaned with pleasure. Holding her breath, Kyle circled Dane's waist and swept her hand up Dane's stomach and over her breasts. The nipples hardened instantly.

"You feel so good," Kyle whispered in Dane's ear, pressing her hips gently against Dane's buttocks.

"One minute more in here and I'll never be able to leave," Dane murmured, her head tipped back on Kyle's shoulder. She wanted to tell her to stop, but she couldn't remember why.

"Who's counting?" Kyle caught an earlobe in her teeth and tugged. Dane turned in her arms with a groan and their lips met. The kiss deepened as tongues gently teased and their bodies melded effortlessly.

When Kyle edged her leg between Dane's, Dane shifted away.

"I...can't."

"Sorry," Kyle sighed regretfully, feeling their tenuous connection break. "I know you have to go." But she wondered as she said it if that was the only reason Dane stopped. Whatever the cause, it was Dane's call. *Maybe that's the point. Maybe she always leads.*

"Besides," Dane continued lightly, working to keep her voice even, "I'm starving."

Kyle shook the water from her eyes and regarded Dane speculatively. "It's *breakfast* that you want, then?"

"Well, actually, it's *you* I want right now, but I have to go."

Kyle sighed again. "Yes, ma'am."

As she stepped out of the shower, Dane laughed. *If only she knew.*

They shared their first breakfast together on the run. While Kyle dressed, Dane poured juice and put bread in the toaster. They munched toast while scrambling eggs and rinsed the dishes as they finished off the coffee. Silence descended as they both gathered their things and prepared to leave.

Kyle zipped her jacket and watched Dane slip a wallet into her jeans, pick up her keys, and grab a leather jacket similar to her own. When Dane finally looked at her, Kyle couldn't read the expression in her eyes. She wasn't sure where to begin, but she was out of time. And she knew if she just walked out the door, all those restless uncertainties would not only return, they'd be worse. Because Dane had awakened *something*. She just wasn't sure what.

"Dane," she ventured softly.

"Yes?"

"Will I see you again?"

"I don't know." Dane averted her gaze. She hadn't expected this. "Do you want to?"

"Yes." Kyle's answer was swift and sure.

"Maybe you should think about it a while," Dane responded carefully, meeting Kyle's eyes. "What happened last night—the way we were together—it might not be what you really want." She hesitated for a second. "And it *is* what I want."

Kyle answered just as carefully, sensing that Dane would withdraw at the slightest misunderstanding. "You'd know I was lying if I said I understood why last night felt right to me. But it did, and I'm not turning my back on that. For no reason I can clearly explain, I want you to touch me again."

"You'd better be sure what it is you want, before you find yourself somewhere you don't want to be." Dane's expression darkened, and for a moment, she lost herself to memory.

"And do you know exactly what it is you want?"

Dane reached for the door. She spoke so softly Kyle almost didn't hear her words.

"I thought I did—until now."

Dane drove the familiar route to her kennel lost in thought. The image of Kyle, resplendent in black leather, riding away on her motorcycle was still fresh in her mind. It had been a strange encounter, not because it hadn't gone well, but because it had. She had enjoyed the night with Kyle more than any she could remember recently. Kyle was surprisingly receptive to her brand of lovemaking, and it had been easy to fall into a scene with her. Still, she was wary, appreciating that Kyle was on the threshold of a new sexual arena. And knowing from experience that the process of adjusting was a long and complicated one, she wasn't sure she wanted to be Kyle's teacher. Teachers were usually replaced as time went on. When the lessons were over, novices moved on, leaving their initiators drained if they were lucky, broken if they had been foolish enough to care. Her life of casual encounters suited her. Comfortable with the limitations as well as the freedom such anonymous liaisons afforded, she hadn't wanted more than one night with anyone in a very long time. Kyle, she realized, might be capable of awakening needs that she had learned to ignore.

As she pulled her van into the small gravel lot beside a low, sprawling building bearing the name Daneland Kennels, she resolved to let the issue rest. *I'll probably never see her again anyhow.*

She got out of the van and stretched. It was a full-blown spring morning and the clear air and blue skies lifted her spirits. She whistled a little as she let herself into the office via a side door.

"Hi, boss," a voice called as she closed the door behind her. "There's someone out back to see you."

"Hey, Anne." Dane walked into a small office where a counter in the middle of the room separated a tiny waiting area with a few chairs and a coffee table from the space where a desk and computer and her assistant sat. "Sorry I'm a little late."

"Well, it is Saturday morning." The tanned young redhead, casually dressed in a plaid flannel shirt, canvas carpenter pants, and heavy work boots, smiled as she swiveled on the stool in front of the desk. "*I* understand that, but I'm not sure our friend outside does."

Dane's heart lifted. "Is my boy here already?"

"He and *my girl* got back about half an hour ago. He's very sassy, too. If he gets any more pleased with himself, there'll be no living with him."

"Where's Caroline?"

"She went out for coffee." Anne's expression softened as she spoke of her lover. "She'll be back in a minute."

Dane headed toward the rear door.

"Tell her I'm out back. I want to talk to her."

Behind the building, secluded from the highway, were fenced-in runs where the dogs could be safely let out to exercise or train. As Dane stepped into the largest area directly behind the office, a Rottweiler at the far end of the run turned in her direction. Dane laughed happily as she saw the familiar face. "Baron!"

The powerful animal raced toward her, barking excitedly. She braced herself as he approached, used to his exuberant greetings after each of their separations. When he pushed his head into her chest, she rubbed his ears and heavily muscled neck vigorously. He tried to return her affections by licking her neck, threatening to topple her over with his weight.

"Enough!" she commanded after a moment, staggering back. He sat immediately, his eyes fixed on her face, his body still trembling with excitement. She moved to the top step and said quietly, "Baron, come."

He responded instantly, pressing close up against her left leg. "So you did it again, huh, boy? I sure missed you while you were gone, but you have to do this once in a while. You're too good to just stay home and keep me company. Besides, I know you love getting out there and strutting your stuff." She ran her fingers through the soft short fur on his back, enjoying the comfort of his solid, uncomplicated affection. "Not letting it go to your head, are you?"

He put his heavy block-shaped head on her knee and half closed his eyes as she petted him. She smiled, remembering how small and cuddly he had been as a puppy. It was hard to believe that he had grown into such a magnificent animal, his conformation nearly the perfect standard for his breed. Despite her pride in him as a champion show dog, she loved him best for his gentle, loyal spirit. He was special to her far beyond his worth as her kennel's premier stud dog. He was *her* dog, before all else. Contentedly, she closed her eyes and relaxed.

When the door opened behind her, Dane smiled at the sturdily built woman with the salt-and-pepper hair who sat down beside her. "Glad to be back?"

"Oh God, yes," Caroline Matthews replied vehemently. "I'm getting too old for the circuit. Sleeping in vans and eating at McDonald's is killing me, to say nothing of my home life. Anne threatened to take a lover if I went on another road trip before June."

Dane laughed and slung an arm affectionately around Caroline's shoulders. Caroline, her friend for over ten years, was not only her business partner, but also the only person she'd trust to handle her dogs at shows. Although only six years older than Dane, she often bemoaned the fact that she was the oldest of the three friends.

"After all this time you don't really think Anne would stray, do you?" Dane queried teasingly.

"We're only coming up on three years, you know, and that isn't very long, as these things go." Caroline sighed and studied her boots. Like Dane and Anne, she was dressed for kennel work in jeans, construction boots, and a tattered black cotton sweater. "I know you don't think it matters, but I *am* twelve years older than she is. I still worry about it. I don't think I could start all over one more time."

"You could, and you would, if you had to." Dane placed her hand lightly on her friend's knee and squeezed. "But Anne is a lot more mature than her age suggests, *and* she's had enough experience to know what she wants."

"You should know about that," Caroline retorted good-naturedly.

"Jeez, are you *ever* going to forgive me for getting there first? After all, it's *you* she chose to be with." Dane didn't mind a bit that she had lost a lover to her closest friend. It happened all the time, and as much as she had enjoyed Anne, she hadn't cared when Anne had left her to be with Caroline. It had avoided complications.

"Oh, I forgive you," Caroline said, meaning it. "I still can't figure out what she saw in me, though—especially compared to you."

"Oh, I can," Dane replied seriously. "You loved her—I didn't."

Caroline looked sharply at Dane, surprised by the coldness in her voice. "You sound like you have something against love."

"Not so," Dane said, twisting her fingers in Baron's rich coat. "I don't have any problem loving this guy."

"Small wonder," Caroline snorted. "He's an absolute sweetheart. He'd die for you, and he never asks for any more than a few strokes." She scratched his black muzzle and smiled. "He just gets better and better. The judges pretended to look at the others this time, but there was no real competition. He just presented himself and stole their hearts."

"It scares me when I realize how really great he is," Dane confided. "Sometimes I forget he's a lot more than just my dog."

"So how have things been around here?" Caroline asked.

"Nothing much new. Just the same old routine," Dane replied nonchalantly. "Oh, I did put in a bid for a puppy bitch out of Kitty Graham's new litter. I thought we were ready for a little expansion."

Caroline nodded her assent. She had a large financial investment in the kennel, but she was totally comfortable with Dane making all the decisions regarding their breeding program. Her own talent was in training the dogs for the show ring and handling them in competition.

"Sounds good. But I didn't mean on the dog scene. I've been gone six weeks. What's been happening with you?"

"Not much."

"Come on, handsome. This is me, and you know I love details." Caroline gave Dane's shoulder a little bump. "Something, or someone, must have happened while I've been away. Give me a break. I'm dying for a little gossip."

Ordinarily Dane didn't tolerate any intrusion in her private life, but with Caroline, she couldn't put up much of a fight. They had been friends too long, and as much as she hated to admit it, sometimes she needed to talk to someone.

"Well," she began cautiously, "the club scene hasn't changed much. More new faces all the time. There's so much leather everywhere these days, *I'm* not sure who's for real and who's just there for the show."

"I know what you mean." Caroline laughed. "Maybe women are just getting more comfortable with it—and more and more are thinking about it. That's some kind of progress."

"Yeah, I guess," Dane muttered. "I met this woman—a real novice, totally uninitiated. And she was so cool about the whole thing. She'd thought about it, and then went out and tried it. Just like that."

"Well, what's wrong with that? That's what we've been saying all along, right? It's just another way that people relate. Not for everyone—but so what?"

"Yeah, but this was different." Dane's voice was contemplative. "She wasn't some kid out for an adventure—she *thinks* about what she's doing. And she talks about it."

"She sounds interesting," Caroline observed, hoping to appear nonchalant when her heart was racing. Dane hadn't talked about a woman in years.

"Yeah, she was."

"Not just a nice body in your bed for a night, huh?" Caroline asked lightly.

Dane looked at Caroline, surprised once more by her old friend's ability to understand her. "I guess you could say that."

"So, what did you do with her?" Caroline had always hoped that Dane would get serious about someone again, but it just never seemed to happen. Dane kept her feelings deeply hidden, even from Caroline.

"Nothing."

"Nothing?"

Dane smiled ruefully. "Well, I brought her home, of course."

"Of course."

"Cut it out," Dane protested. "I'm not that much of a stud, you know. It's not like I have a different woman in my bed every night."

"I know. But you don't do too badly. So, then what happened?"

"She left. And I came here to see you and Baron."

"This was last night?" Caroline's voice rose.

"Uh-huh."

"Well, come on, woman—*tell* me." Caroline jumped up and faced Dane, her hands on her hips. "What's she like?"

"I don't know, just a woman."

"Nuh-uh. Not good enough." Caroline nudged Dane's boot with hers. "There is no such thing. Is she young, old, tall, short, fat, thin, butch, femme, right, left—"

"She's gorgeous, actually." Dane grinned despite her intention to appear unaffected. "Black hair, dark gray eyes, and a great body. Rides a motorcycle, likes leather, and she has a brain."

"Sounds nice." Caroline grinned. "Actually, she sounds major-league hot."

"Yes."

"So..."

"So what?" Dane asked, pretending not to understand.

"So what do you plan to do about it?" Caroline couldn't resist pressing. She was in love, and she wanted her best friend to be just as happy. "Do you have her number? Are you going to call her?"

"No, I don't have her number." Dane was silent for a moment. "And no, I'm not going to call her."

"Why the hell not?" Caroline demanded impatiently.

"Because I don't feel like it," Dane replied with irritating casualness as she stood up and stretched. Baron got up immediately and looked up at her expectantly.

"I think I'll take Baron through his paces," Dane said as she walked away. "He's been taking it easy too long."

"And *you've* been hiding too long," Caroline muttered at Dane's retreating figure.

CHAPTER FIVE

K yle closed the door gently behind her and surveyed her workshop with a sigh of contentment. Benches, piled high with half-finished pieces and dismantled forms, lined the walls beneath peg-boards that held small tools. Paint cans and brushes were neatly stacked in one corner, and a central worktable lay buried under current projects and power tools. A fine layer of wood dust covered everything, and particles big enough to touch floated on the still air.

She slipped on her coveralls and tuned the radio to a station that played a mix of country and rock and roll. As was often her habit when she had something on her mind, she sought refuge in work. She began hand sanding a tabletop, her thoughts drifting as she fell into the well-practiced rhythm of the work. Scenes from the previous night kaleidoscoped in her mind, and she plummeted back into the smoke-filled club, immersed in the music and the heat and the thrill of desire. She saw Dane standing nearly astride her thighs, imperious and aloof, just a hint of a smile lifting the corner of her sensuous mouth. Then they were dancing, and Dane's hands were on her hips, arousing her passion. The moments flickered by too quickly as she recalled the cold ride on her bike through the dark early-morning streets and the hot press of Dane's hands on her body. The memory of their silent entrance into Dane's house and the unfamiliar yet exhilarating physical encounter left her both excited and uncertain. She knew she wanted to feel that sharp edge of awareness, both physical and emotional, again. And she wanted to experience it with Dane. She could still feel her hands, her breath, her body. She could still feel herself coming for her. She groaned softly and stared at the virgin grain surfacing beneath the varnish she had just striped away, but she was seeing Dane's face.

What if I never see her again?

It was impossible to deny that something had shifted inside her—or been awakened—because of her night with Dane. Usually her sexual affairs were casual and pleasant, but they rarely engaged her emotionally in any lasting way. She never missed the deeper connections—she had friends for that. But with Dane, even though they had been strangers, their joining had not been casual. By allowing Dane to restrain her, and then to control her, she had granted Dane a degree of trust she'd never shared before. Why she had instinctively trusted Dane she couldn't say, why she'd allowed Dane to top her didn't matter—all that mattered now was that she *had* done it. By the very nature of their interplay, she had been changed. And she had been touched in some way so fundamental to her being that she wondered if she would ever be content again without that kind of intensity. She feared Dane had released a hunger that could easily consume her, and worse, she feared that it might be *only* Dane who could assuage it.

Sighing, Kyle switched to a finer grain of sandpaper and worked until the varnish was gone. When she applied a light oil, the wood took on a dark warmth before her eyes. She set the piece aside to dry and began on another. She worked steadily for most of the morning, humming to the old familiar tunes in the background. When she finally straightened up, she grimaced at the cramp in her lower back and knew it wasn't caused by her work.

Definitely not used to last night's activity. She smiled. *But God, it was worth it.*

The wall phone rang just as she reached for the next item on her list of projects for the day. She grabbed it and hiked one hip onto the nearby counter.

"Hello?"

"Hi," a familiar voice asked. "Where are you?"

"Hey, Nance. I'm in the shop."

"Oh no, you don't. Not on a beautiful Saturday afternoon. The wine is chilled, the sun is coming around to the deck, and I have been deserted. When can you be here?"

"Where's Roger?"

"Roger who?"

Kyle laughed, picturing her friend and business associate sitting out on her redwood deck in some impossibly skimpy outfit, bored and restless. "That guy you live with."

"Oh, him. He has some terribly important something or other to do at the hospital. I've written him off for the day. So are you coming over, or what?"

"Well, I'm right in the middle of finishing that table."

"It doesn't have to be done until next weekend."

Kyle sighed. "I know, but..."

"Ky—yle!"

"Oh, all right." She could almost *hear* Nancy pout. "I'll be there in an hour."

"Thirty minutes."

Kyle laughed again. "Okay, okay. I'm leaving now." She hung up the receiver, pulled off her coveralls, and headed for the door.

Twenty miles south of Kyle's coastal community, Anne pulled the jeep out onto the highway and reached for Caroline's hand. "I'm so glad you're home."

"So am I, babe." Caroline squeezed Anne's fingers lightly and smiled over at her. "I missed you."

"Oh yeah?" Anne deftly negotiated the heavy expressway traffic, smiling softly.

"Mm-hmm." Caroline's voice was a low purr. "Your sparkling conversation, your great dinners, your wonderful backrubs, and..."

Anne spared her lover a quick glance and a raised eyebrow. "And?"

"And your tender services."

"Let's talk about that some more," Anne said lightly as she drove off the exit ramp and into their neighborhood.

"I've got a better idea." Caroline stretched across the gap between their seats and rested her hand on the inside of Anne's blue-jeaned thigh.

Anne looked down, then quickly back to the road. A flush rose to her neck. "What idea would that be?"

Caroline smiled. "Let's not talk at all."

Silently, Anne nodded, pulled into a parking space in front of their apartment building, and switched off the ignition. Then they walked to the rear of the vehicle, grabbed a suitcase each, and carried them inside.

"I'm going to take a shower," Caroline announced quietly as she dropped her suitcase just inside the bedroom door. She turned to Anne, who stood just behind her. Deliberately keeping her eyes on her lover's, Caroline unbuttoned the top button on the faded blue-checked shirt, brushed her hand beneath the soft material, and slowly caressed Anne's breast. The corner of Caroline's mouth lifted in satisfaction as she saw Anne's sea green irises flicker and dilate. She rubbed her fingers over Anne's nipple until it hardened, then withdrew her hand. As she walked away, she murmured, "Why don't you get ready, too."

Anne took a long shuddering breath, then went directly to the kitchen. She removed the bottle of champagne she had placed in the refrigerator that morning and opened it. Listening to the shower running in the other room, she arranged cheese, crackers, and fruit on a plate, poured champagne into iced glasses, and placed everything on a tray. Then, the pulse of excitement in the pit of her stomach beating faster with each measured movement, she carefully folded linen napkins, slid them into small silver rings, and completed the arrangement with tall, thin candles. Finished, she carried the tray to the bedside table in their room and sat down on the edge of the bed to remove her boots.

"The shirt can go, too," Caroline remarked softly as she walked in with a towel draped around her body and knotted just above her breasts. "Leave your jeans on."

Anne stood, unbuttoned her shirt, and stripped it from her chest to expose her soft, pale breasts. Caroline crossed the room to her, leaned down, and gently kissed each nipple. Then she pulled off the towel, handed it to Anne, and turned her back. "Don't hurry."

Slowly, meticulously, Anne dried Caroline's back, gently rubbing the plush cotton over the curve of her buttocks and down the length of each leg. Then she made the leisurely trip back up, catching each lingering bead of moisture on the inside of Caroline's thighs with the towel. Finished, she simply stood still and waited. When Caroline pivoted to face her, Anne lifted her gaze and, finding her lover's eyes hazy and heavy-lidded, she swallowed a small groan.

Caroline's lips parted into a lazy smile, and she took a long, languorous breath. "You may finish."

Wordlessly, Anne lovingly traced each inch of her lover's body, her hands trembling beneath the towel with the need to feel the warm skin. Stomach tight with want, she folded the square of cotton neatly and placed it on a chair.

"Why don't you pull the drapes." Caroline stretched out on the satin comforter covering their bed and reached for a glass of champagne. She sipped slowly, her gaze traveling appreciatively over Anne's body. "And light the candles."

Tasks completed, Anne looked at her questioningly.

"Would you like some of this very nice champagne?"

Anne nodded, not moving.

Caroline patted the bed by her knee. "Let's see if you can earn it."

As Anne sat, her eyes fixed on Caroline, Caroline dipped a finger into the iced wine, then touched the glistening golden drop to her left nipple.

"Mmm," Caroline sighed, idly rolling the swiftly firming nub between her fingers. As she repeated the process on her other breast, she watched Anne's breathing speed up and saw her shift restlessly on the bed. She wanted to tease her, to make her break the silence, but she wasn't sure how long she could wait. They'd been apart six weeks, and she was dying to feel Anne's clever mouth on her achingly swollen flesh. Struggling to keep her expression neutral, she ran her fingers down her abdomen, then parted her legs a fraction.

Anne was about to beg. Watching Caroline flick a fingertip over her clitoris and seeing her lover's hips jump at the touch that wasn't hers, she had to bite down on her lower lip to stifle a cry of protest. Unconsciously, she fisted a fold of satin and twisted it urgently. The blood pounded so fiercely in her head, her vision dimmed.

"Are you thirsty, baby?" Caroline asked, her husky voice thick with need.

"Oh God, yes."

Caroline touched a passion-scented finger to Anne's lips. "Be good."

Anne carefully stretched out on the bed between Caroline's parted legs, resting her face softly against the inner curve of Caroline's thigh. With one hand, she reached up to cradle Caroline's breast. When she heard Caroline moan, she involuntarily pressed her hips hard against the mattress.

"I said be good," Caroline chastised with a faint laugh. Then she laced her fingers through the curls on top of her lover's head and guided her face forward. As Anne kissed her softly, Caroline closed her eyes and took another sip of the cool, bubbly liquid. *Yes, it's very good to be home.*

Kyle turned her motorcycle up the tree-lined drive that led to a contemporary wood and glass structure nestled at the top of a knoll. The house commanded a view of the ocean in the distance while blending imperceptibly into the hillside where it stood. She walked around the side of the house to the redwood deck in the rear. Mounting the steps to the raised platform, she found her friend stretched out on a recliner in the sun. She shook her head at the almost too thin brunette in tight black Capri slacks and white scoop-necked lycra top designed to outline her full breasts to perfection.

"Aren't you worried about freezing those gorgeous tits off?"

"I never realized you noticed them," her friend said piquishly, shading her eyes with one well-manicured hand. "Could you pour me some more wine?"

"Sure." Kyle grinned. The wine bottle stood chilling in a gold-plated bucket, and an empty cut crystal glass stood beside it on the tray. She refilled the half-empty glass by Nancy's chair and then poured one for herself. "And of course I noticed. Just because I haven't drooled on them—"

"I hate that you have scruples," Nancy complained. "Just because I'm straight—"

"*And* married, don't forget," Kyle pointed out as she settled into the adjoining recliner.

"I don't see why either of those little details should be a deal breaker."

"No foolin'." Kyle snorted. "Then let's just say I love you, I value your friendship, and I'm content to lust after you from afar. End of story."

"Liar." Nancy grinned, then fixed Kyle with a probing look. "So, where were *you* last night?"

Kyle stiffened. "What do you mean?"

"I called the house at eight this morning—I know you never sleep late. And no one answered. Therefore, you must have been out somewhere last night."

"How do you know I didn't get up early and leave this morning?"

"Kyle."

"God, you're fun to tease." Laughing, Kyle relented. "All right. I spent the night in the city."

"Oh?" Nancy inquired, arching her neatly contoured brows as she sat up a little straighter. "A little wanderlust?"

"Is it all right if I go out once in a while, Nance?" Kyle asked sharply, suddenly not certain she wanted to talk about her evening.

"Of course." Nancy ignored Kyle's warning tone and her sudden frown. She'd known Kyle too long to be worried about her quick temper. She flashed hot and burned fast and she never held a grudge. "I'm always trying to get you to go out."

"You mean you're always trying to fix me up with someone." Kyle shifted, irritated, and leaned over to put her glass down on the deck. She wasn't really interested in drinking.

"Well, what's wrong with that?" Nancy feigned a hurt look and reached for a cigarette. She looked expectantly at Kyle, who reached into her pocket on cue and pulled out her lighter.

"Don't be dense, Nancy." Kyle leaned forward and touched the flame to her friend's cigarette, catching the twinkle in her eyes. She shook her head when Nancy held out her slim gold cigarette case to Kyle. "Trying to quit. As to you *fixing me up*—first of all, I can get my own dates. Secondly, half the time the people you're trying to fix me up with are men."

"So?" Nancy drew deeply on her cigarette and looked out over the two acres of her prime coastal property. "Men aren't all that bad, you know."

"Nance, we've been having this conversation since our freshman year in college." Kyle sighed. "I never said men were bad—I just don't feel the same way you do about them."

"I can remember when you didn't mind sleeping with them."

"You have a long memory, then." Kyle could tell her old friend was in a mood to bait her. Whenever the subject of Kyle's sexual preferences came up, they went through the same arguments. Nancy argued that Kyle's choice of partners was limiting, but Kyle was never sure who Nancy thought was limited by them—Kyle or herself. "You know it has nothing to do with sleeping with men or not. It's that I prefer women. There is a very real difference. Women are not substitutes, alternatives, or second choices for me. They're—"

"A positive first choice," Nancy finished for her. "Did you read that somewhere, or are you writing propaganda for all the lesbian groups in the area?"

"Are you trying to piss me off? Because it's working."

"Oh, all right," her friend replied contritely. "I know, I know. It's important to you—that distinction. I just don't see why you have to be so hard-line about this gay thing. You could settle down with some nice, unassuming guy, get a few of the advantages it would bring, and have a lover on the side."

Kyle tried for the hundredth time to explain. "I wouldn't want to live with someone I didn't love. *If* it ever happened, I'd want that person to be the only one. And I don't intend to hide who I am."

"Isn't that a little unrealistic? After all, people aren't perfect, you know. No one person would ever be enough."

"I'm not you, Nance." Kyle knew that her friend had affairs outside her marriage, and she also knew that Nancy's husband, Roger, was aware of them. Roger and Nancy had agreed years ago that both were free to explore as long as they weren't serious about anyone. It seemed to work well for them, and Kyle respected that. She shook her head stubbornly. "It's not right for me."

"Oh, Kyle," Nance said in exasperation. "You're impossibly romantic."

"No, I'm not." Kyle smiled and refilled Nancy's glass.

"Do you think you're going to find the woman of your dreams in those bars you go to when you can't stand the silence of your own home any longer?"

"It's not quite as easy for me to meet people as it is for you, you know." Anger flashed in Kyle's eyes. Her friend was getting a little too close to the quick today, of all days. "*I* can't just go to some respectable society function and pick someone up."

"Touché," Nancy replied softly. She leaned back in her lounge chair and sipped her wine. "All right. So did you meet someone?"

"Yes."

"Is it any different this time than all the other times?" Nancy knew she was pushing Kyle's limits, but she didn't care. She had watched Kyle struggle with her loneliness for years, and she truly wanted to see her friend find some kind of happiness. Maybe she wanted Kyle to be happy because she couldn't seem to find any satisfaction in her own life. "Did you find someone you can stand to be with the next day?"

"Can *you* always stand them the next day?" Kyle retaliated.

"Usually I don't have to worry about it." Nancy grimaced. "They have to go home to their wives. Besides, I asked you first."

"The wine is gone."

"In the kitchen. I put more on ice." Nancy followed her friend's muscular form into the house, noting with a practiced eye the powerful but graceful way she moved. She thought about how Kyle's body would feel on top of hers, and she knew she would like it. She also knew Kyle would never consider such a thing with her. Roger and Kyle were friends, and Kyle, unfortunately, was a woman of integrity.

Kyle returned carrying a fresh bottle of chilled white wine. She removed the cork, filled Nancy's glass and half of her own, then leaned back against the railing in the sun, her ankles crossed in front of her.

"Nancy," she said seriously, "why are you always going on at me about this? I don't bother you about your life, do I?"

"Why should you? I have a great home, plenty of security, all the money I need, and a husband who doesn't mind my...ah...flirtations."

"I don't believe for a second that's all you want. You're intelligent, talented, warm, and loving. All those nice *things* you have can't be enough, or you wouldn't be sleeping with every horny guy you meet."

"I haven't slept with all of them, Kyle," Nancy said demurely. "Not yet."

Kyle laughed. "Oh hell, I give up."

"Good. Now tell me about your latest. *Was* it any different?"

"Yes." *For me at least.*

"Well?" Nancy waited expectantly.

Kyle turned to look down across the bluff to the ocean and was forced to shut her eyes against the brisk wind that brought tears to them. Behind closed lids, she saw Dane's face. "I went to a leather bar last night."

Nancy sat up straight in her chair. "Do you mean an S/M club?"

Kyle nodded, her back still turned.

"Really." Nancy was intrigued. "So, tell me."

"I met this woman and I went home with her. A lot happened. I felt differently with her than I've ever felt before. I felt things about *myself* I've never felt before."

"Did she beat you or something?" Nancy asked in amazement.

"No, it wasn't like that." Kyle turned and regarded Nancy calmly. "It was like being in another world. We were making love, except so much more was happening. I almost didn't know myself. It was physical, and emotional, and something else, too."

"What else?"

"I don't know." Kyle ran a hand through her hair in frustration. "And I don't know how I'm going to find out."

CHAPTER SIX

Three weeks later

K yle put down her stripping knife and sighed. "Nance."

"Hmm?" Nancy replied absently, her mind on the design she was outlining on the door of an armoire.

"About that party tonight—"

"Yes," Nancy murmured, still engrossed in the stencil.

"I don't think I can make it."

Nancy looked up quickly. "Bullshit. You just don't want to."

"It's not that I don't want to." *Well, not totally anyway.* "I just don't feel like meeting a lot of straight doctors."

"Well, all those straight doctors have wives, you know. Well, at least the men do." Nancy waggled her brows and came to stand beside Kyle. "And maybe some of the women, too."

"I don't want to meet somebody's *wife*," Kyle stated with exaggerated emphasis. "I don't even want to meet the doctors who happen to be women. Roger does know a few female doctors, doesn't he?"

"There might be one or two, but *I* don't usually notice." Nancy gave Kyle a beseeching look. "Please come?"

"Well—"

"It's been nearly a month since you went into the city. I know—I've checked the calendar. You must be ready for a little diversion by now."

"Actually, there was something else I wanted to do tonight," Kyle replied with uncharacteristic hesitation. "There's this meeting I read about—kind of a...a discussion group. I thought I might go."

"A meeting? Like AA or something?" Nancy sounded horrified.

"No, nothing like that. Besides, drinking's never been my problem. I *am* down to a few cigarettes a day, though, so don't pick a fight."

"Ooh, cranky, are we?" Nancy nudged Kyle's hip with hers. "So what then—what's this group about?"

"It's about how we use power in our lives."

"Power." Nancy shot her a probing look. "You mean sexual power—the S/M thing again, right?"

"That's part of it." Kyle tried not to sound defensive. Nancy was often a pain in the ass, but Kyle had never known her to be prejudiced about choices that differed from her own.

"You're really serious about this thing?" Nancy narrowed her eyes. "I thought maybe you'd gotten it out of your system after that one night. You never said anything else about it."

"I'm serious about finding out about it."

"Have you seen her again—the woman you spent the night with?"

Kyle shook her head.

"You want to?" This time Nancy's question was gentle. She'd seen a shadow of sadness pass across her friend's face. She hated it when Kyle hurt.

"Yeah." Kyle picked up her knife and turned it aimlessly in her hand. *I still think about that night. I still see her. I still feel her.*

"And I suppose calling her and asking for a...date...is out of the question?"

"I don't know." Kyle grimaced. "I'm not sure what's supposed to come next. But, even if I wanted to call her...I don't know her last name *or* her number."

"Well," Nancy remarked with a hint of sarcasm, "I can see you two spent a lot of time *talking*."

"No, we didn't." Kyle regarded her without ire. "But we *shared* a lot."

"And you think going to this meeting will help how?"

"I'm not sure it will." Kyle shrugged. "But I need some kind of answers, because just *wondering* about it all the time is making me a little nuts."

"Why not just go back to the club and..." Nancy flashed on an image of Kyle in the arms of a mysterious stranger and felt an irrational surge of jealousy. She forced herself to say what she thought Kyle needed to hear. "Well, find her again or someone else to...be with."

Because she's the one I want. Kyle tossed her stripping knife back onto the counter. "I don't think she's interested in someone who doesn't have a clue about what's going on."

Nancy picked up her brush and turned back to her design. "Well, I suppose I'll have other parties."

Dane strode rapidly across the room, her voice tight, her back stiff with the effort to contain her anger. "There is no way, no *way*, that I'm going to some discussion group tonight."

Caroline sighed resignedly and led the dog into the open crate.

"Why not?"

Dane's blue eyes flashed.

"Because it's always the same thing. A bunch of intellectuals sitting around discussing the *politics* of power and what they think about it. It's always what they think, never what they feel. It's an academic discourse by people who are afraid to do more than just *talk* about it. And they always have such a superior attitude about anyone who actually does something to find out what it's like."

"That's not fair, Dane." Caroline looked at her friend in surprise. The vehemence in her voice was startling. Dane was usually so cool. "Anne and I are going—and we do more than talk about it."

"Good. You can be the guinea pigs, then."

"How do you expect women to discover how they feel if no one who knows something will get it out in the open? It's like refusing to talk to heterosexuals about being gay." Caroline crossed her arms and sat down on the corner of the desk. "Ignorance doesn't go away by itself."

"Let them come to the club, then. Let them go to a scene party," Dane persisted. *Let them take a chance.*

"Maybe they're afraid to," Caroline said quietly. "It's as threatening for some people to go to a leather bar or a scene party as it once was to go to a regular gay club. Just because you had to find out by yourself doesn't mean it still has to be that way. Maybe you can help other women understand."

Dane stared at Caroline stubbornly. "I don't feel like telling a bunch of strangers what I do in bed."

"You don't have to, and you know it." Caroline couldn't hide her exasperation. "But you could talk about *why* you do what you do in bed. Come on, Dane, what are you afraid of?"

"I'm not the one who's afraid."

"Then why not come?"

"Christ, you're persistent."

"How do you think I got Anne away from you?"

Dane grinned reluctantly. "I'll *think* about it, okay?"

Caroline smiled at the glimmer of progress. "Okay."

Kyle checked her reflection in the mirror for the tenth time, astonished at how nervous she was about going to this meeting. It wasn't as if it was exactly a foreign experience. She'd been a member of the gay and lesbian group on campus when she was in college, and even after that, she'd spent some time at the gay and lesbian community center. It had been fun tossing ideas around and being part of the social community. Tonight felt different, though. She was a newcomer and not at all certain what to expect. Still, she wanted to go, needed to know more about her own feelings and if other women shared them.

The memory of that single night with Dane haunted her in a way no other encounter ever had. She thought about the way she'd lain helplessly bound, her body on fire, waiting, praying, for Dane to set her free. She touched herself and imagined Dane's hands teasing her until she was wet and hard and ready to explode. When she ached to come, she heard Dane's voice tell her to wait, and she tried to recapture that sharp edge of brilliant desire. Most often she failed, although her climax was often so powerful it left her weak and trembling. *Yeah, she's provided more fantasy material than anyone else I've ever known. But I can only get off thinking about her for so long.*

Despite the profound pleasure she had experienced with Dane, Kyle had to admit that the drive to explore those new feelings went beyond her desire for sex. She felt that an essential part of herself needed to be expressed...and that perhaps sex was just one means of communicating something far more fundamental than just physical pleasure. She regarded the woman in the black jeans and leather vest staring out at her from the glass. The face and the body were familiar. Tonight, however, she wasn't entirely certain she knew who looked back.

But she intended to find out.

When she pulled her bike between several cars at the address she'd noted for the meeting, she realized it was a private residence. She hadn't expected the meeting to be in someone's apartment. That seemed far too personal and a great deal more intimate than she wanted to get. She'd been hoping to find a back seat somewhere and just listen. She hesitated at the bottom of the steep wooden staircase that led up a shrub-covered slope to the slightly ramshackle house.

Maybe this isn't such a good idea.

A younger woman wearing a tight black T-shirt, denim jacket, and blue jeans ripped in decidedly provocative locations passed Kyle and started up the steps. She stopped, turned back, and gave Kyle a friendly smile.

"You coming up?"

"Uh...I don't know. I saw this notice about a discussion group."

"Right," the woman said, extending her hand. "I'm Joan. This is the place."

Kyle shook the petite blond's hand. She was appealingly boyish-looking with short spiked hair and red high-tops. A thin braided leather bracelet encircled the wrist she thrust forward.

"Thanks, I'm Kyle." When she hesitated the other woman gave her a questioning look. "Uh—you know, I'm not sure I should be here. I mean, I don't know much about it."

"That's the idea." Joan grinned while taking in Kyle's heavy black motorcycle boots, black jeans, and leather jacket. "No one will *know* you don't know anything, and no one will ask you anything. You can talk or just listen. There won't be a test or anything."

Kyle laughed and willed herself to relax. "Okay, I'm with you then."

She followed Joan to a second floor apartment where they were admitted by a well-muscled Asian woman with a warm smile, a hearty welcome, and a bone-crushing handshake. From there, Kyle found herself in a comfortably appointed living room where five or six women were already seated. To Kyle's relief, they all looked like regular dykes to her, the kind of women she might meet in any club. Several glanced at her and nodded before returning to their conversations.

Finding a place on the floor, Kyle rested her back against the arm of a couch that looked like it had seen better days and surreptitiously took stock of the room's other occupants. The women ranged in age from early twenties on up. Denim, boots, and leather were plentiful, but a couple of women wore skin-tight tops displaying more than a tease of cleavage, even tighter hip huggers showing plenty of enticing skin, make-up, and decidedly feminine jewelry. Kyle caught one, a pretty brunette wearing a narrow leather strap on her left wrist, eyeing her with frank speculation. When Kyle met her gaze, the woman raised an eyebrow and gave Kyle a sultry look that had her blood racing. The response was totally involuntary, but for one brief instant, Kyle pictured herself on her knees in front of the slender brunette and imagined the glint of candlelight reflecting off the handcuffs that bound her own wrists. *Jesus Christ!*

Quickly, Kyle averted her gaze, but she swore she heard a soft, throaty laugh. To her relief, a woman entered carrying a six-pack of beer and another of soda.

"Hi, everyone. I'm Dana, for those who don't know me. Help yourself to the drinks." She passed the cans around and sat next to

Joan on another sofa across from Kyle. "And for the benefit of those who haven't been to one of these meetings...a group of us have been getting together the last six months or so to talk about how we perceive power in our lives."

"You mean S/M, don't you?" one woman asked.

Dana nodded. "Basically, yes. Except that term is sort of limiting, because not everyone has the same idea about its definition. Some take it to mean BD—bondage and discipline, some see it in terms of rigid roles...master/slave or dominant and submissive. Some of us just like to explore it in sex play. There are lots of different ways for power to be expressed." She laughed. "Which is as good a place to start as any, I guess. Before we talk about specifics, I think we should find out how we see the central issue—power."

Kyle was surprised to hear the diverse opinions of the group members regarding the role of power in relationships. At first it seemed as if each woman had a different idea, but as time went on, it became clear that everyone agreed on one thing: all relationships were based on some kind of exchange of power, no matter whether it was defined that way or not. Sometimes it was very subtle, like who made the first move in lovemaking, while other times, it was more obviously based on role playing.

As the conversation flowed back and forth, Kyle was struck by the wide range of concepts and apparent experience. It was obvious that for some women the issue was sociological or political, and for others much more a lifestyle or sexual issue. Two women across from her, obviously a couple, talked easily about their own relationship and how they perceived the exchange of power in their lives. They admitted that it was an important part of their sexual expression.

Kyle listened with interest as the older of the two, an attractive, athletic-looking woman in worn chinos and a frayed cotton shirt, responded to the claim that too much emphasis was placed on sex by power-oriented women.

"I think that sexual feelings are a much bigger part of any relationship than most of us care to admit," Caroline suggested calmly. "It's not just how you make love, or how often, but how you react physically to everything around you. Appreciating the way your lover looks in leather is sexual. Fantasizing about strangers in the subway is sexual. Feeling strong and confident when you wear boots is sexual. Those feelings are there all day long; it's just that we don't call them sexual."

"Are you saying that women aren't sexual enough?" Kyle asked, intrigued by the woman's train of thought.

Caroline smiled at Kyle, who had been silent up until then.

"I'm saying that women are much *more* sexual than we appreciate, because we put too much emphasis on definitions. And our definition of sexual is very narrow...most of the time we think of it only as what we do in bed." Caroline shrugged. "I think we are sexual, and sexually powerful, all the time."

Other women picked up the thread, and Kyle soon discovered she had more questions than answers. Nevertheless, as she listened, she felt she was making contact with an important part of herself. She was surprised and disappointed when Dana announced that it was after eleven and time to wrap it up. The date and place of the next meeting was decided, and Kyle made a mental note of the information. Once outside, she found herself on the stairs just behind the couple who had been across from her all evening.

"Excuse me," she said, catching up to them on the street. "I really liked what you two had to say tonight."

"Thanks. It was a really good group." Anne smiled. "I'm Anne, by the way. And this is Caroline."

"Kyle Kirk." Kyle stopped in front of her motorcycle, and they stopped with her, apparently in no great hurry. "I'm glad that women want to get together and talk about it."

Caroline laughed and slid her arm around Anne's waist. "Some of us even like to do more than talk."

"Yeah." Kyle grinned. "I got that impression."

"We're going to unwind at the club for a while. You?" Caroline asked.

"I was thinking about it," Kyle replied. Then, because she felt comfortable with them after listening to them talk about their lives, she added, "I'm still not sure what this all means for me."

"There's no hurry, you know," Caroline said kindly.

Kyle heard Dane's deep voice. *I'm not rushing you.* She shrugged. "Maybe not. But the way I feel sometimes..." She shook her head sheepishly. "Sorry. I'm probably not making any sense."

"As a matter of fact," Anne said with surprising gentleness, "you are. I remember how confused I was for a while."

Caroline gave her lover a quizzical look. "And it's just a club. Besides, the only way to find out about anything is to go find out."

"Don't get her started," Anne said with obvious affection as she gave Caroline a quick hug. "Really, though, Kyle, you can meet us there. We can all have a beer or something."

"I don't have anywhere else to be," Kyle admitted. She made a decision and nodded. "I'd like that. I'll see you there—Leathers, right?"

Surprised that Kyle knew the club, Caroline nodded. *Not such a novice then.* She took Anne's hand. "Yep. See you soon."

"Will do."

As Kyle buckled on her helmet and started her motorcycle, she admitted to herself that she was hoping to run into someone else there. She might not have all the answers. She might not even understand all that she felt. But she knew what she wanted, and what she wanted was to spend another night with Dane. Thinking about it called the heat to her blood and her stomach quivered with the first lick of arousal. *God, let her be there. And let her be alone.*

CHAPTER SEVEN

Kyle parked her bike at the end of the line in front of Leathers just as Caroline and Anne were getting out of a green camouflage-painted Jeep Wrangler. She called out a greeting, and they met on the sidewalk in front of the club.

"I take it you've been here before," Caroline probed.

"Once. A few weeks ago."

"And?"

"I had a great time." Kyle shrugged a little sheepishly.

Caroline looked as if she was about to ask another question, but Anne tugged her arm to quiet her. "Come on, hon. Don't put her on the spot."

Kyle laughed and Caroline joined in.

"She's right," Caroline acknowledged as they walked toward the entrance. "I never know when to quit. It's not that I'm nosy—"

"Yes, you are," Anne interjected.

"Okay—I am," Caroline swatted Anne's butt affectionately, "but I'm also really interested in how women feel about these things."

"I don't mind the questions," Kyle remarked as she paid her cover charge and got the back of her hand stamped with a small red X. "And I feel the same way—interested, I mean—in what others have experienced. If I didn't, I wouldn't have come to the group tonight."

"See," Caroline crowed, giving Anne a victorious look. "She said I could be nosy."

Anne shook her head at Kyle. "You're in trouble now."

As they went through the ritual of forging a path to the bar through tightly pressed bodies, getting the harried bartender's attention, and staking claim to one of the few remaining unoccupied tables, Kyle scanned the room. It was filled with women, but she saw no one she recognized. The wave of disappointment that followed was keen, but, at the same time, her pulse stirred with anticipation. She'd been lonely, she realized, these last few weeks—lonely for the company of those who understood her struggles without need for explanation or excuse.

She loved Nancy and once, long ago, had thought she'd been in love with her. But they'd never slept together, probably because every time they'd come close, Nancy had been drunk. Kyle had worried that it was alcohol and not affection that had fueled her friend's ardor, and she'd held out for a time when Nancy would reach for her out of clear-eyed desire and not just dazed lust. That moment had never come, and then Nancy had met Roger, and it was time to move on. Kyle had always known that Nancy's friendship was something she could count on, even if half the time Nancy's volatile temperament drove her crazy. Still, there were some critical issues Nancy could not understand, because they were too far beyond the realm of her experience. Being an outsider was one of them.

Kyle looked around the room and sensed a kinship with these strangers that she did not share with her best friend—the one woman in her life she loved. If she dwelled on that irony too long, she'd *want* to drink just to forget it.

Instead, she shook the dark thoughts away and studied Anne and Caroline, who sat close together across the tiny table crowded with their glasses, bottles, and a shallow saucer doubling as an ashtray. Anne's hand was curled around the inside of Caroline's thigh barely an inch south of decorum. The subtle show of possessiveness intrigued Kyle. She'd been trying to figure them out all evening. Caroline—older, seemingly more aggressive— gave off top vibes, but Anne—decidedly more butch *looking* than her lover—seemed anything but submissive. Kyle flashed to the brunette at the meeting, anyone's picture of femininity, and knew without a doubt that she would be dominant in a scene. *And I bottomed for Dane, and I'm hardly passive* or *femme. Oh, hell. So looks can be deceptive. Like that's news?*

Smiling inwardly at her own unconscious stereotyping, Kyle asked, "How come you two went to the discussion group?"

"What do you mean?" Caroline's expression was curious and not the least bit defensive.

"Well, you're obviously not newcomers to the scene, so why bother?"

"I think it's because we still have things to learn about ourselves and our relationship." Anne looked at Caroline, who nodded in agreement. "Sometimes sharing ideas, questioning our unconscious assumptions, makes us see our own lives in a different light."

"We end up exploring new aspects of our life together," Caroline noted, grinning at Anne, who pretended to roll her eyes. "How about you, Kyle? Did it help?"

"Sometimes, I almost feel like I'm coming out all over again." Kyle regarded the crowded room pensively. "I haven't given my own life much thought for a long time. I've pretty much been going along, never considering whether I *liked* the way it has worked out." She shrugged and grimaced faintly. "That sounds a little feeble, doesn't it?"

"Not at all," Caroline said quickly. "It just sounds honest."

"And you're here now," Anne added, "and that's what counts."

Feeling suddenly much lighter at heart, Kyle reached for her untouched bottle of beer. "Yeah, I guess that's true."

After a minute, Anne turned to her lover. "Are you planning to ask me to dance?"

"Is that what you want?" Caroline asked casually, regarding Anne with a tilt of her head and an appraising glance. She dropped her eyes to the hand in her lap, then lifted them to meet her lover's steadily.

Anne's lips parted, as if in surprise, and then she said quietly, "Yes, it is."

Caroline leaned close and whispered something against Anne's ear that Kyle could not hear. Whatever it was, Anne's quick flush of color was visible even in the hazy light tinted blue with smoke and dust. She nodded once, got up from the table, and disappeared into the mass of milling people.

When Caroline glanced at Kyle, Kyle shrugged. "Sorry. Didn't mean to stare."

"Really?" The corner of Caroline's mouth lifted slightly. "You don't like to watch?"

Kyle carefully swallowed the mouthful of beer she'd almost choked on. "Ah—well, I...ah, fuck." She laughed and ran a hand over her face. "Are you inviting me to?"

"No," Caroline's smile grew, "but if you're into that, I can point you in the right direction."

"Why do I get the feeling you're enjoying my not-so-blissful ignorance?" Kyle complained good-naturedly.

"Because," Caroline answered seriously, "I have a feeling you're in this for real, and I don't think you'll be ignorant for long. Plus I like you." She stood and her eyes traveled around the room. "Now, I've got to go."

Her voice had dropped a notch, and Kyle caught a glimmer of heat in her eyes.

"I have a woman waiting to be taken care of."

Kyle watched her slip away in the direction Anne had gone and couldn't help but imagine just how Caroline intended to do that. She didn't think about it too hard, because just being in the club had ignited the low hum of arousal in the pit of her stomach. She didn't need any *more* stimulation; she was already distractingly aware of the pressure between her thighs.

"Back again, huh?"

The voice close to Kyle's ear was unmistakable, and her stomach convulsed. Kyle turned to regard Dane, who looked better than Kyle had remembered in the throes of her frantic fantasies. Tonight Dane was dressed in full leathers, from her pants to the vest that covered her otherwise bare chest.

"Hello." Kyle's throat was suddenly dry, and she hoped she wasn't staring like a fool. Or grinning like an idiot. *God, she is so hot. And so much better than any memory.* "Yeah, here I am."

"This your first time back?" Dane sat down in the empty chair next to Kyle, drained her bottle, and absently passed it from hand to hand. *Have you found other lovers? Has someone else touched you the way I did?*

"Yes," Kyle said, watching Dane carefully. She seemed distracted, distant, unapproachable. And beneath the cool façade, Kyle thought she might have looked unhappy. She resisted the urge to touch her, and realized that she'd done that a lot the last time they'd been together. Wanted to touch her and hadn't.

Dane looked up suddenly and caught the tail edge of a question in Kyle's eyes. "What?"

"Do you ever let anyone top you?"

For a few desperate seconds, Kyle thought Dane would get up and leave. A curtain fell across her sharply sculpted features, which became completely still and totally unreadable. Kyle held her breath, feeling slightly sick. *Don't go. Tell me to fuck off. Tell me it's none of my business. Just don't go.*

Dane smiled slightly and pushed her bottle out in front of her. "Want another beer?"

Kyle drew a shallow, shaky breath. "I'm still working on this one."

"So why are you here?"

Looking for you. But she wasn't about to risk saying anything else that might drive Dane away. As close as they'd been during those few intense hours, she couldn't seem to reach her now. "I was at a meeting earlier, and I came over after with some women I met."

"Oh, man, not you, too."

"What do you mean?" Kyle asked carefully. Dane seemed edgy, restless, and a little angry, although Kyle sensed that the anger was not directed at her.

"Oh, my friends were trying to get me to go to one tonight." Dane sighed and looked around the club. "Not for me. I'm tired of all the talk." Her expression said she was more than tired.

"Dane?" Kyle stepped onto uncertain ground, knowing a mistake here would cost her. Cost her perhaps the one person she really wanted.

"Hmm?"

"It's pretty tough to talk in here anyway."

Dane narrowed her eyes. "I thought you liked to talk?"

"Sometimes I'd rather listen."

Dane pushed her chair back from the table, and Kyle watched her stand, her heart pounding. When Dane shifted out of sight, Kyle wasn't certain she hadn't left. Disappointment sliced through her, sharp enough to draw blood. Then warm, strong fingers brushed the side of her neck and slid beneath her collar. A thumb traced the muscle along the edge of her jaw. Fingertips glided over the surface of her collarbone. Kyle sat very still while a hot fist of desire formed in the pit of her stomach.

Warm breath against her skin, soft lips against her ear. A low, husky voice.

"Let's dance."

It was like the first night, but slower, almost torturously slow. They danced to one song after another, not talking, while Dane's hands on Kyle's hips guided her against Dane's body. Kyle massaged the muscles in Dane's back while they moved to the music, remembering the way she had clung to Dane as she'd come in Dane's arms. She groaned involuntarily.

"Are you always so ready?" Dane murmured, her own breath hitching as the sound of Kyle's excitement tore through her. *Do you ever let any one top you?* The question had taken her by surprise—no, more than that—had stunned her with its audacity. And the response that had leapt unbidden to her lips had terrified her. *I might let you.*

"You make me want to come just looking at you."

Dane bit Kyle's neck and drew another groan. "You need to learn a little discipline."

"All right." Kyle's vision was already hazy.

Dane stepped away because she was in danger of losing control—of pushing Kyle into the corner and feasting on her. "I need a beer."

Kyle nearly protested. Her legs were leaden, her arousal so keen she ached. She saw Dane's eyes, brilliant in the dim light, fixed on hers. *You know I'm about to come apart here, don't you?* She saw something else in those blue depths, too. She saw need and want as sharp as her own. The power she experienced knowing that Dane wanted her made her daring. She turned so that no one nearby could see and ran a hand slowly down the center of Dane's chest, over her stomach, and down the tight rise of leather over her crotch. She sensed rather than felt Dane shudder. "What about my lesson?"

Dane grasped Kyle's wrist and pressed the questing hand hard between her legs before pulling it away. Her expression didn't change even when a spasm of pleasure rippled down her thighs. "If you can manage to be good, I *might* let you pay for that impertinence later."

Kyle met Dane's eyes for an instant and then, unaccountably, looked down. "Whatever you say."

"I *say*," Dane managed to repeat evenly, "let's get that beer."

When they reached the table, Caroline and Anne had returned.

"Glad you could make it to the group tonight, Dane," Caroline said sarcastically before Dane and Kyle were even seated.

"Ran short on time," Dane replied tersely as she settled into a chair.

"I'll bet."

Confused by the sudden tension, Kyle regarded Dane and Caroline uneasily. *So—they're friends. I guess.*

Anne, also clearly uncomfortable, tried for a change in subject. "I see you two have met," she began.

"Yes." Dane answered quickly, clearly disinclined to explain anything further. "I'm going for beers? Anybody need one?"

When Caroline failed to answer and Anne got a panicked look on her face, Kyle half turned in the direction they were both staring. Someone she'd never seen before—a woman with keenly honed features and slicked-back raven hair—stood just beside her. Everything about her was austere and razor-sharp—from her tight-fitting black leather pants that accentuated her thin, rangy figure to her perfectly ironed white shirt with sleeves rolled to mid-forearm, exposing sinewy tendons and taut muscles. Long, slim fingers hooked loosely around a wide black leather belt.

"Hello, Anne, Caroline." Her voice was smooth, yet somehow dangerous.

To Kyle, she appeared dangerous in a way that Dane, for all her cool aloofness, never did. *It's her eyes.* The stranger's eyes were flat, black disks that showed not the slightest trace of warmth.

Caroline looked anxiously at Dane and then over at the new arrival. "Hello, Brad."

"I thought you might introduce me to your new friend here," the cool, husky voice continued, her hand now resting lightly on Kyle's shoulder.

Kyle shifted in her seat, surprised by the unanticipated contact, but the hand remained firmly on her shoulder, massaging lightly. She glanced at Dane. Dane's face was set, her jaw tight, and Kyle noticed a slight tremor in the hand that held an empty beer bottle.

"This is Kyle, Brad," Anne interjected in the sudden silence. "Kyle, this is Terry Bradley—Brad to most of us."

"Hello, Kyle," Brad said softly. Suggestively. Then she pulled a chair from an adjoining table and sat down on Kyle's right. Stretching her legs out, her thigh against Kyle's, she tipped back slightly in her chair and slowly studied Kyle's face. Then she dropped her gaze, lingering on the tanned triangle of skin exposed by Kyle's open-collared shirt before moving downward.

Since no words seemed required, Kyle simply nodded a greeting, acutely aware of Dane's stiff silence. She tried to catch Dane's eye, but Dane stared fixedly ahead, her expression inscrutable.

Brad smiled slightly, a crooked grin that might have softened her features if it hadn't held a hint of cruelty. Just as quickly, the smile disappeared, and she turned her attention to Dane as if seeing her for the first time. "And how is the legendary Dane Jorgensen these days?"

Dane acknowledged Brad by tipping her bottle infinitesimally in her direction, but she did not meet her eyes. "Same as always, Brad. Fine."

Brad laughed, her gaze shifting to Anne and Caroline. "I haven't seen much of you two lately. Is the dog business keeping you busy?"

Her words seemed friendly, but Kyle detected an edge of condescension in her voice.

"Don't you keep up anymore?" Caroline replied nonchalantly. "Business has been great." She looked pointedly at Dane, trying to gauge her friend's response to Brad's presence. She knew very well that Dane went out of her way to avoid Terry Bradley. And she knew why. "We've all been working hard, and we just wanted to come out to unwind tonight."

"Oh, yes," Brad remarked slowly. "I *did* notice that Baron took best in show in Georgia. Things can't be too bad. Still a one-dog show, though."

Dane stared at Brad, her face tight. "Baron deserves it, and you know it."

"Oh yes, I know it." Brad dismissed Dane with a shrug and dropped her hand onto Kyle's leg. "And how about you, Kyle? Are you into dogs, too?"

"No—furniture." Kyle didn't have much room to maneuver around the crowded table, and when she edged away as much as she could, Brad only slid her hand higher on her thigh.

Dane rose suddenly, her body tense. She looked down at Kyle and Brad, her eyes as dark and impenetrable now as Brad's. "You should be careful how you choose your company, Kyle. Some people aren't worth the effort."

Kyle jerked in surprise. *What the hell is going on?* "Dane—"

"What's the matter, Dane?" Brad asked, a hint of challenge in her voice. "Lost your competitive spirit?"

"I'm not competing with you, Brad." Dane smiled tightly. "I don't have to." She turned abruptly and within seconds had disappeared into the crowd.

Anne and Caroline both stood. Caroline looked pointedly at Kyle. "We're leaving soon, Kyle. You're welcome to stay at our place tonight, if you don't want to drive."

"Thanks, no," Kyle said quietly, stunned by the quick turn of events. "I haven't had much to drink. I'd rather just head home, too."

Brad's grip tightened on Kyle's leg. "You don't have to leave so early, do you?"

Finally able to move, Kyle twisted out from under the table and rose. "I'm afraid I do."

"Some other time, then," Brad said congenially, draping her arm over Kyle's now empty chair.

"Perhaps." Kyle nodded once, then followed in Caroline and Anne's wake toward the exit.

Brad sipped her drink slowly and watched Kyle leave, smiling to herself in satisfaction.

CHAPTER EIGHT

"Do you ever let anyone top you?"
"What's the matter, Dane? Lost your competitive spirit?"

Dane drove rapidly through the city, her mind careening from image to image—Kyle, her eyes tender and warm, awakening by her side; Brad, arrogant and cool, a possessive hand on Kyle's shoulder, taunting her as only Brad could. It had been so good to see Kyle, better than she'd remembered, and she'd let down her guard. When they'd danced, she'd allowed herself to imagine not just the hot flood of passion when their bodies joined, but the peace that would follow in the aftermath. A serenity she'd felt with Kyle and no one else—not in years. And then Brad had appeared, and she'd put her hands on Kyle.

Swearing under her breath, Dane switched on the radio, hoping the music would drown out her thoughts and block the images she couldn't forget. It had been months since she had last seen Brad, but the response Brad provoked was undiminished by time. She had only to see her cool black eyes, to hear her smooth, seductive voice, and she was flooded with impotence and rage, and beneath that, fear. Brad was always so damn sure she could have anything she wanted, and in her heart, Dane still believed that she probably could. Hating herself for her inability to control her emotions at these moments, faced with her own undeniable weakness, she wanted only to escape. Anger and self-loathing simmered close to the surface, eroding her hard-won sense of balance.

Why can she still do this to me?

Abruptly, she swerved into an empty space at the curb, realizing for the first time that she had driven unconsciously to a familiar neighborhood she hadn't visited in almost half a year. She sat for a second staring at the three-story Victorian set back from the street. A single light, almost a beacon, flickered in a window tucked high under the eaves. Dane saw the light, but she was thinking of a place without windows, without sound, without thought.

Even as she hesitated, she knew what she would do. There were too many emotions tearing at her—anger, helplessness, despair—memories so painful it hurt to breathe. She couldn't stop the images pounding in her head, and there was only one sure way she knew to push them away. She carefully locked her car and tucked the keys into her front pocket. With a determined stride, she crossed the darkened street, climbed the steps to the front door, and knocked firmly.

A moment passed, a moment when Dane could have changed her mind, but she had already stopped thinking. Had already surrendered. A large woman, her broad features accentuated by short, close-cropped hair, opened the door. Her sharp dark eyes searched Dane's face, undoubtedly noting the agitation Dane tried to hide. Wordlessly, she stepped back, motioning Dane in with a barely perceptible nod of her head. Her smile was of satisfaction, not welcome.

"It's been a long time, Dane. Things must be going well for you these days." Her voice held a bite of sarcasm, because she knew that Dane visited her only when in the throes of some intolerable emotional turmoil. Dane came to her only when driven to it—only when she could no longer endure her own vulnerability. Dane came to exorcise her demons.

Dane had nothing to say. In a bleak, dispassionate way, she hated this woman whose power over her, willingly given, embodied the essence of her own failure. When she could not obliterate her own desperate needs, she sought physical escape. When she could not deny her own weakness, she sought physical punishment.

"What's your safe word?" the woman asked sharply, having no desire for conversation. Already she felt the excitement that

Dane's presence always aroused in her. Dane was so cool, so controlled, so perfect in everyone's eyes. But *she* knew; she knew Dane as no one else would ever know her, for she had seen the depths of her despair. And before long, she would witness Dane's surrender to it.

"The same." Dane's voice was low, tight, curt. *Just do it. God, don't make me wait. I can't stand the way it hurts.*

She suppressed a sigh of relief when the woman turned and headed for the staircase at the rear of the house. She followed without needing to be told. She'd done this before. They climbed to the third floor where a single door faced them at the end of a short, narrow hall. With the sense of being an observer, eerily removed from the events, Dane watched the familiar figure sort through a ring of keys, unlock the door, and gesture for Dane to precede her inside.

Unhesitatingly, Dane entered.

The room was surprisingly warm. Dane stood in total blackness for a moment, knowing that the darkness was enhanced by the absence of windows. Suddenly a dim red glow suffused the room as a switch was flipped on behind her. Reflexively, sweat broke out on the entire surface of her body, and her pulse quickened. She did not turn around when she heard the door close resoundingly. The lights were arranged in recessed ceiling tracks in such a way that much of the space around her was in shadow. There was a deep carpet on the floor and thick insulation on the walls, a combination that absorbed all sound. No one would hear her cries, only the one person who would not care. No one would witness her defeat; only she would know.

Left alone with her thoughts in the womb-like atmosphere, Dane quickly lost track of time. She waited, breathing shallowly, eyes nearly closed.

"Take off your clothes."

Dane jerked infinitesimally at the voice that cut through the silence from somewhere in the shadows. She reached toward her vest.

"Slowly."

With trembling hands, Dane worked each snap open on the damp leather. She pulled it off and dropped it behind her. Bare-chested, she raised first one slender leg and then the other to remove her boots. Next she released the buckle at her waist and freed the buttons on her fly to reveal her naked flesh. The heat, the soft red light, and the stillness closed around her as she pushed the smooth leather down her legs to bare herself completely.

The woman in the shadows smiled triumphantly. Dane stood physically exposed, helpless and without protection. Soon she would be emotionally naked as well.

"Close your eyes."

Moments passed and still Dane stood unmoving in the center of the room. Her mind slowly emptied of all thought as the sound of her own heart beat louder and louder in her ears. She tensed slightly at the touch of a hand on her back, but she did not turn. The darkness became total as a soft, close-fitting leather hood was pulled over her head and fastened snugly around her neck. Her eyes were completely covered, but there were ample spaces for her nose and mouth, making it warm inside but allowing for easy breathing. Something was pressed to her nose.

"Inhale," the voice directed.

For the first time, Dane resisted, but a firm hand at the back of her neck squeezed until she gasped involuntarily and breathed in the acrid scent. Almost immediately, a wave of heat washed through her, and the red that had been the room was now inside her. Her head pounded and her skin tingled. Nausea surged and then passed, leaving an uneasy arousal in the pit of her stomach. She was aware of being pushed roughly forward, her body seeming to move without her guidance. The hood blocked her keenest senses, her sight and hearing, and isolated her from her surroundings. She was forced now to experience events through her skin—to open the natural barrier of her body and to feel through it—beyond it to her core.

She was jerked to a stop, and thick, soft straps were buckled around her wrists and ankles. Her body was pulled off balance, first one way and then another, as her limbs were secured to a scaffold. Once she was suspended, her feet barely touched the floor, and the leather restraints stretched her arms taut over her head, the tension just verging on painful. She floated in the silent void while pain and fear and desperate anticipation coalesced in her depths.

Her master walked softly to the side of the room, sat on a stool at a small bar, and studied her handiwork with satisfaction. Dane's finely muscled back and small, firm buttocks looked tantalizing in the muted red light. She imagined those tight muscles clenching at the first strike of the lash, and lust surged in her loins. Forcing herself to wait, knowing this would enhance Dane's sense of disembodiment, she poured brandy into a glass and sipped it slowly. The anticipation would make her own pleasure all the more acute as well. She resisted the urge to press a hand between her thighs. There would be time for that later, when she was alone, remembering.

Finally, she opened a small cabinet set into the wall and removed the largest of her braided cats, a treacherous whip when wielded by someone less practiced than she. When her hand closed around the heavy, leather-wrapped handle, she felt a thrill of excitement course from her center. Then she took a deep breath and focused her entire being on the pale, naked figure before her.

Dane had drifted so far into her own inner world that at first she did not recognize the odd sensation on her thigh. When the second blow, harder than the first, landed across her buttock, her head snapped up in response. She forced herself not to tense her back muscles, knowing from experience it would make the cutting strokes more painful. She tried to focus on the way her skin felt after the blow had landed and the immediate flash of pain had passed. There was a tingling heat left behind that resembled a bright, sharp light in the night. Soon she lost count of the strokes that fell more rapidly and harder across her upper back and shoulders. Her consciousness, devoid of ordinary sensation, became subsumed with the cumulative agony of the blows. There were no barriers to the surfacing of her deeply buried terror and remorse. As she opened herself to the physical anguish and absorbed the manifestation of her emotional torment into the fiber of her being, the pain seared through her mind with a cleansing flame and flickered out.

Gasping with the effort not to cry out, Dane clung to consciousness by a thread, still aware enough to know that the woman would not stop the blows until bidden. Only someone as experienced as Dane would dare to go so far, or to ask so much of her body. Still, she pushed herself, taking more punishment than she ever had before. She held on until at last she felt purged of all feeling except absolution. One single sensation—pure and without regret. Only then did she utter the safe word, agreed upon by both of them long ago.

Hearing that word, barely audible since Dane's voice was so hoarse, the woman wielding the torturous whip pulled herself up short. Heart pounding, she was stunned to realize how close she had been to losing control. She'd been delivering her blows in a near-frenzy, and now, looking at Dane slumped within the confines of her restraints, she was forced to acknowledge a grudging respect for her. It was only her own practiced discipline that had guided her during the last few minutes, and her considerable skill with the cat that had prevented the whip from flaying open Dane's back. Still, she knew that the deeper, delicate blood vessels had burst. Dane's back was a mass of welts already beginning to darken from the blood pooling in the wounded tissue beneath the skin. Nevertheless, Dane had been silent throughout, as she always was, and her master could not help but admire her.

Her head clear once more, the woman dropped the whip and strode quickly across the room. She released the restraints and caught Dane as she fell, then laid her on her side on the floor. She removed the hood, checked Dane's pulse, and found it steady and strong. She left Dane curled on the floor, naked, to find her own way out whenever she regained consciousness.

The highway flashed beneath Kyle's bike as the headlights cut a swath through the darkness. She raced along the treacherous, twisting road by instinct, fleeing from her disquiet and disappointment without thought to her destination. When she swerved abruptly from the road into a steep driveway, gravel flew behind her rear tire, and the bike only stayed upright as a result of its own momentum. She nearly skidded out and got a leg down at the last second, barely managing to avoid crashing into the last car in a line of pricey vehicles parked along both sides of the long drive. Visible through the trees, the elegant house on the hilltop was ablaze with light. Sweating, guts churning, Kyle ground the bike to a halt and took a long, shuddering breath.

She hesitated. The party was in full swing. *What in hell am I doing here?* But she knew, or her unconscious did. She was hurt, and she wanted comfort. Or at the very least, not to be alone with her pain.

Avoiding the brightly lit front entrance, she made her way along the winding flagstone path between well-tended shrubs to the rear deck, seeking the relative privacy of the shadows there. It wasn't until she reached the top step that she saw two figures in the midst of a frenzied embrace in the semidarkness of the nearby corner. A woman pulled away from her partner at the sound of Kyle's step.

"Jesus," Nancy cried. "Kyle! Is that you?"

"Yes." Kyle halted quickly. "I'm sorry...I'll just go back dow—"

Pushing the young man with her toward the house, Nancy whispered, "Go inside." Then she took Kyle's arm and pulled her across the deck, away from the view of the people just inside. "What are you doing here?"

"I don't know." Kyle slumped against the railing. "Fuck, I'm sorry—I just ended up here."

"That's okay. Never mind." Nancy brushed her fingers through Kyle's hair. "Are you all right? What happened?"

"Everything is crazy, Nance. I started out the night at a discussion group and ended up in the club. Just for a bit of fun." Kyle rubbed her face vigorously, trying to clear her head. Trying to erase the memory of Dane's face, furious and cold. "Is there anything to drink?"

"Of course. When isn't there?" Nancy searched Kyle's face with concern. "Come inside."

"No," Kyle said quickly. "I didn't mean to crash your party."

"Don't be stupid," Nancy said in exasperation. "It's a bore, anyway."

Kyle laughed despite her discomfort. "I could tell you couldn't find anything to do with yourself."

"Oh, him. Just a diversion. Roger is deep in some heavy conversation somewhere." Nancy shrugged dismissively. "Sit down. I'll be right back."

Kyle sighed and sank gratefully into one of the deck chairs. The moon was out and the surf pounded somewhere far below, but the vision that should have been beautiful only left her feeling empty. She closed her eyes, too weary to think any longer.

"Here," Nancy said, settling herself at the foot of Kyle's chair. "Drink."

Kyle reached for the glass and moved her legs to make room for Nancy. "Thanks."

They sat close together for a while in the moonlight. Finally, Nancy placed her hand on Kyle's arm.

"So, what happened? Did your discussion group turn into a free-for-all?"

"No. It was fine." Kyle spoke softly, her head tilted back as she watched clouds drift across the face of the moon. "I went to the club afterwards and *that's* when it turned into—I'm not sure what. Dane was there, and at first it was...great. We danced..." She took another gulp of wine, her throat tight, but not from thirst. *It was so good. For a few minutes it was perfect.*

"And then?" Nancy refilled Kyle's glass and her own, then shifted closer to Kyle on the chair. The night *looked* gorgeous, but the air was rapidly turning cold.

"But then Brad turned up and everyone started acting really strange. Brad came onto me...sort of, I think...and Dane got pissed and stormed off."

"My, my. Sounds like fun." Nancy's voice held the merest trace of envy. "Who's Dane? And *who* is Brad? I thought you'd quit men."

Kyle laughed, drinking without really tasting it. "Dane is the woman I told you about—the one I met last month. And Brad is a woman, too."

"Clearly, I missed the real party." Nancy picked up the bottle and leaned back against Kyle's side, her head against Kyle's shoulder. "So why did you dash madly out here?"

"Because everything went to hell. Something seriously bad was going on and I didn't know what. Dane turned to ice as soon as Brad showed up, and Brad was..."

"What?"

"Insistent."

"And you weren't interested," Nancy finished for her. "Was she crude and unattractive, or what?"

"Oh, she's attractive. It was more than just the way she looked—which was great. She was so damned confident. The way she came on to me—like how could I possibly resist?" She remembered the hand on her shoulder. There had been more than a hint of ownership in Brad's touch. "She got my attention, at least."

Nancy looked intrigued. "She was really something, huh?"

"Yeah." Kyle sighed. "*Something.*"

"So, why are you here, instead of somewhere with her? You're not getting all moral, are you? After all, you never minded one-nighters before."

Kyle thought about it seriously and had to acknowledge her involuntary attraction to Brad. That kind of physical aggressiveness and confidence *was* exciting.

"I don't know. Maybe I would have, if it hadn't been for seeing Dane first." *If I'd never been with Dane.* "But it was Dane I wanted," she admitted as she drained her glass and automatically refilled it. "And I never got a chance to really connect with her before Brad showed up. Then everything changed. Christ, Dane acted like I would automatically want Brad, just because Brad wanted *me.*" Suddenly angry, she started to sit up and found that Nancy had curled up so close to her she couldn't move. With a sigh, she slumped back. "The two of them acted like I was some prize to be taken by the strongest. Like I couldn't choose for myself. Fuck them."

"Oh well. Who needs any of them anyway?" Nancy smiled and snuggled under Kyle's arm, happier than she'd been all evening. "Men or women—it's all the same. One pain in the ass after another."

"Things aren't going so well for you either tonight, huh?" Kyle stroked Nancy's shoulder absently.

Nancy's laugh was tinged with bitterness. "Oh, you know. Typical party. The men are all getting quietly drunk and eyeing every female in sight. And the wives are sitting off by themselves bitching about their husbands."

"Why do you bother with it, then?" Kyle's question was serious, because she knew Nancy could change things if she wanted to. Her friend had everything going for her—looks, brains, and a strong will. She had never understood why Nancy continued in a life she obviously didn't find fulfilling.

"Oh, it has its rewards," Nancy replied, her tone unconcerned.

"Sure," Kyle responded, "that's why you were out here in a clinch with some—what was he, a med student?"

"Busboy," Nancy answered. "And don't go getting so high and mighty with me, Kyle Kirk. You're not all that much different from me. We're both casting about in the dark for something we can't see."

Surprised at Nancy's perceptiveness, Kyle sighed. "You're right. Great partners, aren't we?"

"We might be," Nancy said quietly. She carefully slipped an arm around Kyle's waist. Kyle's body felt so solid, so good against hers. *Why haven't you ever tried to touch me, Kyle?*

Nancy started to press closer when a male voice called from the darkness, "Nancy? Are you out here, hon?"

For an instant, Nancy hesitated, then replied. "Over here."

Kyle looked up at the man who appeared beside her chair. "Hi, Roger. Sorry, I dragged Nancy away to keep me company."

"Kyle," Roger said in surprise. "I thought you weren't going to be able to make it. Nancy said you were tied up."

"No such luck." Nancy laughed, slightly drunk, and sat up on the side of the chair. "But she wanted to be."

"No, I just had to be somewhere else earlier," Kyle covered quickly, feeling slightly dizzy when she straightened up. She hadn't meant to drink so much. "How are you?"

"Fine, fine," he said heartily. "Great party, isn't it, sweetheart?" He looked at his wife uncertainly.

"Oh, yes, great." Nancy stood up with practiced care and smoothed the soft material of her clinging dress down over her

thighs. "I guess I should go play hostess and check on our guests."
She looked pointedly at Kyle. "You *will* come in, won't you?"

"I'm not really dressed for it, Nance." Kyle indicated her
boots and jeans.

"Oh, bullshit. You're the best-looking thing here."

Embarrassed for Roger's sake, Kyle said hastily, "Okay. In a
minute."

Wistfully, Roger watched Nancy enter the house, then gave
Kyle a genuine smile. "It's good to see you. How have *you* been?"

"Not bad." Kyle wished there was something she could do to
help both her friends. But she knew there wasn't. "Business is
good."

"I figured. Nancy's been spending a lot of time at the shop
lately."

Is that where she tells you she's going? Shrugging
noncommittally, Kyle desperately tried to avoid talking about
Nancy with Roger. She had never wanted to be in the middle of
their relationship, no matter what she thought of it. And when all
the lines were drawn, it was to Nancy that she owed her
allegiance.

"Yeah, well—I guess we've all been busy."

"Oh, you know how it is." He tapped her shoulder
awkwardly. "Why don't you come in?"

"You sure you don't mind?"

"Of course not." He regarded her thoughtfully. "And Nancy
wants you."

There was nothing she could say to that, and nothing she
wanted to think about for long, so she simply grabbed the wine
bottle and followed him inside.

CHAPTER NINE

Anne turned at the sound of a key in the side door. When Dane walked in, Anne immediately noted her pale, drawn complexion and the dark smudges beneath her eyes. She looked close to collapsing.

"Hi. I didn't expect you today." Although alarmed, Anne resisted the urge to take Dane by the arm and lead her to a chair. "Things are really quiet. Why don't you take the day off?"

Dane slowly headed toward the rear of the kennels. "There are some things I want to check."

Anne reached for the cell phone the instant Dane disappeared and hit speed dial. A minute later, she said, "Honey? Are you almost here?...Dane just showed up and she looks...I don't know...bad." She sighed with relief. "Yeah, good...Are you kidding? I didn't say a thing."

Five minutes later, Caroline came through the front door. "She still here?"

"In the back," Anne said quickly.

Caroline found Dane by the exit to the outdoor dog runs. Anne had been right. Dane's face was gray, she was sweating despite the coolness of the room, and her eyes were shadowed with sickness. Carolyn's heart plummeted but she kept her tone casual. "Hi. I thought you were off today."

"Nope." Dane pulled a heavy jacket off a hook by the door. She knew she sounded abrupt, but she was not in the mood for company. Turning her back to her friend, she shrugged into the padded canvas coat, her stomach churning when pain shot through her shoulders and back. The weight of the material against her sensitive flesh was almost more than she could handle.

"Dane—" Caroline began.

"Later, okay? I want to work with Troy some."

Without being invited, Caroline followed Dane outside. When Dane led a two-year-old dog into the large training area behind the building, Caroline sat down on the steps to observe. Dane was one of the few in the country certified to train animals in the difficult skills necessary for the dogs to attain Schutzhund titles. Schutzhund training, popularized in Europe as a method of assessing the ability and temperament of working dogs, emphasized obedience, tracking, and protection. The protection training focused on disarmament and containment, and Dane and her dogs were expert at it.

Dane took the dog, a heavy, well-muscled animal, through some preliminary obedience exercises first. He followed her every move, his calm dark eyes fixed on her face. She had been working with him since he was a puppy, and he had already distinguished himself by earning the Schutzhund I and II degrees. He was by nature an even-tempered animal and had acquired an even deeper level of control by virtue of Dane's careful training.

Caroline, watching them work together flawlessly as Dane signaled her desires by silent hand commands, appreciated once again her partner's expertise. For some reason, though, Dane's timing seemed off. When she signaled Troy to attack, the big dog growled, propelled himself at her, and clamped his massive jaws around Dane's padded arm. As he shook his huge head and pulled with his considerable weight, Dane staggered and nearly fell. Seeing the sweat pour off Dane's face and hearing a grunt of pain, Caroline got quickly to her feet. She doubted she could separate them, and she felt afraid for the first time during a training session.

She breathed a sigh of relief when, panting, Dane commanded the dog to release. He did so immediately, watching Dane with a clear-eyed, expectant expression.

"Good boy, Troy, good boy," Dane gasped. Dropping to one knee, she hugged him and ran her hands over his sleek back. "That's a good boy."

"Here," Caroline said quietly as she approached with Troy's lead in her hand. "Let me take him back for you."

Wordlessly, Dane nodded. The cramps in her abdomen were so sharp she wasn't sure she could get up. Her back hurt everywhere that her damp shirt touched, and a sharp, stabbing pain shot through her chest each time she took a deep breath. Gritting her teeth, she forced herself upright and weaved her way back inside. Then she eased the jacket off slowly, dropped it on a chair, and leaned back against the counter to catch her breath.

"Looks like Troy wore you out," Caroline observed, acutely aware of Dane's exhaustion. Something was wrong. "You okay?"

"Yeah," said Dane, regaining her composure. She continued to lean on the counter and hoped that Caroline couldn't see her legs shaking. "Late night. Just tired."

"Uh-huh." Caroline knew that kind of workout shouldn't have even winded Dane, but she also knew that if she pushed, Dane would just shut her out. Gently, she asked, "When are you going to stop letting Brad get to you?"

Dane glared at Caroline and reached into her pocket for a cigarette. Her hand shook as she lit it. She coughed as the smoke seared her lungs, and the pain in her chest escalated. "She doesn't get to me."

"Oh, sure. That must be why you left in such a huff last night."

"I just don't care for Brad's company, okay? I'm tired of her arrogance and her fucking ego."

"It's been almost three years, Dane." Caroline wanted to comfort her, but held her place. Dane couldn't be touched when she was like this, remembering Brad. "Can't you let it go?"

"I *can't*. Not after what she did." Dane groaned. *She drove me over the edge and then just walked away. No one—no one should do that to someone they love. Or say that they love.*

Caroline needed no reminder of those precarious few months in Dane's life. She hadn't been certain that Dane would survive them, but she had, and Caroline would always respect her for that. "You beat her. You beat her at her own game. You made it without her."

Dane's eyes were bleak. "Did I?"

"You built all this, and she doesn't even show dogs anymore." Caroline waved her arm, taking in the kennel.

"Baron beat her," Dane said quietly. "This kennel is built on him—and she knows it. Before we bred his line, Brad was the big name around here. Now it's us." She shook her head. "But she still thinks she can beat me in everything else." *Maybe she's right.*

"You mean Kyle?" Caroline asked astutely. She'd seen the way Dane and Kyle had danced—the energy, the attraction between them. She'd seen the way Dane had looked at her, too, and there had been more than lust in her eyes. A stranger might not have noticed, but Caroline had. Dane was much more than just physically attracted to Kyle.

Dane tensed. "Kyle is nothing to me."

"Oh, come off it." Caroline didn't even try to hide her exasperation. "What are you so damned afraid of? If you ask me, Kyle is pretty interested in you, too."

Dane turned to stare out the window over the counter. She didn't want to hear this. She didn't want to even think about it. Not today, not when she'd tried so hard not to feel anything. "She doesn't know *what* she wants right now."

"You'd better give her a little more credit. She *does* know what she wants—she just may not be sure *who* she wants."

Dane spun around, her blue eyes flashing. "Well, Brad is the master, right? Who better to show her what she wants!" Another wave of pain rolled through her and her knees buckled. She grabbed the counter for support. "Shit."

"What's the matter?" Caroline cried, moving quickly across the room.

"Nothing. I'm fine." Dane closed her eyes and wiped at the beads of perspiration on her face with her sleeve.

Suddenly, Caroline understood. *Oh God, I didn't think Brad could still do this to her.* Heartsick, she smoothed her fingers over Dane's pale brow. "Oh, Dane. Not again."

Spots danced before Dane's eyes when she opened them, and she feared she might vomit. She was in trouble. "Yeah. I'm sorry."

"Never mind that now." Carefully, Caroline took Dane's arm and draped it over her shoulders. "Just lean on me. We're going to my place."

Anne checked the rear-view mirror and caught a glimpse of Dane's face, but she couldn't tell if Dane was asleep or not. She was slumped in the corner of the back seat, eyes closed, head lolling with the motion of the vehicle. Beside her in the front seat, Caroline stared out the window, her face expressionless. She'd been holding Anne's hand tightly ever since they'd gotten into the Jeep. Neither had said anything since Caroline had helped Dane into the office and announced, "Close up. We're leaving."

As if feeling Anne's eyes upon her, Caroline turned, shook her head slightly, and motioned toward Dane almost imperceptibly. Silently, she mouthed, "We'll talk later."

Anne sighed. *This is not going to be a good day.*

As soon as the three entered the apartment, Anne went directly into the den and closed the door behind her, affording Caroline and Dane privacy.

"Is she okay?" Dane asked hoarsely, looking toward the closed door.

"She'll be all right," Caroline replied quietly. "Come on. Let's get you to bed."

Wordlessly, Dane followed Caroline into the guest bedroom, emotionally and physically too exhausted to protest. She hated to admit it, but she needed Caroline's help.

"Can you undress?"

"I'm getting stiff," Dane admitted, her tone devoid of inflection. She was flushed but shivering. With shaking hands, she unbuttoned her shirt. "If you could just help me with my pants and boots."

"I'll be right back. Sit on the side of the bed." Mechanically, Caroline walked into the bathroom, opened the medicine chest, and pulled out several jars and bottles. She refused to think about Dane's pain—the physical or the emotional. It hurt too much to imagine, and she had work to do. When she returned, she deposited the items on the floor by the bed and reached for Dane's boots. "Where are you hurt?" Her voice was as neutral as Dane's had been, but her stomach was in knots.

"Just my back."

Just. Oh, Dane. Caroline nodded, averting her eyes from Dane's bare breasts. She knew how hard it was for Dane to expose herself, physically or emotionally, and she had no desire to make her friend any more uncomfortable. She wasn't interested in inflicting more punishment. Dane had already taken care of that. As she pulled at the heavy boots, she murmured, "Hold on."

"It's okay," Dane gritted as she gripped the edge of the mattress. Without protest, she lifted her hips to allow Caroline to unbutton her jeans and pull them off. Sighing in relief when she was finally nude, she collapsed onto her stomach with a soft moan.

Looking down, Caroline drew a sharp breath at the sight of Dane's back. The flesh was swollen and discolored from her shoulders to her hips. Ridges of red were crisscrossed with dark purple welts. Thankfully, there were no tears and no bleeding. She pulled up a clean white sheet to cover Dane's buttocks, which were bruised, but not badly.

Knees suddenly weak, Caroline sat down on the side of the bed and placed her hand tenderly on the back of Dane's head, the only place she wasn't afraid to touch. She couldn't imagine the discipline it must have required to accept that amount of punishment. "Why did it have to be so damn much?"

Dane lay quietly, desperately trying to dissociate her mind from her screaming body. "It took that much."

"To do what?" Surprised that Dane had answered and able only to think that Dane was too sick to keep her normal barriers in place, Caroline carefully applied a topical anesthetic lotion to Dane's back. Her ministrations would only help temporarily and would reach only the surface pain, but it would provide Dane with enough relief to sleep.

"So I could forget." The slight pressure of Caroline's hands sent lancets of pain stabbing through her sensitive muscles.

"Forget what?"

"Brad's hands on me." Dane hesitated. "And...the wanting."

Caroline continued to stroke Dane's back gently, closing her mind to the sight of her friend's beautiful body in ruins. "What about when you're with other women? Can you forget then?"

"Once in a while. With Kyle—" Dane stopped, not having meant to mention her name.

"Kyle?" Suddenly things made much more sense. "You've already slept with her?"

"Once." Dane was starting to drift as the pain abated a little.

"So, Kyle was the one you were telling me about last month?"

"Yeah. We...just fit. It was good."

"Why didn't you ever call her?"

"She's a novice. I don't want to bring someone else out." Dane groaned, not with pain this time, but with the absence of it. "I've had enough of that."

Caroline winced. "You mean like with Anne?"

Dane laughed as much as her protesting muscles allowed. "Will you stop? Anne and I would never have made it."

"Do you want to make it with anyone?"

"I don't know anymore. I'm used to the way things are." She turned her head and opened her eyes. Her vision was clearer. "I meet someone, we do a scene, and then it's over. It's easier that way."

"Maybe what's easier isn't always what's best." Caroline hesitated, not sure how far to go. "Maybe if you had someone you could really touch—who could touch you—you wouldn't need this kind of edgeplay."

"I'm afraid I'll always need this." Dane sighed and mustered up a smile. "Thanks, Caro. I feel better."

"Who is she?"

"Caroline—" Dane protested.

"Damn it, Dane. You're my friend. I love you. Why can't you tell me who does this to you?"

Gingerly, Dane rolled over onto her side to face Caroline. "It's personal—and I asked her to do it."

"What about what we share? Isn't that personal?" Caroline blinked away tears.

"I can't." Dane caressed Caroline's hand gently. "I'm sorry."

"She must be something."

"Yeah. A top's top." Dane's voice was at once bitter and begrudgingly respectful.

Caroline leaned down to kiss Dane's cheek. "Right."

"Hey, you. Wake up." Nancy shook Kyle's shoulder firmly. "Come on. It's after noon."

Muttering sleepily, Kyle kept her eyes closed and tried to roll away. "No. It's the middle of the night."

"Wrong." Smiling, Nancy sat on the edge of the bed in the guest room and leaned down, her mouth close to Kyle's ear. In a soft seductive purr, she whispered, "Coffee." She blew in Kyle's ear. "Mmm. Italian dark roast."

Still half asleep, Kyle felt the warm breath steal across her neck and at the same time became aware of a soft weight pressing against her bare arm. *Breast.* Her stomach gave a pleasant roll. *Nice.* She rolled onto her back and opened one eye. Full red lips were poised just above hers. *Holy shit. Nancy!*

Their eyes locked and Kyle saw the undisguised wanting in her friend's hazy gaze. Nancy's hand rested on the sheet over her bare abdomen, and Kyle felt herself respond to the soft caress. Her stomach quivered, and she prayed Nancy didn't feel it. Careful not to move, she asked quietly, "Is the party over?"

"Long over, thank God." Nancy's voice was thick, and her breasts rose and fell rapidly beneath her black silk robe. She broke away from Kyle's intense gaze and glanced down, seeing her own hand, as if it were a stranger's, stroking her friend's body. "And Roger's gone to some meeting upstate until Monday."

"So I guess you want me to get up, huh?" *Don't do this, Nance. We don't have anywhere good to go with it.*

"I want..." Nancy waited for some sign from Kyle. Any indication that her touch was welcome. After a long moment, she eased away, letting her fingers trail over the sheet and off Kyle's abdomen. "I want you to keep me company."

Relieved that the inflaming fingers were gone, Kyle groaned and sat up. She peered at the floor by the bed. "Where are my clothes?"

"I don't know." Nancy feigned ignorance. "Where did you leave them?"

"Nance," Kyle said threateningly. "I had a little too much wine but I remember getting undressed right here."

"All right." Nancy laughed and stood up. "They're in the dryer. I'll have them out for you in a minute."

Kyle fell back gratefully into the pillows. "Good. Wake me up when they're done."

"Oh, no you don't! You're getting up." She pulled a robe from a hook behind the door and tossed it onto the bed. "Here. We're having breakfast, and then we're going to the shop."

"Oh, fun."

"And then we're going out."

Kyle regarded her suspiciously. "Where?"

Nancy gave her a self-satisfied smile. "To that club you've been hanging out at lately."

Shocked speechless, Kyle could only stare.

CHAPTER TEN

Nancy pirouetted before the full-length mirror in Kyle's bedroom. "Well, how do I look?"

"Great." Kyle surveyed the sultry brunette, who somehow managed to look elegant in blue jeans and a plain pale yellow cotton shirt. "And you know it."

"Are you sure I can't wear your leather pants?" Nancy looked over her shoulder to study her backside in the mirror and pursed her lips critically. "God, these jeans don't do a *thing* for my ass."

"No, you can't wear my leathers." Kyle shuddered at the thought. "And your ass doesn't need help with anything."

"You're not wearing them," Nancy pointed out practically. She tilted her head and regarded Kyle's black jeans. "Those *are* hot. Don't wear a shirt over that black T though—it shows off your...muscles so nicely." *And every other part of you, too.* She'd had a hard time all day forgetting exactly how good her friend had looked *and* felt lying naked under just a sheet that morning. She'd always found Kyle attractive, but she'd never been quite so feverishly aware of her physically before. The timing might have had something to do with her own growing dissatisfaction with her increasingly frequent extramarital liaisons, but *that* subject was not something she intended to spend any time pondering. Not when a night of fun lay ahead.

"Thank you for the fashion advice," Kyle said dryly. "I can dress myself."

"Oh, I know." Nancy smiled sweetly as she held the garment in question up to her body, assessing the leg length. "I just want all the girls to be jealous of my date."

"First, my pants are too big for you." Kyle ignored her friend's attempt to distract her from the issue. "Second, I don't trust you in them."

Nancy's eyes grew large as she tried to look innocent. "Whatever do you mean?"

"I don't want the competition. Put them back."

"Ky—yle."

"No." Suddenly serious, Kyle asked, "Why do you want to do this?"

"Why not? We haven't been out together in a long time," Nancy said casually, giving up on the pants but continuing to comb through Kyle's closet in search of a jacket. "And before you say anything, we've been to gay bars before."

"This isn't just *any* gay club, Nance," Kyle reminded her. *This is one game you don't know how to play.*

"How much different can it be?"

Kyle merely shook her head, knowing nothing she said would deter Nancy from her plans. *How much different, indeed.*

Brad saw Kyle the moment she entered. She smiled in anticipation and studied Kyle's pretty companion with interest. *Another new one.* Carrying her beer, she threaded her way through the crowd and settled at the far end of the bar to watch the couple. The sexy brunette looked tasty—ripe for the picking and, from the way her eyes roamed the crowd with eager anticipation, ready and willing. Kyle, Brad noted, looked just as good as she had the night before—the well-built body, great face, and seething sexuality were definitely intriguing. Although Brad rarely had to compete for company, she still enjoyed a challenge. And Kyle represented that and more—she was new to the scene, but had a natural confidence that suggested she would be a versatile and willing partner in bed. Plus, sensing that Kyle was involved with Dane only heightened the thrill. Nothing aroused Brad more than a battle with Dane, especially in the sexual arena.

Since they had parted, Dane's reputation as a demanding but safe top had flourished. Women trusted her to take them unharmed through a scene. Word was, too, that she never let anyone top her, and that only added to her mystique. Brad refused to acknowledge that Dane, intentionally or not, represented real competition, but she welcomed the opportunity to reestablish her own superiority. Seducing Kyle would certainly be satisfying, and if it hurt Dane, all the better. As she slowly sipped her beer, she waited for an opening to make her first move. She was in no hurry; she enjoyed playing the game as much as winning.

She watched as Kyle and Nancy found a place halfway down the bar and ordered drinks. Catching the bartender's eye, she motioned her over with a tilt of her head. The burly woman in a sleeveless white T-shirt that showcased the large tattoos on each upper arm frowned but hurried over.

"Yeah, Brad. Need something?"

"Let me have another beer," Brad said. "And give those two women who just ordered whatever they asked for with my compliments."

The bartender grinned knowingly. "Which one you going for?" When Brad merely stared, her eyes hard and flat, the bartender flinched. "No problem. I'll take care of it."

When the bartender set the bottle of beer and vodka tonic down in front of Kyle and Nancy, she gestured toward the far end of the bar. "From your friend over there."

Following the woman's gaze, Kyle flushed when she met Brad's cool gaze down the length of the bar. She tried to ignore the involuntary surge of excitement stirred by the lean, leather-clad figure. When Brad lifted her bottle in greeting, Kyle nodded in return.

"What's happening?" Nancy watched the exchange with interest.

"We just got drinks—from Brad."

"Yeah?" Nancy regarded the dark-haired woman dressed completely in black leather with open curiosity. Since the woman was staring at *her* in frank appraisal, Nancy saw no reason for subtlety. She smiled slightly and got a lazy once-over in return. Her skin tingled as the hot dark eyes played over her. *You are an arrogant thing, aren't you?*

"Whew," Nancy said throatily, finally breaking away from the woman's hypnotic stare. "She is something."

"Uh-huh," Kyle said, keeping her eyes on her beer while intentionally avoiding Brad. The woman might kick start her hormones, but she wasn't the one Kyle wanted.

"So, now what happens?" Nancy sounded breathless.

"Damned if I know."

"Aren't you supposed to *do* something?"

"What would you like me to do?" Kyle gave Nancy an exasperated shrug. "Take my clothes off?"

"Well, you'd better think of something." Nancy cast a surreptitious glance back down the bar. "Here she comes."

Before the words had even registered in Kyle's mind, Brad was next to her. Standing with legs slightly spread, a bottle dangling from her right hand, she seemed to tower over them even though she was no bigger than either.

"Kyle," Brad said smoothly.

"Brad," Kyle said, meeting her gaze evenly.

"Having a good time?"

Kyle nodded. "Thanks for the beer."

"My pleasure," Brad said, turning toward Nancy and extending her hand. "Hello. I'm Brad."

"Nancy." She gave a small start of surprise as she took Brad's hand. The woman looked so hard, but her touch was not only soft, but unexpectedly gentle. Voice throaty, Nancy added, "It's a pleasure."

"Yes," Brad agreed with a slow smile. "It is."

"Thank you for the drink." Emboldened by the flirtatious tone in Brad's voice, Nancy decided to flirt back. Flirting was something she not only understood, it was something at which she excelled. She let her eyes slip languorously down Brad's body, intending to send Brad the message that she wasn't intimidated in these new surroundings. But her breath caught and she gave a small involuntary start when she saw the unmistakable swelling nestled in Brad's crotch along the inner curve of her left thigh.

To her consternation, Nancy blushed. Brad laughed so quietly that only Nancy could hear, and when Brad cocked her hips forward in a move calculated to tease, Nancy's stomach quivered with excitement. Unwilling to be outmaneuvered, she met the dark eyes boldly. "Is it appropriate for a lady to ask for a dance?"

"Nance," Kyle whispered, reaching for her friend's hand. *What the fuck are you doing?*

"Oh, without a doubt." Brad settled the beer bottle against her thigh and almost laughed again when Nancy involuntarily looked down at her crotch for a second and then dragged her gaze away. What had begun as a tingle of arousal when she'd first seen Kyle and Nancy walk in escalated rapidly to a steady throb. "But I was about to go somewhere with a little more...action." Her eyes held Nancy's. "Perhaps you two would like to join me."

Before Kyle could say no, Nancy's hand closed hard on her arm.

"Sure, why not?" Nancy said quickly.

"I don't know," Kyle objected mildly. "We just got here and it looks like there's a good crowd tonight."

Brad, unperturbed, finished her beer and placed it on the bar. "I just thought you might be up for a change."

"Come on, Kyle." Nancy, fascinated and more than a little turned on, was persistent. "We don't have any plans."

"Okay," Kyle agreed reluctantly. She recognized the "won't take no for an answer" tone in her friend's voice. "Sure, why not."

"Excellent." Brad smiled a satisfied smile. "I'll drive. It'll be easier."

As the three women filed out into the night, none noticed the woman watching from the shadows.

With Nancy perched on Kyle's lap in the cramped front seat, Brad maneuvered her red Mercedes sports coupe through the sparse downtown traffic. Once on a wide avenue running along the waterfront, she picked up speed and glanced at Kyle.

"Ever heard of Encounters?"

"No."

"You'll find it interesting. Your friend here is cool, isn't she?"

Nancy, one arm curled around Kyle's shoulder, leaned forward to catch Brad's eye. Her tone was honey smooth, but there was an edge beneath the charm. "You don't have to worry, Brad, my dear. I'll be just fine."

Brad laughed and flicked her eyes to Nancy. "I'm sure you will be."

The block in the warehouse district where Brad parked was deserted. The broad, pothole-filled street was empty, and all the factory buildings on either side were dark. Here and there a semi stood waiting for its next shipment, but there were no pedestrians and very few vehicles. As she followed Brad down the block, Kyle's initial discomfort blossomed into apprehension. She felt responsible for Nancy, and Brad was a virtual stranger. The only thing she knew about Brad with certainty was that she could be dangerous. If not physically, then emotionally. Her opinion was partly based on instinct and partly on memory—the memory of the confusion of emotions on Dane's face when Brad had appeared. Anger, above all, but perhaps a hint of involuntary lust—and beneath all that, fear.

"Listen," Kyle said hastily when Brad stopped in front of an unlit door marked only by a small sign stating Private Club. "I don't know about this."

"Don't worry." Brad gave a feral smile as she pushed open the door. "You're with me."

There was no time to reply as Nancy hastened after Brad up the dimly lit stairway toward the light on the second floor. Kyle followed.

"Yo, Brad," a small, tight-muscled redhead seated behind a rickety card table at the head of the stairs said. "These..." she looked Nancy and Kyle over with an insolent grin. "...hot items with you?"

"Yeah." Brad grinned back and handed the woman twenty dollars. "My lucky night."

The woman added the bill to a stack in front of her, passed Brad her change, and smirked. "Have fun."

Beyond the narrow entrance hall, unadorned and lit only by a single unshaded bulb on a frayed cord, was a cavernous high-ceilinged room with a bar along one wall and a central stage ringed with tables. Brad pointed to an empty table at the edge of the floor.

"Grab that one and I'll get drinks."

Kyle sat down with Nancy and checked out her surroundings. The room was dim, although multiple spots shone among the pipes and heating conduits overhead. The air was a hazy yellow from the combination of weak lighting and smoke. On the raised platform directly in front of them was a scaffold of some kind formed by stout beams.

"Kyle?" Nancy queried softly, staring at the short chains which dangled from heavy metal hooks embedded in the wood. "Do you think that's just part of the décor?"

Following her friend's wide-eyed gaze, Kyle shook her head. "I don't think so."

"Jesus."

"Look, Nance. We can go—"

"Are you kidding?" Nancy's voice was high with excitement. "I can't believe this place."

Looking around, Kyle had to agree. Most of the tables were occupied, and women jostled three-deep in front of the bar. There were more leather collars, studded bracelets, chaps, and boots than she had ever seen in one place before. More than a few of the woman were obviously packing, the outlines of their generous equipment blatantly displayed beneath tight denim and leather pants.

"Oh my God," Nancy gripped Kyle's thigh, "look over there!"

A small, dark woman standing by the bar with several others wore a thin leather collar around her neck and, except for her shimmering leather pants and boots, she was naked. Her well-formed breasts glinted with small gold rings through each nipple.

Kyle swallowed, her mouth suddenly dry. She felt as if she should look away, but the woman was beautiful and clearly didn't mind being observed. "She's...interesting."

"And I thought *I* was liberated!"

Brad returned with their drinks and placed glasses and bottles on the table before settling into a chair between the two friends. "It's early yet. Things should pick up in a while."

As she spoke, a handsome middle-aged woman in a white silk shirt, impeccably tailored trousers, and matching vest strolled by leading another woman by a short leash connected to wide leather shackles binding her wrists together at her waist. The bound woman's face was obscured by a hood that entirely enclosed her face except for holes over her nose and mouth. She was naked from the waist up.

"You mean there's more?" Nancy said sarcastically as she watched the strange procession.

"Oh, yes—much more." Brad laughed, appreciating Nancy's aplomb.

"They definitely do not charge enough to get into this place."

"What's back there?" Kyle asked, indicating several doorways toward the far end of the room. The shirtless woman with the pierced nipples had disappeared through one of those doors.

"Scene rooms," Brad said, enjoying her role as guide. "There's space for playing—or watching others play. Whatever pleases you."

"And privacy?" Kyle lit a cigarette casually, reluctant to allow Brad to see how affected she was by what she was witnessing. She was disturbed and disturbingly aroused at the same time. The idea of blatantly dominating or being dominated in the manner of some of the women she had observed did not particularly excite her. But she had to admit that the very atmosphere of unapologetic physicality *did* stir her.

"If you want that, you can go upstairs." Brad laughed. "Very private. But then again, that's all part of the fun—getting to watch."

The overhead lights dimmed, the huge space grew dark, and conversations dropped away to a background hum. In the eerily quiet space, a single unfocused spot blinked on to highlight the center stage as three women approached.

"I think you'll get the idea in a minute," Brad observed, anticipation stirring in the pit of her stomach.

CHAPTER ELEVEN

The elegant woman in the stylish suit led the hooded woman to the platform with a practiced tug on the leash.

The manacled submissive, subtly guided up the three steps by another woman who appeared from the shadows, stopped in the spotlight and waited docilely.

"Who is the third woman?" Nancy whispered, leaning close to Brad. She eyed the new arrival with curiosity and just a bit of envy. The surprisingly feminine brunette was attired in figure-hugging black silk pants and a laced bustier that barely restrained her full breasts. *She's beautiful, and she knows it.*

"An attendant." Brad brought her mouth close to Nancy's ear, enjoying her decidedly female scent. "She'll help with the scene. The top will tell her what she wants done or what equipment she needs."

"Fun job," Nancy muttered dryly. Brad chuckled, and her warm breath caused Nancy to shiver.

In response to a quick nod from the top, the attendant directed the submissive to the scaffold and efficiently secured her ankles to the strategically placed hooks with soft loops of leather. Then the top handed the brunette a key, and she released the wrist cuffs, raised the hooded woman's arms higher up on the frame, and bound each wrist to it with the short lengths of chain. When finished, she stepped away, unobtrusively awaiting her next instruction.

Kyle stirred uneasily, uncertain about witnessing what was obviously to come. Even though these women had chosen a public forum to act out their desires, she still felt like an interloper in something that should be private. And she wasn't at all sure that she wanted to watch one woman inflict pain on another, even when it was consensual. As much as she enjoyed the *idea* of expressing emotional dynamics through physical demonstration, she found neither the delivery nor the acceptance of punishment arousing. With Dane the exchange of power had been very real and very erotic—she could still feel the surge of excitement at being restrained—but she'd had no need or desire to experience pain.

She brushed Brad's shoulder to get her attention. "Is this for real?"

Dark eyes flashing with sardonic amusement, Brad shifted closer and pressed her thigh along the length of Kyle's. "You tell me, Kyle. What is real?"

Unsure how to reply, Kyle was drawn back to the haunting tableau on the stage. The pressure of Brad's thigh, added to the memory of her night with Dane and the inexorable sexual stimulation of everything that was happening around her, was having an undeniable effect. Despite herself, she was throbbing and wet, and she struggled to ignore the insistent pressure mounting between her legs.

"Do you know them?" she asked at last, hoping her voice sounded steady.

"Seen them before." Brad placed her hand gently on Kyle's tightly muscled leg. It might have been a casual, friendly gesture, but her touch was just a little too purposeful to be anything other than possessive. As her fingers trailed lightly up and down the rough denim, she answered, "The dominant and submissive are a couple. The attendant is a friend of theirs, maybe a sometime lover, too."

"Why are they doing this—up there, I mean. It seems..." Kyle's stomach tightened as the steady rhythm of Brad's hand sent shivers racing along her spine, and then she forgot her words of protest as the top directed the attendant to open a large canvas bag. Behind the two, silhouetted in shadow, the hooded woman remained silent, suspended by her arms.

"They want us to see because our pleasure heightens theirs," Brad murmured, her eyes fixed on the scene, her fingers sweeping up and down Kyle's thigh. "Don't disappoint them."

The room was eerily quiet as all eyes focused on the stage. The attendant drew out a short, stout-handled crop from which dangled many long, thin strands of leather, and, keeping her gaze down, held it out. The top walked deliberately to her and took it with a quiet murmur. Nodding, the attendant stepped out of the light, leaving the two lovers alone in the center of the stage.

Kyle jerked when the top arched her arm and the sharp crack of the whip broke the silence. The bound woman stiffened with the blow, but still she made no sound.

"Jesus," Nancy breathed in surprise, leaning across Brad to grab Kyle's arm. "Let me have a cigarette, will you?"

"I thought you quit." Kyle's voice was hoarse and tight. Nevertheless, she shook one out of the pack on the table with hands that trembled, passed it to her friend, and flicked her lighter to the tip. When she shifted position to reach Nancy, Brad leaned in to her more closely and simultaneously slid her hand higher. Kyle caught her breath in surprise at the sudden increase in pressure against her already straining flesh, and her stomach rolled. She bit back a moan. "What are you doi—"

The crop arced a second time, and Kyle forced herself not to jump again. Brad cupped her lightly now, her hand an unrelenting presence against the material stretched tightly across her crotch. The touch was so intense that Kyle felt naked. Senses on overload, she didn't think to move Brad's hand, even though the attentions were uninvited. She couldn't look away from the stage.

The lash continued to rise and fall, accompanied by the sharp snap of leather through air heavy with excitement, and it was another minute until Kyle realized that the stinging blows were actually falling against the bound woman's leather-covered hips rather than her bare back. Still, the effect was staggering. The act of dominance was real; the act of submission, no matter how staged, was real. The absence of true physical punishment was immaterial. The scene had been set, the roles defined. The stark declaration of power exchanged was inescapable and compelling. Kyle stared, transfixed, her mind clouded with lust. With every fall of the lash her pulse quickened; her clitoris twitched in response to Brad's repetitive strokes.

"Stop," she choked out, unable to bear the enticing promise of Brad's touch any longer. Breathing hard, she pulled back in her seat, easing herself away from the exquisite torture. Eyes slightly unfocused, she looked into Brad's face and saw her supremely satisfied smile. "Move...your hand."

With a smile that was almost gentle, Brad softly stroked the line of Kyle's jaw with one long, delicate finger. "You all right?"

"Fine." Kyle shivered, a part of her wanting nothing more than for Brad to continue touching her, to take her over that edge and make her come. She was so agonizingly close. She inched further away. Her body might have short-circuited, but her brain still worked. Barely. "Just...don't."

"Keep watching." Unperturbed by Kyle's resistance, Brad leaned back in her seat, but not before she squeezed Kyle's crotch one more time. "There's more."

The scene continued for what seemed like hours, the crop falling in metrical cadence, slicing with dizzying speed through the cone of light that isolated the central figures. The bound woman silently endured the blows, her body straining with each strike. Finally, as precipitously as it had begun, the punishment stopped. The attendant moved quickly out of the darkness and deftly released the restraints, supporting the submissive with an arm around her naked waist as she led her to where the top waited. As the attendant slipped away, the top released the straps at the back of the woman's hood and pulled it off. She ran her fingers gently over the woman's damp face, then dropped her hands to the submissive's shoulders and pushed her to her knees. Once kneeling, the submissive eagerly pressed her face to the vee between the standing woman's legs and wrapped both arms tightly around her. She guided the top's slowly thrusting hips against her mouth until the standing woman threw back her head and shuddered with orgasm.

Someone at the table groaned.

Mesmerized, Kyle hadn't realized she was holding her breath or that Brad had returned her hand until the quiet voice behind her caused her to exhale explosively and jerk back to awareness.

"You never give up, do you, Brad?"

Three heads turned as one toward the woman behind them. Dane stood looking down at them, cold fury turning her eyes to steel. Kyle noted the quick smile on Brad's face.

"Did you expect me to?" Brad smiled thinly and motioned to the fourth place at the small round table. "Join us. I'm sure there's more entertainment to come."

Dane hesitated briefly before deciding that Brad would not best her so easily. She sat on the opposite side of the table from Brad, between Nancy and Kyle, her eyes sweeping over Kyle's face without a trace of emotion. She'd seen Kyle shift away from Brad a moment before, but not before she'd also witnessed Brad's hand against the damp fabric of Kyle's crotch. Kyle's dark eyes were *still* hazy with arousal and Dane's insides churned knowing that Brad had put that look in Kyle's eyes.

Nancy broke the silence by standing up. "I could use another drink. Kyle?"

Kyle nodded gratefully. "Please."

"And what are you drinking, Dane?" Nancy asked.

Dane stared at Nancy in surprise, wondering how the attractive brunette knew her name. "Scotch."

"I'll just get us all a refill." Nancy rested her hand on Brad's shoulder. "Want to help carry?"

Brad grinned and rose. "I'm always ready to help a lady."

In the awkward vacuum that remained when the two women left, Kyle studied Dane, who had still not met her gaze. Released now from the hypnotic pull of the scene, she was beginning to think clearly again, although her body still pounded with arousal. After another long moment, tired of the tension and confused by Dane's icy behavior, she asked warily, "What's going on?"

"Don't you know?" Dane spat out. *Jesus, she practically had you coming in your pants at the table!*

"No, damn it, I *don't*," Kyle replied angrily. She shook her head in frustration. "You were angry last night, and you're still angry."

Finally, Dane looked at her, and she couldn't prevent her expression from softening. Kyle's intensity, and her honesty, were impossible to resist. "Sorry. I guess you couldn't be expected to understand. It's something between Brad and me."

"I gathered that. But what has it got to do with me?"

"I'm not sure," Dane confessed, suddenly almost too tired to continue. Her body ached; her heart ached; and, always, there was Brad—reminding her of the dark roads she had traveled and how easily she could lose herself there again. "Brad just seems to keep turning up in my life—just when I think I'm rid of her."

"I don't understand. Maybe someday you'll tell me." Kyle's tone was compassionate because she sensed Dane's turmoil and pain. "But don't put me in the middle of it. I'm not the enemy, and I don't want to be."

"Then what *do* you want?" Dane's eyes flashed with renewed emotion. "Brad?"

"I don't even know Brad," Kyle protested.

"You don't know me either."

"You're right. But I've touched you." Kyle leaned across the table, her fingers brushing Dane's hand where it lay fisted on the battered surface. "I've held you and been held by you. I've trusted you with my body—with my feelings. To me, at least, that counts for something."

Dane regarded Kyle in wonder. "Does it?"

"Yes."

"You let her touch you." Dane couldn't keep the bitterness from her voice. If she hadn't been so beaten down, physically and emotionally, she never would have admitted that she cared who Kyle fucked, or who she let fuck her. "Christ, she was about to make you come."

"Maybe. But I didn't intend for any of that to happen." Kyle refused to apologize, but she wanted Dane to understand. "I got caught up in what was happening..." She gestured toward the stage. "Up there. I...I was a little crazy watching it..."

Dane nodded despite her anger. "Yeah. That happens."

"When I could think past my hormones, I told her to stop."

"Fuck," Dane muttered, rubbing her face and leaning back in her chair with a sigh. "You don't owe me an explanation."

"I know," Kyle answered, "but *you* should know that what got me started was thinking about you. That's all I've been doing since that night we were together."

"Yeah?" Dane's voice dropped. "So what do you want to do about that?"

Before Kyle could answer, Nancy and Brad returned with drinks. As they sat down again, Nancy sidled close to Brad, and Kyle sensed that Brad's attention had been diverted during the drink run. She barely glanced at Kyle or Dane.

"Well," Nancy said, taking a large swallow of her drink, "wonderful party. I'm so sorry I'm not properly dressed." She looked mischievously at Kyle. "Leather pants would have been so nice!"

"You look just fine," Brad murmured.

Nancy smiled brilliantly and rested her fingertips on Brad's wrist while looking at Kyle. "I've talked Brad into giving me a tour of those intriguing rooms in the back. Want to come?"

"I'll pass," Kyle said quickly. *I don't want to be anywhere near another scene with Brad.*

Dane gave Brad a hard stare. "Look, Brad—"

"No need to worry, Dane," Brad said lightly. "Nancy will be quite safe with me."

"Oh, leave them." Nancy rose, pulling Brad's arm. "They're no fun."

Brad shrugged as if to say "What can I do?" and allowed herself to be led away by the hand.

"Oh, boy," Kyle said, watching her friend disappear. "That's Nancy."

"She okay?" Dane asked.

"Ordinarily, she can take care of herself. But tonight?" Kyle just shook her head. "I'm not sure *she* knows what she's looking for."

"Well," Dane expelled a long breath, "I can guarantee she has no idea what she's getting with Brad."

They sat in silence, a silence that intensified until Dane leaned forward.

"I want you to come upstairs with me."

Kyle studied her—the fierce eyes, the chiseled features, the simmering emotions. She remembered tenderness and power and just a little danger. She remembered the freedom of being led down paths new to her, but not foreign. She remembered Dane trembling in the aftermath of orgasm, helpless and, for an instant, hers.

"Yes."

When Nancy stepped through the doorway into the surprisingly wide hallway beyond, she slowed, suddenly uncertain. It was nearly black, much darker than the large main room had been, and the air was warmer, thicker, heavy with the scent of arousal.

"Come over here," Brad murmured and moved against one wall, pulling Nancy back against her. She slid her arms around Nancy's waist from behind, settled Nancy's hips in the bend of her own abdomen and thighs, and nestled her cheek in the curve of Nancy's neck. Her lips brushed Nancy's ear when she spoke. "Just watch."

While Nancy waited for her eyes to adjust to the gloom, she was acutely aware of the firm prominence against her buttocks and saw again the unmistakable form nestled along Brad's thigh. Brad's hand, the fingers splayed wide, rested on her abdomen just below her breasts. Nancy could feel the heat of that hand through her clothes and astonishingly, felt arousal flow in response. She was no stranger to anonymous sex, but lately the couplings had left her not only unsatisfied, but often had failed even to excite her. Nevertheless, she was used to being in control. Determined to maintain the upper hand, she shifted her hips suggestively into Brad's body as she slowly became aware of the activity around her. Then, she couldn't prevent a small gasp of surprise.

Behind her, Brad chuckled and softly kissed her neck.

Across from where they stood, two women reclined on a small sofa in a recessed alcove. One lay on her back, her head lolling against the upholstered arm as the other woman knelt between her open thighs, bringing her to orgasm with her mouth.

"God," Nancy whispered, giving an involuntary start. The figures were indistinct, their features pale and fluid in the murky light. Nevertheless, she could see that the woman being ministered to was about to come. Her spine was arched, her left hand clenched on the edge of the sofa while her right stroked fitfully through her lover's hair. Nancy could hear her soft moans.

"She knows you're watching," Brad whispered. "She wants you to feel her come."

A hot flush coursed through Nancy's body, and she was suddenly dizzy. She imagined being in the woman's place; she imagined the hard urgency in the pit of her stomach as she climbed toward climax; she imagined the stroke of a firm tongue and the pull of soft lips on her screaming flesh. She flashed on Kyle's face and imagined her friend as the source of her pleasure. Trembling, she found Brad's hand and pushed it down her body toward the terrible need pulsing between her thighs.

"She'd like it if you came with her." Brad traced her lips along the curve of Nancy's ear. She resisted the pressure on her wrist and raised her hand instead to Nancy's breast, finding the hard knot of nipple through the blouse. When she squeezed, Nancy arched in her arms.

"Please," Nancy choked. She turned her head until her mouth was against Brad's neck. "Please touch me."

"Touch yourself." Brad brought her other hand to the opposite breast and worked both nipples steadily, keeping Nancy upright when she felt her sag from the onslaught.

Nancy's body burned and her mind was a confusion of sensation—desperate arousal undercut with anger. Brad had stolen her control, her ultimate weapon, and despite the painful demands of her body for release, she would not give Brad the satisfaction of dominating her. She would *not*. With one hand, she reached back and pressed her palm between Brad's thighs, closing her fingers over the swelling she found there. Through the mists of her own wild need, she heard Brad gasp.

"You're used to leading men around by their dicks," Brad grated, ignoring the exquisite pressure against her screaming nerve endings. First touching Kyle, now Nancy, had fueled her own excitement to the point where was she poised to explode.

Nevertheless, she steadied her breathing and, with supreme effort, kept her voice from trembling as Nancy continued to massage her. "You won't be able to do that with me."

"I know...you like it," Nancy gasped. Across from her, the woman reared up, screaming as she came. Nancy almost climaxed just from witnessing her pleasure.

"You're right." Brad shifted from behind Nancy until she was standing next to her, one arm still around Nancy's waist, her own back to the wall. She dropped her free hand, unzipped her fly, and in a practiced move, extracted the phallus. She gripped it, warm and pliant from the heat of her body, in the palm of her hand. "I like it very much."

When Nancy reached for it, Brad caught her wrist and held her hand away. "No."

To Nancy's stunned amazement, Brad gestured instead to a stranger who had stopped in front of them to stare. Without a word being spoken, the woman dropped to her knees and took Brad into her mouth. When Nancy looked down, all she could see were the familiar motions of an act she had performed countless times herself, but this time it held a fascination she had never experienced. The act was real, powerfully so, and she heard Brad's breath catch on a groan as her hips jerked. The sound sliced through Nancy like a knife.

"You *bitch,*" she seethed as she placed her hand on Brad's abdomen, her own stomach tightening as she felt the board-like muscles convulse. "You're going to let *her* make you come."

"Yeah." Brad tipped her head back, closed her eyes, and tightened her grip on Nancy's waist. Her legs quivered uncontrollably, and she fought not to moan out her pleasure as the rhythmic motion of the woman's mouth on the phallus was transmitted to her clitoris. "Yeah."

For the first time in her life, Nancy was not only stone-cold furious but also insanely jealous. Brad had beaten her in an arena where *she* had always reigned victorious, and she vowed that it would not happen again.

CHAPTER TWELVE

Darkness cloaked them as Kyle pushed Nancy's sleek Ferrari through the tight turns toward home. She was in no mood for conversation, and, gratefully, Nancy was strangely—and uncharacteristically—subdued. Keeping her eyes fixed on the road, Kyle grappled with the roller-coaster events of the evening. So much had happened, physically and emotionally, and then—abruptly—it had simply ended. When the two couples had returned coincidentally to the table after their separate excursions, the conversation had consisted of nothing more than terse, formal goodbyes. Dane had left abruptly, pointedly ignoring Brad completely and murmuring only "I'll see you" to Kyle. As Kyle had watched Dane walk away, she'd been left wondering when, if ever, that might be.

Still no phone number. No mention of next time.

Brad had then chauffeured Nancy and Kyle back to Leathers, the short trip passing in silence. Just before Nancy climbed from the car, Brad had whispered something to her that Kyle hadn't been able to hear.

"Cigarette?" Nancy asked softly, jolting Kyle from her reverie.

Kyle reached automatically into her jacket pocket and fingered two from the pack. She handed them across to Nancy, who lit both from the lighter in the dash.

"I'm trying to quit," Kyle said after a moment. "You starting again is not helping."

"Sorry." Nancy blew out a thin stream of swirling smoke and sighed. "Looks like I fell off all the wagons tonight."

"You okay?"

"Yeah. Just feeling a little weird." For some reason, she didn't want to recount the details of her experience with Brad. She sensed that Kyle would not approve. It had never bothered her before when Kyle was critical over her dalliances with men, perhaps because those interludes hadn't meant anything to her. She could brush away Kyle's censure as easily as she could banish the memory of the empty couplings. And although she didn't completely understand what had happened with Brad, of one thing she was certain. It mattered. "How was *your* night?"

"I'll tell you about it some other time." Kyle gripped the wheel more tightly, welcoming the aching tension in her fingers. The pain helped dampen her emotional turmoil. Her reactions to the night, and to her experience with Dane, were still too raw and painful to relive. She needed to put some distance—if not emotionally, at least temporally—between herself and those few intense minutes before she shared them, even with Nancy.

Appreciating Kyle's deep sense of privacy, Nancy didn't push, but *she* wanted to talk nevertheless. If she talked, she wouldn't have to keep thinking about Brad. She wouldn't have to feel angry and excited and fascinated and disturbingly unsatisfied. She wouldn't have to acknowledge the insistent thrum of arousal deep inside that was making her just a little crazy. And most especially, she wouldn't have to think about that bastard Brad's parting words.

"Later—when you make yourself come—you'll imagine me touching you. Just when you're about to scream, you'll see my face."

Nancy shifted irritably in her seat. "Bitch."

"What?" Kyle glanced at her, frowning.

"Nothing." Nancy took a long breath and gathered the reins of her control. *I am not going to be played by an arrogant asshole like Brad, no matter how fucking sexy she is.* "God, what a place. Is it always like that?"

"Like what?"

"Everyone—everything—was so intense. So exposed." She shivered, uncomfortable with the memory of how close to the surface her needs had surged, nearly overwhelming her. That kind of loss of control just didn't happen to her. "It was as if I didn't have a private thought—or feeling."

"I've never been anywhere like that before. Most of the time—in the usual clubs and the bars—it's just a whole lot of strangers trying to find one face, one soul, in the crowd to connect with. You know that picture." Kyle's voice was hollow, her expression bleak. "That place tonight...that whole scene is designed to strip away the trappings of self. The *people*—who we are or who we care about—don't count. It's just about the sensations."

"What the hell happened to you in there?" Nancy asked sharply, a little frightened by the bitterness in her friend's voice. She had come to count on Kyle's optimism, on her core belief in the possibility of romantic passion. She needed Kyle's refusal to settle for less just so she herself could hold on to a kernel of hope.

"I found out that I was just another person who didn't count."

"Are you talking about Dane?" Nancy laughed. "Oh, I don't think so. I saw the way she looked at you."

"And all of a sudden you're an expert on what people are feeling?" Kyle's anger boiled over. "Since when? People are just bodies to you anyhow, right? You said it yourself—men or women, it doesn't matter. It's just another experience."

"Not fair, Kyle." Nancy refused to lash out, even in defense, when Kyle was so obviously hurting. "*You're* not just another body." She hesitated. "Neither is poor Roger. Believe it or not, I try not to hurt him with my...extracurricular activities."

"Fuck." Kyle turned into Nancy's driveway and braked sharply. Hands still wrapped around the wheel, she stared straight ahead, forcing herself to step back from the pain. "I'm sorry, Nance. It's not your fault. I wanted someone to be pissed at, and you were just handy."

"Uh-huh. I know." Nancy reached over and stroked the top of Kyle's hand. "Let's go inside, make a fire, and commiserate."

"Sounds perfect." Wearily, she followed Nancy into the living room with its huge windows and million-dollar ocean view.

"The fire's set to go. Just strike a match and get comfortable on the sofa," Nancy instructed. "I'll find us something to nibble on. You want wine?"

"Maybe a little." As directed, Kyle lit the tinder beneath the carefully stacked split logs, and in a minute, the fire was blazing. Despite the heat that quickly suffused the room, she shivered. The chill, she feared, was somewhere inside herself, and she wondered if the cold would turn her heart to stone. Tears, unnoticed, danced on her lashes and sparkled brightly in the light from the fire. She closed her eyes and drifted, lost and uncertain, until she felt a finger tracing the single damp trail down her cheek.

"Tell me, sweetheart. What is it?" Nancy murmured gently, sitting softly on the opposite end of the sofa.

"I can't." Kyle opened her eyes and shrugged helplessly. She took the glass Nancy offered but set it down on the floor by her feet, the wine untasted. "I'm not sure what I feel right now."

"Tell me what happened, then." When Kyle remained silent, Nancy stated the obvious. "Something happened between you and Dane."

Kyle laughed shortly. "Yeah."

"Something you didn't expect...something you didn't like...something you didn't know how to han—"

"Okay, okay. Jesus, you never let up." Kyle dropped her head back and stared at the ceiling. "After you and Brad left to go exploring, we went upstairs to one of the private rooms. We made love—no, that's not right. We had sex."

She stopped, tasting bitter disappointment as the irony of her words struck her. The first time she and Dane had touched, they'd been strangers, but their physical connection had been more than sex. Hours ago, it had been as far from making love as anything she could imagine.

"I've always wondered about *that* distinction." Nancy spoke lightly, sensing Kyle's struggle and hoping to help.

"You know there's a difference." Kyle turned her head, catching Nancy's gaze. "Even though you like to pretend there isn't."

"Well, maybe the first couple of times. Then, after the romance dies, it's just two bodies looking for a little satisfaction."

"I don't have anything against two people having sex for no other reason than mutual pleasure." Kyle grimaced. "Obviously.

But when you're with someone you...care about, being together should mean more than that."

"I know. That's your problem." Nancy sighed. *You expect the honeymoon to last forever. And you're heartbroken when it doesn't.* Nancy lifted Kyle's jacket from the nearby coffee table and found the cigarettes in the inside pocket. She helped herself and settled back, waiting for Kyle to do the honors. "So tell me— what was wrong with what went on with you two?"

Frowning, Kyle searched her pants pockets and then the jacket for her lighter. It was one of those little possessions she thought of as a talisman, and she carried it even when she wasn't smoking. "Damn. I lost my lighter."

"Never mind. I've got a light." Nancy walked over and used one of the wooden fireplace matches, then returned to the sofa. "Come on. What happened? Did she hurt you?"

Finally, Kyle capitulated to the relentless questions. But in remembering, the images, the feelings, returned with aching clarity.

Dane moved unerringly through the crowd, her fingers laced through Kyle's. At the far corner of the room, a narrow opening led to a steep flight of stairs that seemed to climb into a void, it was so dark above them. Dane started up, and Kyle followed unhesitatingly.

At the top of the stairs, a dim light flickering from beneath a shaded fixture provided just enough light for Kyle to make out a series of doors on either side of a long hallway. Several stood open, but most were closed. Beneath her feet the floor vibrated with the pulse of the music and the many bodies below. Here, though, the air was still and close. A light sweat broke out on her skin, but she didn't think it was from the heat. She heard a soft moan emanate from behind one of the closed doors as they passed, and her pulse quickened.

The room they entered was even darker than the hallway, lit only by a weak red bulb set high up in one corner. A narrow metal-framed cot with a bare mattress was pushed against one wall. A wooden chair sat beside it. As her eyes adjusted to the murky light, Kyle noticed stout eye-hooks screwed into the wall at various heights. Otherwise, the room was empty and bare of adornment.

Uncertain as to what to do, Kyle remained motionless as Dane closed and locked the door. She waited for some sign, some word to connect her to the silent stranger. She gave a small jerk of surprise when Dane carefully pulled her T-shirt from the waistband of her jeans.

"Dane—"

Dane pressed her fingers to Kyle's mouth, stilling the words before lifting the shirt all the way off.

Her sudden nudity left Kyle feeling vulnerable, and, seeking some comfort in connection, she reached for Dane. But Dane avoided her touch and moved quickly behind her. Kyle stiffened when both arms were drawn back and handcuffs closed firmly on each wrist. Then, soft fabric was drawn over her eyes and she was left in total darkness.

Her breathing escalated with a combination of apprehension and excitement. She trusted Dane—yearned for her touch—but the restraints and the effects of the silent blackness left her disoriented. She felt isolated and disconnected, and the sense of being so alone was unexpectedly painful. Where are you? Why won't you let me touch you, hear your voice?

She moaned quietly when soft lips traced the curve of her neck and then gentle hands cupped her breasts. As minutes passed, the fingers methodically teasing her nipples became the only connection to the woman behind her. Her entire focus settled into those small throbbing points of pleasure, because only there could she forge some fragile link to something outside herself. But even as she struggled to feel Dane, her awareness of anything beyond her own need was slowly eclipsed by the effect of the insistent caresses. She lost track of time, lost track of who was touching her, until she knew only the exquisite excitement that spread from her breasts through her belly and deep into her core. She'd been on the verge of coming more than once that evening, and now she surged rapidly to the edge of release.

She moaned, hips thrusting against empty air, desperate for a touch—any touch—to send her over.

"Please. Please."

A warm hand slid down her bare abdomen and a sharp tug at her waist opened her jeans. When fingers dipped inside, she whimpered and fought for breath. When the contact stopped short of where she so desperately needed to be stroked, she begged.

"Touch me. Touch me. Please."

Abruptly, Kyle sat forward and rubbed her palms angrily across her face. "She restrained me, then she made me come. She took her time and after a while, I didn't care that I couldn't see or touch her. I just wanted her to keep touching me. I wanted her to be everywhere—inside of me, all over me. I didn't care who she was, I only wanted it to go on."

"Jesus," Nancy muttered, draining her glass, "that sounds good to me."

"God, you're an unsympathetic SOB." Kyle wanted to be angry, but it was difficult. Somewhere in the midst of the memory, she had felt Dane's tenderness.

"Was she rough with you?"

"Not physically, no."

"Then what—"

"She made it so she could have been *anyone.*" Kyle's voice broke. "*I* could have been anyone. She made it mean nothing."

Nancy's throat tightened. *I could have been anyone. She made it mean nothing.* The words sparked sudden, painful understanding. *Yes, I know how* that *feels, because that's Brad's game.* When Nancy spoke, her voice was devoid of her usual levity. "For someone so smart, I think you have everything backwards."

Kyle turned her head and eyed her friend irritably. "What does that mean?"

"Uh—forgive me for being indelicate, but wasn't Brad getting pretty familiar under the table tonight?"

"Fuck." Kyle blushed. "You saw that?"

"Well, the entertainment on stage *was* pretty riveting, but when a hot woman like Brad is doing my best friend—"

"Shit. *Okay.*" Kyle held up a hand to halt further description. "That place got to me."

You're not alone there. Nancy's laugh was hollow. "That seems to be the intention."

Kyle sighed. "I should have stopped her—wanted to stop her...sort of—but I was so caught up, I just didn't."

"Kyle, sweetie—I'm not criticizing. You're both adults. That's not where I was going." Nancy slid closer, wrapped her arm around Kyle's waist, and rested her cheek against Kyle's shoulder. "Do you love Brad?"

"Christ, no."

"Like her?"

"Not particularly."

"But, even so," Nancy gave her a squeeze, "she had you about to co—"

"Nance," Kyle interrupted threateningly.

Nancy grinned. "Well—*that* was impersonal sex."

"Yes." Kyle reached down, recovered her glass, and sipped the warm wine. "Your point is?"

Tilting her head, Nancy regarded Kyle with unusual seriousness. "You really want to know?"

Kyle nodded.

"You...like Dane, right? Have a thing for her."

Again, Kyle nodded.

"What you told me about you and Dane tonight—it's what you've been looking for. You've been wanting someone to make love to you that way."

"What do you mean?" Kyle asked warily.

"You went to that club in the first place because you were interested in exploring power, or S/M, or whatever it is you all call it. You wanted to relate to someone differently—more basically, more physically, more real-ly. Is *real-ly* a word?"

"I guess so," Kyle said in frustration. "So?"

"So, that's what you got. That's what Dane did. She dominated you. She defined you for however long you two did what you did. She said, 'You are this and I am something else—I am the controller, the one responsible for your pleasure, the'— what do you guys call that?"

"The top."

"Yeah—that sounds right. The *top*. You told her somehow to be that, and she was. Your call. She did that for you." Nancy reached for another cigarette and flourished it dramatically. "But you let that happen with *her*—not Brad, not some stranger—*her*, because of who she is to you. Because she means something to you."

Kyle looked at her. "How did you know all that?"

"I read a lot. Now get me a light."

"I can't stand you."

"Mm-hmm. I know."

Kyle stood to retrieve the fireplace matches. *You let that happen with her...because she means something to you.*

"Feel better?" Nancy asked as she accepted the light.

"Some." Kyle paced. "It bothers me that she won't let me touch her."

Nancy's brows rose. "She doesn't come?"

"Ah...that's not what I said." Even through the cloud of her own climax, she'd heard the slide of a zipper, the harsh sobbing breath, the muted groan.

"I don't suppose you'll tell me?" Nancy's heart picked up speed as a panoply of images from Encounters came flooding back. The restless unease in the pit of her stomach resurged as well.

"No." Kyle rested a hip on the arm of the couch.

"Maybe she needs more time." Nancy's voice was surprisingly gentle.

"Yeah." Kyle smiled gratefully, then leaned down and kissed Nancy's cheek. "Thanks. I need to crash."

"It's late. You know where the guest room is."

"Yeah. Thanks."

"Mmm. See you in the morning." Nancy watched Kyle walk away and slowly finished her cigarette, thinking about what she had seen that night and what she wanted now. She hesitated a minute outside the guest room, listening at the half-open door. She heard nothing from the darkened room and finally walked on.

When she stretched out alone beneath cool crisp sheets, when she revisited the sights and sounds of the evening, she tried to think of Kyle, a woman she trusted and loved. But when she came, she saw Brad's face. When she turned on her side, still gasping with the wrenching pulsations, she remembered Brad's hands—and ached to feel them again.

CHAPTER THIRTEEN

Dane awoke to a cold nose in her ear.

"Go away," she muttered, ineffectually pushing at the huge head with one arm. She tried to regain her dream, an erotic collage of soft, tanned skin, warm tender lips, and fiery caresses. Just as she began to drift into Kyle's enticing embrace once again, the covers were roughly tugged off, leaving her bare and shivering.

She bolted upright, blinking in the harsh sunlight. "Damn you, Baron."

The big black dog sat happily at the foot of her bed, the blankets in a tangle around him. He almost seemed to smile at her as he panted excitedly.

As Dane swung her legs over the side of the bed and reached to retrieve the covers, the phone rang. Snarling, she snatched up the receiver and snapped, "What!"

"Well, a nice hello to you, too," Caroline replied. "Are you awake?"

"No!" Dane shouted. "The only one up around here is Baron."

Caroline laughed. "It's seven o'clock. We'll be set to go in an hour. Are you alone?"

"Yes. *Like I've been every night for the last two weeks.* She hadn't been out to the clubs since the night she'd been with Kyle at Encounters. She kept telling herself, night after restless night, that she just wasn't in the mood for a scene, or even for a quick vanilla sex fix. But she couldn't avoid the truth, especially when she dreamed. The only person she wanted to see, to touch, was

Kyle. And that scared her. Wanting someone made you careless, made you vulnerable—and being vulnerable was what had led to her downfall.

Just thinking about Kyle made her stomach clutch.

"I'm alone." Dane dropped back against the pillows and closed her eyes against the start of a headache. Reaching out blindly, she fumbled on the bedside table for her cigarettes.

"Then you shouldn't have any trouble being ready on time. See you, sunshine."

"Is she up?" Anne asked as she walked into the bedroom from the bathroom, toweling her hair.

"Sort of." Caroline had heard nothing but a click as Dane had unceremoniously severed their connection. "Sounds like she's in a bitchy mood, though."

Anne sighed. "So what else is new?"

"Does she seem that way to you, too?" Caroline shed her robe and stepped into underwear, then pulled on khaki chinos.

"Excuse me? These last few weeks she's been unbearable." Anne pulled on a blue T-shirt with Daneland embroidered in yellow above the image of a dog's head and scowled over at her lover. "I don't think I've done one thing right around the kennel in days. I can't even answer the phone properly."

"You know it's not you, don't you?" Caroline tucked in a blue polo shirt—one that matched Anne's T—as she crossed the room to her. When she wrapped her arms around Anne's waist, she was surprised to feel her lover pull away. For an instant, Caroline's heart faltered, ambushed by her barely contained fear that her young lover would someday leave. "Anne?"

How can I know it's not me when no one tells me anything? Even you? Anne struggled with the frustration of the all-too-familiar sense of being left out of what was happening around the kennel. The personal closeness between Caroline and Dane didn't help. Still, hearing her lover's uncertainty was enough for her hurt to give way to tenderness. She kissed Caroline very lightly on the lips before settling into the embrace and resting her head on

Caroline's shoulder. "I know, but it still bothers me. Do *you* know what's wrong with her?"

Involuntarily, Caroline stiffened slightly. She never liked to discuss Dane's personal life. "I—"

"Oh, *sorry.*" Angrily, Anne stepped back and turned away. Her eyes brimmed with tears despite her resolve not to give in to the hurt. "I didn't mean to infringe on your *special* relationship with Dane."

"Babe," Caroline whispered softly, sadly. Carefully, she rested her hands on the younger woman's tense shoulders. She hated it when Anne was unhappy, but she owed it to Dane to guard her confidences as well. Faced with failing one of the two women she loved, she bled.

Anne kept her back turned, not even certain why she cried.

"Hey, babe," Caroline repeated as she slowly drew Anne around to face her again. The confusion in her lover's eyes broke her heart. And made her decision. "Dane hates to have anyone know what's going on with her. It takes a long time for me to get anything out of her."

"I know that." Anne wiped her eyes. "It's just that sometimes I feel like such an...outsider."

"Anne, oh, baby." Caroline hugged her tightly. "You are the most important thing in the world to me—don't you know that yet?"

Anne wrapped her arms tightly around Caroline's waist and smiled faintly. "Is this where you tell me I'm being stupid?"

"No, because you have a point." Caroline sighed and rested her forehead on Anne's. "My relationship with Dane is special because we're old friends and we have a lot of shared history. Even so, I would never want that to take anything away from you and me." She kissed Anne's forehead. "Sometimes I don't think about that as much as I should. I'm sorry."

"I'm a little jealous, I think," Anne confessed quietly.

"Jealous?" Caroline's tone was incredulous. "God, don't you know you're everything to me?"

Anne tilted her head, studied Caroline's face. "Yeah?"

"Oh yeah." Caroline kissed her again, this time on the mouth. And this time with the passion and desire that she had failed to convey with words. When she finally relinquished Anne's mouth, her breathing was shallow and Anne's eyes were misty. She trailed her fingers over her lover's cheek. "I'm sorry that I haven't done a very good job of letting you know that you're my whole life."

"No, you do," Anne protested, brushing her fingers through the wisps of gray at Caroline's temples. "Sometimes, I forget."

Caroline smiled tenderly. "Then I'll just remind you more often."

Anne pressed close for one last instant of physical connection, then reluctantly stepped away. "We should finish getting ready. We still have to pick up the van, load the dogs, and get the reluctant king."

"Mmm." Caroline gathered her wallet and keys. As she followed Anne downstairs, she mused, "You know, if I knew what was bothering Dane, I'd tell you. But I don't. She's stopped talking to me, too—ever since that night a few weeks ago when she left here to go out to the club." *The night after she let someone beat her until she nearly bled. God, what is hurting her so much?*

"Is she seeing someone?" Anne locked their door and the two headed toward their Jeep.

"Not that I know of, but I certainly wish she would. She needs someone."

Anne laughed shortly. "Dane?"

The genuine disbelief in Anne's voice reminded Caroline how young she really was. "Probably more than most of us."

Dane climbed into the back of the van, leaned up against one of the dog's crates, and asked abruptly, "When are we showing?"

Caroline glanced at her friend in the rear-view mirror. "Good morning. We're fine, thanks." Expecting no answer and getting none, she glanced irritably back at the road. "We show at one o'clock. The Schutzhund exhibition is at three."

It was the biggest specialty show of the season, and they all knew it was important that their kennel be well represented. Breeders and buyers followed the results of such shows religiously, and if Daneland Kennel's dogs finished well, it would mean more business. Caroline was scheduled to show three of their own and another of Baron's sons from another kennel over the course of the afternoon. But she was especially edgy because Anne was showing one of their new bitches in a point show for the first time. Anne displayed talent for showing, and now that their kennel was expanding, Caroline needed help. Still, she was nervous, and she counted on her more-experienced friend to get them all through the day. "Dane? You are going to show, aren't you?"

"I have to." Dane stared moodily out the window. She'd entered Troy in the advanced obedience exhibition later that day. "Troy is counting on it."

"We're all counting on it," Anne murmured, her own anxiety showing.

Dane turned to where Anne sat in the front passenger seat as if seeing her for the first time. Fleetingly, her eyes lost their chill, and tenderness softened the hard edges of her expression. "All set for the big day, Chicken?"

Caroline drew a sharp breath but kept her gaze forward. Dane had not called Anne that in what seemed like an age. Twisting in her seat, Anne searched Dane's face, trying to find the strong, compassionate woman who had led her so gently into awareness just a few years before. But by the time she looked, all she found were the trails of Dane's pain etched across her face and the scars of many wounds hardened in her eyes.

"Yes, I'm ready." Anne's smile was sad, her heart aching for the woman who had held her so long ago, and whom she had loved so fiercely in return.

Silently, Caroline watched the exchange from the corner of her eye, seeing for the first time not the much-younger woman she had fallen in love with, but the mature woman her lover had become. She reached over and grasped Anne's hand.

"Do you know that I love you?" Caroline asked softly.

Anne squeezed her hand. "Yes."

The showgrounds were chaos. Anxious owners and keyed-up handlers milled around the judging rings with their dogs, half of whom barked at every other passing animal. Latecomers rushed about in search of the appropriate rings, and harried judges struggled to keep the events on schedule. Dane watched from a ringside chair as Caroline brought out the first of their young bitches in the open class. Maia, a Baron daughter, was just two years old and in perfect condition. Dane was especially proud of her, for she represented one of the first products of her own breeding program.

"Nice-looking bitch," a cool voice said from behind her chair.

Dane stiffened imperceptibly and turned to look up at Brad, who stood with one hand in the pocket of her jeans and the other loosely clasped around black leather driving gloves. Purposefully Dane met the slightly mocking gaze for an instant, despite the churning in her stomach, and then deliberately looked back at the ring. "Thanks."

"So, how have you been, Dane?" Brad placed her hand lightly on Dane's thigh as she knelt down beside the chair to watch the event. She smiled to herself as Dane pulled her leg hastily away.

"Fine." Dane kept her eyes on Caroline and Maia, determined not to let Brad see her discomfort. She broke out in a sweat and her heart thudded almost painfully in her chest.

"Seen much of Kyle lately?"

"No." Dane stared straight ahead, her jaws clenched so tightly they ached.

"Too bad. She's quite a woman."

The brittle walls of Dane's defenses snapped. "How would you know?"

"Well, I admit I've only had a taste." Brad laughed. "I haven't had the pleasure of quite *all* of her yet. But I will."

Dane turned her head, her blue eyes hot with fury. She and Brad were close enough to kiss. "Are you so sure of that?"

"I might not be, if it were anyone else but *you* she wanted." Brad lifted a shoulder. Her dark eyes were smoky, her voice husky. "You're too much of a fool to know what to do with her. But I'm not. She'll come around."

Dane rose quickly, catching Brad unaware. She looked down at her, nearly choking with rage, hands clenched tightly at her sides. And wanting nothing more at that moment than to drive Brad's insolent face into the ground.

"You're wrong about her, Brad. She's too good for either of us." She stepped quickly around Brad's surprised figure and stalked away from the ring.

Brad laughed at Dane's retreating back as she straightened up.

"Why don't you leave her alone?" Caroline asked angrily. She'd seen the end of their encounter as she had led Maia from the ring.

"Why, Caroline," Brad soothed, hands raised in supplication. "What have I done?"

"You know damn well what you've done. You bait her and push her whenever you can. Why don't you just let her be?"

"Because she's too much fun to let go of." Brad's voice and expression had hardened. Her tone was glacial. "Besides, she needs to learn some discipline."

"You bastard." Caroline quivered with rage. "You tried that once and nearly killed her."

Brad shrugged, the corner of her mouth curling in cool amusement. The memory both pleased and aroused her. "Don't forget, she asked for it."

"Not like that, she didn't. What you did to her—"

"You don't know what she asked for, do you?" Brad leaned close, her tone sharp as a lash. "But you know what she likes, *don't you,* Caroline."

Nearly blind with anger, Caroline took a quick step toward Brad, who had turned to leave, but was brought up short by a tug on her arm.

"Honey, let her go," Anne said quietly. "You can't change her. Dane will just have to find her own way to deal with her."

Caroline gazed from Brad's retreating figure to her lover, allowing her anger to dissipate. "My God, when did you grow up? Have I missed it all these past few years?"

"I think you've been so worried about my age," Anne laced her fingers through Caroline's and smiled a little ruefully, "and that I might run off in a frenzy after someone else, that you never noticed it was *you* I've always been crazy about."

"All right, lover, you win. I am a jerk on any number of levels." Caroline closed her eyes for a second, breathing in Anne's scent and drawing comfort from her solid presence. Then she sighed and met Anne's worried gaze. "I'm okay. But we have two more dogs to show, and..."

Anne took a deep breath, "You'd better go see to Dane."

Caroline kissed her swiftly. "You're right again. I'll catch up to you later. And I won't forget what I have in mind for you."

"Just maybe *I* have plans for *you.*" Anne ran her fingers down Caroline's arm. "I'll take Maia. Go."

Five minutes later, Caroline found Dane at the van, sitting on the tailgate smoking a cigarette. She sat beside her and slipped her arm lightly around Dane's waist. The whip-slender body felt tauter, more honed than she remembered. A steel wire strung to the breaking point.

"Maia won, Dane."

"Good. She deserved to."

"Anne's showing Tara next. I know she'd like you to be there."

Dane nodded, her face set. She stared blankly ahead, every muscle tight. "I will be."

"Can't you just close *her* out, instead of the rest of the world?" Caroline asked softly.

"I can't." Dane's voice was bitter, heavy with resignation. "Not when she reminds me of what I am—or what I'm not anymore."

"*No,*" Caroline objected. "She does not make you who you are—she can't do that." She risked putting her free hand on Dane's arm. She wanted to gather her close, to rock her until the pain was gone. "You were nearly destroyed, but you've come back from it. I *know* what that took. I was there, remember?"

"It doesn't matter." Dane shook her head and glanced down her own body as if it were a stranger's. "There's nothing left of me. She wants Kyle, and she'll have her, because I have nothing to offer."

"Oh, Dane—you're so wrong. Won't you try, *just try* with Kyle?"

"I can't, Caroline. I can't fight Brad for her—besides, I don't care enough anymore to try."

"You mean you don't want to care anymore."

Dane merely shrugged, her face revealing none of the despair that threatened to choke her.

"Come on, let's go watch Anne show them how it's done."

CHAPTER FOURTEEN

Kyle sat on a shady knoll above the show ring with her back against the trunk of a weeping willow. For the last hour she'd strolled the grounds, watching the events and trying to figure out what was happening. It didn't take long to discern that the animals were grouped by sex and age, and that males were called "dogs" and females "bitches." She found the term "puppy bitch" unexpectedly endearing and grinned every time one of the ring announcers said it. But exactly what made one animal a winner eluded her. They each looked perfect, and the fact that they all looked exactly alike—to her eye at any rate—did nothing to dispel the confusion.

Nonetheless, the obedience trials now being held in the ring below were much more interesting to her than the conformational competition had been. The dogs were given a series of commands, sometimes separately and sometimes in a group. As one, they responded with flawless control. The dogs, so powerfully built and obviously intelligent, appeared perfectly attuned to their handlers' commands. Kyle found that bond of mutual respect and discipline between animal and master exciting. It seemed so much deeper than love alone.

As she watched the choreographed routines, she flashed on her last night with Dane, recalling the painful distance that had loomed between them even as they seemed so intimately connected physically. Nancy had been right about a lot of things that had initially bothered her about that scene. She *had* wanted Dane to top her. But what she had desperately missed, even as her body responded sexually, had been some emotional link to connect them even in the midst of their separate roles. If Dane had touched her after it had ended, or had at least allowed Kyle to touch her, she would not have felt so alone.

Thinking about it over and over is not going to change what happened. Only seeing her again, trying again, will help. And that seemed unlikely to happen. She had not seen Dane since that night, despite her hope that Dane would appear at Leathers.

Kyle sighed, lit her second cigarette of the day, and was reminded of her lost lighter. It still aggravated her to be parted from it. Relaxing in the heat of the late afternoon, she lost track of time until the sudden sight of a familiar figure approaching the ring brought her upright in surprise. An announcement was made, but she lost the words in the wind. Dane's figure, however, was unmistakable.

She wore black jeans and a short-sleeved, open-collared white shirt. Close to her side was a very handsome, heavily muscled dog. Kyle watched, her attention divided between the beautiful animal and Dane's equally beautiful face, as Dane put the animal through some preliminary maneuvers. The crowd murmured with appreciation at the dog's split-second responses to Dane's commands. Even from a distance, it was clear that Dane controlled him purely by hand signals.

The dog remained in place, tensely alert, as Dane walked slowly away. Kyle observed a man enter the far side of the ring and rapidly approach Dane from behind, his raised arm wielding a short club, poised as if to strike. Kyle's heart sped up as alarm coursed threw her. At a signal from Dane, the dog instantly attacked. Kyle drew a sharp breath as the dog raced toward the man, only to exhale quickly as the powerful animal drew up short between the stranger and Dane. He held the man at bay with threatening growls and short rushes toward him, but he never touched him. At Dane's command, the dog slowly herded the intruder toward the judges' table, whereupon Dane called him back to her side.

The sound of applause drifted to Kyle as Dane then walked to the side of the ring and returned with a heavy protective garment covering her left arm. At yet another signal from his master, the dog launched himself ferociously at *her,* all semblance of restraint gone. Kyle shuddered as Dane's slender body rocked from the shock of contact. The dog clamped heavy jaws around her arm as he brought his considerable weight to bear, pulling savagely against her. Their struggle seemed endless as woman and dog joined in a contest of strength and will. Then, as quickly as it had begun, it was over. Dane raised her right arm, and the dog immediately released to sit with his eyes fixed on Dane's face. She praised him with a vigorous pat on his solid shoulder as she led him from the ring.

Without considering the wisdom of her actions, Kyle stood and hurried down the hill toward the ring. She walked up to Dane just as she was finishing a conversation with one of the judges.

"That was very impressive," Kyle said softly as the judge turned back to the ring.

Dane's brows rose in surprise. "What are you doing here?"

"Just happened to be in the neighborhood?"

"Uh-huh." Dane smiled, but her eyes were cool blue slate. "Way out here?"

Kyle shrugged. "Actually, Caroline mentioned the show last week after one of our group meetings."

Dane grimaced. "Still going to those, huh?"

"When I can."

"Learning anything?" Dane asked, starting to walk away. Kyle followed.

"Some. You'd be surprised at the things that women think about—and do, for that matter."

"Would I?" Dane stopped to look at Kyle. "There's not much I haven't seen."

"Oh, I'm sure of that." Kyle was not intimidated by Dane's curtness. "I only meant to suggest that a lot of women who might never act on their feelings about power nevertheless *do* think about it. And recognize some of those same elements in their own lives."

"Great," Dane replied, reaching for a cigarette. "I'm *so* happy that more women appreciate my lifestyle." As she lit her cigarette, she was startled by Kyle's quick grasp on her wrist.

"That's my lighter." Kyle's voice was sharp, more with surprise than anger.

"I know." Dane stared at the black and gold lighter in her hand, then nonchalantly dropped it into Kyle's palm. "You left it upstairs at Encounters when we were there."

"Why did you keep it?"

"I don't know—a souvenir? My bedpost is already full." *Because it's yours and it's all I have.*

Kyle jerked as if struck, quickly searching Dane's face with dark, angry eyes and finding only the blank wall she'd come to expect. "You son of a bitch." She turned her back and started away.

Dane looked after her for a split second, then called out before she had a chance to think. "Kyle, wait!"

When Kyle turned back, Dane saw that her face was pale. *Fuck, Jorgensen, what is wrong with you? It's not her fault.*

"Look, I'm sorry." Dane wanted to explain that it had soothed her just to reach in her pocket and find that small memory of Kyle there. She just couldn't bring herself to say the words.

Kyle sighed and walked back. "Why do I feel like you're always trying to push me away? Do I have to humiliate myself by telling you I want to see you?"

Dane continued staring straight ahead, acutely aware of Kyle's body so close to her own. "I thought you'd have other things to occupy your time by now."

"Do you think I spend all of my time looking for a bed partner?" Kyle asked quietly, determined, this time, to get through to this woman.

"When you aren't busy fighting off the offers." Dane laughed.

Kyle laughed, too. "I do go out—mostly just to see if what I've been thinking about feels real to me when I'm actually living it. But I don't need to sleep with someone to find that out."

"Jesus." Dane sighed as she put Troy into his crate in the van. "You think way too much, Kyle."

"Sometimes. Are you done here today?"

"Just waiting for Caroline and Anne to come back."

"Tell them you're leaving with me. Come to my place." Kyle surprised herself with her own words, but she knew she wanted more from Dane than occasional sex. "I'll make dinner."

"Today?" Dane's voice rose in surprise.

"Right now."

Dane laughed and shook her head. "Why do you think I'd want to do that?"

"I don't." Kyle held her gaze. "I just know *I* want you to."

Unable to read anything in Kyle's deep gray eyes except honesty, Dane wavered. There were so many reasons to say no. One of the biggest was how badly she wanted to take Kyle's hand and just go.

"Say yes, Dane." The words came softly, with an undercurrent of tender welcome. "Say yes."

Answering the need that burned brighter than any fear, Dane nodded.

"Yes."

Dane relaxed behind Kyle on the large motorcycle as they roared down the highway. The wind felt good in her face, as did the softness of Kyle's leather jacket under her hands. She wasn't thinking about anything, didn't have to think, and it was a surprising change. Even more astonishing than that, she was content to let Kyle lead the way.

They turned up a gravel-covered side road into the woods. As they rounded a turn, a house unexpectedly appeared, tucked unobtrusively into the hillside. There was a second smaller building behind the main house, with a neatly stacked pile of firewood under the sloping side roof. Kyle pulled her bike under the shelter of the overhanging eaves.

"This is home," she said simply.

"It's beautiful." Dane climbed off and took a deep breath of pine-scented air, then turned completely around. She didn't see another house. She grinned. "Nice."

Kyle smiled shyly, enjoying Dane's obvious pleasure. "Thanks."

"Have you lived here long?" Dane asked as Kyle lifted one denim-clad leg over the bike and stood. Although she was truly interested in the answer, a close-up look at Kyle after two weeks of dreaming about her hit hard in the pit of her stomach, and she found herself unable to concentrate on anything but the image of the woman before her. Beneath the jacket was a ribbed T-shirt that hugged every inch of her chest and abdomen, tucked into button-fly jeans that were frayed in some very interesting places. Dane swallowed hard imagining what might have worn the fabric so thin it was almost transparent just to the right of Kyle's fly. Through the rapid buzzing in her ears she heard Kyle speaking. "What? Sorry."

"Three years," Kyle repeated, following the drift of Dane's hungry gaze. Smiling inwardly, she felt herself twitch in response. Her voice was thick as she finished. "But I didn't finish it until just this year. I moved from room to room as I built."

Dane regarded her with genuine admiration as well as barely contained desire. "It's great."

"Can you build a fire?" Kyle unlocked the side door and led the way inside. "It gets cold up here as soon as the sun goes down."

"I can manage."

"Good. There's wood by the fireplace. Start it up while I get us a drink." Kyle pointed in the direction of the living room. "You hungry?"

More than I realized. Dane shook her head. "I can wait."

Kyle grinned. "I'll be right back."

Dane surveyed a spacious living room that seemed much larger than it really was, primarily due to a large wall of glass that looked out onto the surrounding woods. The sitting area, down several steps and centered on a large natural stone fireplace, contained two oversized leather chairs and a low table of finely crafted wood. She got the fire going easily and settled into one of the large, comfortable chairs. She was amazed at how relaxed she felt, and how unconcerned she was at being there. She tried to remember the last time she had been in another woman's space, other than Caroline and Anne's, and couldn't.

Kyle came in quietly and handed Dane a glass. "Brandy okay?"

Dane nodded silently and took the heavy glass filled with dark, swirling liquid.

"As soon as I unwind a little, I'll fix us some food." Kyle settled in front of Dane on a large cushion on the floor, her back resting lightly against Dane's knee, and stretched her legs toward the warmth of the fire. "Hope you like simple cooking."

"Sounds great. And there's no rush." Dane looked down at Kyle's face in profile. The dancing flames created a chiaroscuro of the bold planes of her face, softly framed by her tousled hair. "I like the fire."

"Yeah." Kyle nodded and leaned a little more firmly against Dane's leg. "I'm glad you came."

"Are you?" Dane murmured, mesmerized by the flickering red glow of the fire and the warmth of Kyle's back against her leg.

"Uh-huh." Kyle reached up and curled an arm softly over Dane's thigh. The brandy was relaxing her, and she didn't want to lose contact with Dane's presence. She replenished their glasses from a bottle by her side as they sat in companionable silence.

Dane shifted her legs a little, and Kyle pushed closer, her head coming to rest gently against Dane's inner thigh. Without thinking, Dane reached down and curled her fingers into Kyle's thick hair. Running the soft strands through her fingers, she leaned her head back against the worn leather and closed her eyes. She drifted in the soothing heat from the fire and the warmth of Kyle's body against her, peaceful and pleasantly, if distantly, aroused. When startled by a soft caress on her neck, she opened her eyes to discover Kyle kneeling upright between her legs, looking down at her with an expression both tender and intense.

"Did I wake you?" Kyle stroked the sharp edge of Dane's jaw, then let her fingers trail down her neck again.

Dane smiled slightly, not moving. "Wasn't sleeping. Just drifting."

"Good." Kyle smiled gently. "Close your eyes again."

Enjoying Kyle's gentle command, Dane did as requested. Kyle's hands tenderly traced her face and throat, stirring her blood to race wherever they touched. When Kyle leaned forward, the heat from her body scorched through the denim covering Dane's thighs.

Pulse pounding, Dane barely stopped herself from reaching out to draw Kyle closer. So exquisite was the slow rise of her desire that she didn't want to hurry. But when Kyle tugged her shirt free and gently opened the buttons over her breasts, Dane couldn't prevent herself from sliding her hands along Kyle's hips to pull her near. She wanted, needed, more of her. She opened her eyes to see Kyle's gaze upon her, cloudy now with desire that equaled her own.

"Uh-uh." Lowering her head, Kyle nipped at Dane's lower lip then drew quickly back. "Keep your eyes closed."

Dane's lids flickered with a surge of arousal that beat hard through her belly, and she knew that her need must show clearly in her face. Not caring that Kyle could see how much she wanted her, she did as she was bidden and closed her eyes, relinquishing control. She wouldn't have done it for anyone else. There was no one she trusted that much.

Gently, Kyle pushed the shirt down Dane's shoulders, tethering her arms in the tightly stretched sleeves. She pressed her mouth to Dane's ear. "Don't move."

Dane knew she could free herself easily if she tried, but the effect of being restrained by Kyle was not unwelcome. She wanted to be hers.

"Ohh." Dane moaned as Kyle brought soft lips to an exposed breast, and as Kyle's tongue ignited the sensitive skin of her nipple, Dane's head grew light. She arched her back and tried to push more of herself against the warm mouth. Even as lips and teeth worked her nipples, Dane felt a hand pull open the buttons on her jeans. She lay unprotesting, holding her breath, as Kyle slipped an arm under her to push down her clothing. The warmth of the fire caressed Dane's bare thighs as Kyle once again lay gently down upon her.

The denim of Kyle's jeans was rough against Dane's skin, and as Kyle insinuated herself more firmly between Dane's legs, Dane gasped at the contact of the material against her swollen flesh. She couldn't prevent herself from thrusting her hips, seeking even more contact. A cry escaped her tight throat, and Kyle quickly pulled away, breaking the exquisitely tormenting pressure.

"What is it?" Kyle gasped.

"Oh God, Kyle, don't stop." She needed Kyle's touch; more, she needed Kyle to release her. When she started to lift her head, Kyle held her back with one hand firmly in the hair at the base of her neck. "Please. Help me. Touch me."

"Wait, Dane—wait," Kyle whispered as she carefully slipped her free hand between Dane's legs.

Dane cried out again, strangling on her own desire, as Kyle's fingers, feather light, stroked her, drawing Dane's passion forth in a flood upon her hand.

"I can't. Oh, please, I can't." Dane moaned, hips writhing, urgently seeking to bring Kyle inside. Her breath caught in her throat as Kyle finally entered her in one full, deep thrust. With the weight of Kyle's body bearing down upon her, she sought Kyle's kiss hungrily. When Kyle filled her mouth as deeply as she filled her body, Dane cleaved to her, mind and body exploding.

Kyle waited until Dane's breathing quieted and her body ceased to quiver before gently slipping free, drawing forth another soft moan. Exhausted, content, Kyle rested her head on Dane's chest.

Dane pulled her arms free of the shirt sleeves and held Kyle tightly, keeping her warm, keeping her safe. They lay together wordlessly until long after the fire had burned to flickering embers.

"Fire's almost out," Dane whispered into Kyle's hair.

"Yours or mine?" Kyle murmured against Dane's skin.

"Ours." Dane laughed and pushed herself up on her elbows. "Needs more wood."

Kyle looked around and got up with a sigh. "I'll get it."

Dane watched as Kyle bent to throw more logs on the fire, wanting her close again. When Kyle returned and settled into her arms, she asked, "So where did you learn to do that?"

"What, make love?" Kyle smiled at the memory. "God, that was good."

"It was." Dane shook her head. "But I meant take control so easily. If I didn't know better, I'd say you just topped me."

"Mmm. Didn't I?"

"Top *me?*" Dane kissed her. She took her time, exploring the surface of Kyle's lips, the velvet smooth inner edges, the hot welcome of her mouth. As she teased with her tongue, she caressed Kyle's breasts through the thin fabric of the T-shirt, one thigh edged between Kyle's. When Kyle moaned, Dane slowly pulled away. She was panting softly, and Kyle's eyes were glazed. "Hmm, I *guess* maybe you did. You learn that at one of those meetings of yours?"

"Uh-uh. Some things I come by naturally."

Dane laughed and fit her body more closely to Kyle's. They kissed again, not hungrily now, but with the afterglow of pleasure shared. Eventually they slept, safe in one another's arms. And as they did, the fire burned brightly.

CHAPTER FIFTEEN

"Uh."

"Mmm."

"Hey," Kyle murmured, shifting in the cramped quarters until she could see Dane's face. Smiling, she brushed her knuckles lightly along the edge of Dane's jaw and was rewarded with a kiss skimmed over them in passing. "How you doing?"

Dane blinked and grinned lazily. "I just spent the night half-naked in a chair the size of a generous picnic basket." *With the hottest woman I've ever met.*

"Bad, huh?" Kyle had had the presence of mind to pick up a nearly threadbare couch blanket on her way back from feeding the fire, so at least they hadn't frozen.

"No." Dane stretched out on Kyle, her legs insinuated between Kyle's. She braced herself on her arms and rocked her hips, enjoying the rise of color to Kyle's neck. "It was good." She dipped her head, caught Kyle's bottom lip in her teeth, and tugged gently before releasing it and licking the small bite. "Very good."

Kyle's blood ran hot, starting at her heart and settling into a fiery fist in the pit of her stomach. "Are you..." She gasped when Dane pulled her shirt up and lowered her mouth to Kyle's breast. "...surprised?"

"No," Dane said softly as she moved to the other breast. She hesitated, trying to place the unfamiliar sensation. "Happy. Take your shirt off."

When Dane eased back, Kyle arched away from the chair and stripped the shirt over her head. Her nipples were hard from Dane's attentions, and she slid her hands over her breasts, rubbing the sensitive tips. Her stomach quivered with the answering echo between her thighs.

"Feel good?" Dane's blue eyes darkened to purple, and her voice dropped to barely a growl.

"Yes." Kyle gritted her teeth as Dane pumped a tight hard thigh against her crotch. It was so good it almost hurt.

"Keep working them, then." Dane slid down until she was kneeling on the floor between Kyle's spread legs. Deftly, she opened Kyle's pants, hooked her fingers over the waistband, and yanked. "Kick off your boots...no, don't let go of your nipples. I want you to keep them hard."

Breathing erratically, Kyle watched through half-closed lids as Dane laid her bare. Dane was still naked from the waist up, her jeans open from the night before. Kyle wanted to touch her, wanted to stroke the soft curve of her breasts and drag her fingers down the center of her taut abdomen. The more her eyes feasted, the faster she squeezed her nipples, until the pressure was one long wave of pleasure. She moaned, back arched.

"Harder." Dane spread her fingers over the soft, sweet skin of Kyle's inner thighs, very near the focus of her desire. She pressed and opened her—thumbs tracing the full, ready folds already damp with arousal and fragrant with yearning. Dane's hips jerked. No one had ever made her want to lose control so badly. All she wanted was Kyle coming in her mouth.

"I...want to come," Kyle gasped, eyes closed now. Every muscle was so tight her back barely touched the chair.

"I know you do, baby," Dane whispered. "But you can't yet."

Dane placed a palm low on Kyle's abdomen and pressed the rigid muscles as she caught Kyle's passion on her tongue. She held Kyle down when she would have reared up at the first touch. Then she slowly took Kyle into her mouth, sucking gently because her clitoris was already too hard, too close to going off. When Kyle thrust against Dane's face, demanding more, Dane used her teeth to carefully back her off, controlling her steady climb to orgasm with soothing strokes of her tongue and the maddening pull of her lips. Only when Kyle began to whimper and then beg did Dane increase the tempo and pressure of her mouth on the ready-to-burst flesh.

"I'm coming," Kyle cried, half sitting up as the first wave struck.

Dane groaned as the sharp pulsations of Kyle's orgasm played across her lips and brought her own excitement to a fever pitch. She drove her hand against the denim between her thighs and rubbed her clitoris through the material, coming instantly.

Trembling, struggling to focus through the roar in her head, Dane kept up the teasing motion of her tongue until Kyle jerked away.

"Can't," Kyle gasped. "Jesus. I'm going to have a heart attack."

Still shuddering with the last spasms that rippled down her thighs, Dane rested her forehead against Kyle's abdomen. "I think...I already did."

Kyle laughed shakily and dropped her hand onto the back of Dane's head, cradling her face against her body. "Did I feel you come in there somewhere?"

"Oh man, yeah."

"Mmm. Damn, I missed most of it."

Dane laughed softly. "Sorry. Couldn't wait."

"Sounds like you could use some discipline," Kyle said playfully.

You could use some discipline. Brad's voice, Brad's face, flickered through Dane's mind, and her stomach lurched dangerously. Taking a long breath, she lifted her head and gazed at the woman regarding her with soft, sated, tender eyes. She blinked and focused on Kyle's face. "You offering?"

"Yes." Kyle wasn't certain what had just happened, but Dane's eyes were wounded, her voice raw with some old pain. She stroked Dane's cheek. "But I won't hurt you."

"What if I...want you to?"

Kyle kept her fingers lightly on the side of Dane's neck, resting on the pulse that skittered and jumped just below the skin. "Do you?"

"Sometimes I like...rough." Getting the words out was hard. She hadn't let anyone top her, really top her, since Brad. At least not when she wanted pleasure. What she sought in the dark moments of her despair was neither sex nor satisfaction; it was absolution.

"Rough I can handle," Kyle murmured, trailing her fingertips over the delicate arch of Dane's collarbone. "But I won't make you bleed."

"I don't want you to." Dane sighed and closed her eyes, feeling as if some great weight had been lifted from her heart. *I don't want you to hurt me.*

"Then we don't have a problem." Kyle massaged the tight muscles in the back of Dane's neck until she felt them loosen up. Until she felt Dane relax completely in her embrace. "Hungry?"

"Yeah, I think." Dane sighed, eyes still closed. "Need a shower, too." She raised her head. Grinned. "Wanna come?"

Kyle shook her head, grinning as well. "Yes, but I'm not going to. You go ahead, and I'll cook something."

Dane leaned back, still kneeling, and ran her hands briskly over her face. "You go first, then cook."

"Deal."

While Kyle showered, Dane wandered about the house.

"What's in the other building out back?" Dane asked as she rejoined Kyle in the kitchen after her own shower.

"My shop."

"Can I see?"

"Uh-huh. I'll give you a tour after breakfast."

Kyle carried plates into the adjoining dining area while Dane walked to the windows for another look at the view. Her hair was still damp from the shower, and she wore one of Kyle's old shirts. Despite the fact that it was too loose on her, it didn't conceal the fine lines of her shoulders and back. The top three buttons were open as well, and the rise of her breasts was evident with every movement.

Kyle watched her, startled to feel the swift surge of desire. She cleared her throat.

"Dane?"

Dane turned, smiling, her eyes bright. "Hmm?"

She appeared younger somehow, and only then did Kyle recognize that the dark shadows in her eyes were gone. *You're so beautiful, so much more tender than I ever imagined. Why do you hide it?*

"What?" Dane raised an eyebrow, uncertain of the look in Kyle's eyes. "Kyle?"

"Will you please come over here and eat?" Kyle's throat was tight, her voice husky. "Because if you don't, I'm coming over there, and I promise you, the eggs will get cold."

"I love cold eggs." Dane cocked her hips and crossed her arms over her chest with a defiant grin. "Your call."

Kyle took three swift steps and drove her hands into Dane's hair, crushing her mouth to Dane's. While her tongue plundered the hot recesses of Dane's mouth, she fisted her fingers in the soft cotton at Dane's throat and wrenched the shirt open. Buttons flew, spinning off the window glass like tears. For the first time, they took one another in the sunlight, grappling furiously on the soft carpet, first one on top, then the other. Hands jerked at clothing, limbs tangled, lips devoured taut nipples and sweet flesh. Moans of pleasure, sharp cries of surprise, satisfied shouts filled the air. In what seemed like only moments, they lay gasping on their backs, staring dazedly at the ceiling, side by side.

"Fuck."

"Uh-huh."

Dane turned her head, the only part of her that would move. She could still feel Kyle's weight pinning her down while she'd driven into her and driven her to a climax that had left her sobbing. "You have a nice bite on your neck."

Kyle reached up weakly, fingered the sore spot, and grinned. "Bet you do, too."

"Feels like a couple."

"You make me lose my mind." Kyle shifted with a faint groan and regarded Dane with a grimace. "I can't come any more. Something's going to fall off."

Dane laughed. "That sounds like a challenge."

"Fact."

"We'll take a rest break."

"Deal." Kyle levered herself to a sitting position. "I'm *still* hungry."

Dane grinned. "I doubt the food has had time to cool off."

After breakfast, Kyle took Dane out to her shop.

"How could people cover this beautiful wood with paint?" Dane asked as she ran her hand over the dark grain of a sideboard that Kyle had just finished stripping.

"It's easier than maintaining it naturally, I guess. I'll never understand it."

"So, this is what you do, huh?" Dane leaned back against the work counter, thinking about the places in her body, and far deeper, that Kyle had awakened with her touch. "You bring things back to life."

Struck by the seriousness in Dane's typically bantering tone, Kyle searched her face questioningly. Dane's eyes, usually so inscrutable, appeared vulnerable and sad. For an instant, Kyle glimpsed the fragile woman beneath the impenetrable exterior. Propelled by a wave of tenderness, she put her arms around Dane's waist and her head on Dane's shoulder. Softly, she said, "Sometimes if I'm lucky, I find a treasure that has just been waiting for someone to look beneath its surface. It doesn't often happen, but when it does, it's like a gift."

Dane kissed her hair and sighed. "What if there's so much of a barrier built up over the years that the heart is...gone?"

Kyle didn't raise her head but pressed her lips gently into the hollow at the base of Dane's slender throat. "The heart may be buried, but it can always be found if you work slowly and carefully. And I'm very patient."

"How can you be sure?" Dane lifted Kyle's chin and softly kissed her lips.

"I can feel it."

Dane closed her eyes and wished that she never needed to relinquish this woman, this peace.

Kyle hummed softly as she rubbed the coarse wire brush over the surface of the oak desk, recalling the pleasure she'd felt at having Dane in her home.

The door to the shop burst open, and Nancy flew in, shattering her reverie.

"Hi," Nancy called, flinging her sweater over a chair.

"Hi yourself."

"You look wonderful today." Nancy pulled coveralls over her designer jeans and scoop-necked lycra top. "How come?"

"What, do I usually look like a troll?"

"No, you just don't usually look..." Nancy cocked her head. "So content. Did you have a nice night?"

Kyle nodded. "Uh-huh."

"And?"

"And it was nice," Kyle said, returning to work.

"I hate it when you keep secrets," Nancy pouted. She began to arrange her brushes and paints, then cast Kyle a sly grin. "*I* had a nice evening, too."

"I'm glad."

"Brad says hello."

Kyle stopped in mid-stroke, her heart seizing. "When did you see *her?*"

"Last night."

"Where, for Christ's sake?"

"At the club, of course." Nancy shrugged dismissively. "Did you think I had her out to the house for dinner?"

"*You* went to the club? Where was Roger?"

"Home. I told him I was coming over here."

"Damn it, Nancy," Kyle exploded, "what if he'd called here looking for you?"

Nancy smiled sweetly. "You would have thought of something."

"I can't believe you!" Kyle ground her teeth, half outraged and half ready to laugh. "Jesus. Why?"

"Why what?" Nancy asked, deliberately obtuse.

"Why did you go there?"

"I don't know, really," Nancy answered seriously. "I just wanted to. It's different and exciting, and I felt like having fun. Brad *is* a lot of fun." *And I couldn't stop thinking about the things I saw, the way she made me feel.*

"Oh, sure," Kyle said sarcastically, recalling her own encounters with Brad. "I don't trust her, Nance."

When Nancy didn't respond, Kyle's eyes narrowed with sudden suspicion. "Did you sleep with her?"

Nancy was silent for a long moment, and then she sighed. "Not exactly. We went to a party."

"A party?"

"Uh, it was a house full of women getting it on." She faltered, remembering the sex play, the bondage scenes, and the way that Brad had fondled her absently as they'd strolled about watching other women come. She'd wanted to be one of them, but Brad had never touched her intimately enough for that to happen. She'd been frustrated and oddly humiliated. She wasn't used to potential lovers turning her down. Still embarrassed and unrelentingly horny, she pushed those thoughts away. "Brad's a little hard to read. Sometimes it felt like she wanted to, but she never pushed. It's not like with men—they're so single-minded sometimes. So easy."

"Nancy," Kyle began, deeply uneasy where Brad was concerned. "I don't think you know what you're getting into here. You can't toy with Brad the way you do with men. She's into some very heavy sexual trips. I'm not so sure it's safe."

"Oh, come on." Nancy snorted. "You know I can handle myself. Do you think I've never had any experience with kinky sex?"

"This is different, and you know it. Promise me you won't get into anything with her without talking to me about it first, okay?" Just the thought of Nancy and Brad together made Kyle nervous.

"Yes, Mom." Nancy acquiesced to alleviate Kyle's obvious concern and decided that it would be wise not to mention that she'd already made another date with Brad. *And this time I'm not going home until I'm satisfied.*

"Thanks," Kyle muttered, wondering why she didn't feel reassured.

CHAPTER SIXTEEN

Without calling attention to herself, Dane slipped out the back door of the kennel. She leaned against the wall, watching Anne work with one of the dogs they were going to show soon. As the young woman took the dog smoothly through his routine, showing his good points to advantage and downplaying his few faults, Dane nodded in appreciation. *Caroline's right. You're a natural, honey.*

"Don't stretch him out quite so much—he's long enough as it is," Caroline called, studying her lover's moves with a critical eye. "And keep his head up—it shows off his shoulders more."

Dane observed for a few more moments and then walked down to join her friends. "Hey! Who's watching the desk?"

Anne looked over, Ramsey at her side, and smiled. "I plugged the phone in out in the back room and left a note at the front desk telling anyone who came in to walk back outside and yell."

Dane laughed. "All bases covered. You look good, too. There's only one problem."

Both Caroline and Anne regarded her with concern.

"What?" Caroline appeared ready to come to her lover's defense.

"Who's going to take care of things around here when you both go off to a show? You know I can't be trusted. I'll have all of our appointments screwed up in no time."

"Well, actually," Anne began, "I have this friend who needs a job. I thought maybe I could teach her the desk, and she could help out cleaning the runs and things."

Dane arched her brows and looked from Anne's expectant face over to Caroline. "I guess she's got it all figured out."

Caroline shrugged. "Looks that way."

"Tell her to come see me," Dane said, "and we'll talk about it."

"Great." Anne hurried toward the kennel, passing the dog off to Caroline. "I'll go call her."

As she rushed off, Dane laughed again. "Getting to be quite the businesswoman."

"Getting to be quite a woman, period." Caroline's face glowed as she led the dog into his run and then returned to join Dane on the rear steps. She studied Dane's profile, noting that her friend looked more rested and relaxed than she had in a long time. "I haven't seen much of you since the show last week."

"I've been in and out. I guess we just missed each other."

"Oh come on." When Dane remained silent, Caroline jostled her shoulder. "Tell me what happened, damn it."

"When?" Dane leaned back on the step and slid her hands into the pockets of her denim jacket. Frowning, she pulled out an unexpected object and stared at it. *Kyle's lighter. She must have put it there the night I spent at her place.* A slow smile played over her face.

Caroline followed Dane's gaze. "Present?"

"Nope. A souvenir."

Caroline looked exasperated. "Dane, why are you making me beg? What happened after the show?"

"I told you. I went to Kyle's for dinner."

"And?"

"And we ended up having breakfast, okay?"

"Okay!" Caroline felt like dancing. "So are you seeing her again?"

"She's coming into town this weekend." Dane tried to keep a lid on the excitement that swelled just at the thought of seeing Kyle again, but failed. She couldn't think of much else. "I told her I'd meet her at Leathers."

"Progress at last." Caroline sighed happily.

"Don't jump to any conclusions, Caro." Dane's expression was solemn. "We're just going to have a drink. I told you before—I don't want anything serious. Besides, I don't really know how she feels about all of this yet. She might decide it's not right for her."

"Dane," Caroline began carefully, knowing how sensitive Dane was about the issue of sexual expression, "you've changed a lot in the last few years. We all have. You're more flexible than you used to be."

"What do you mean?" Dane was suddenly wary.

"I mean that none of us is wholly power oriented all the time. Sexually there's a broader range of interest."

"The needs are still there," Dane said quietly. "Those still have to be satisfied, especially for me."

"What makes you think Kyle can't meet those needs, that she doesn't want those things, too? Is she only into vanilla sex?"

"Hardly." Dane laughed, thinking about the ease with which Kyle could take control. "She surprised me the other night."

"Oh?" Caroline asked expectantly.

"She brought me back to her house, she set the scene, she topped me." Dane hesitated, still amazed at how good it had felt. "More than once."

Caroline was uncharacteristically subdued. "You let her do all that?"

Dane nodded silently.

"Well," Caroline said as she slung her arm around her friend's shoulders, "she gets my vote. And I suppose that's all you're going to tell me?"

"Yep," Dane replied.

"So, where's the problem?"

"I'm still not convinced it's an important issue for her."

"God, you're stubborn. The woman shows up at Leathers on her own, because she's interested. She comes to the discussion groups regularly, because she's interested. She takes you home, she makes love to you the way no one else can. Besides that, she's gorgeous. What more do you want?"

"I don't know." Trapped on the precipice between disappointment and desire, Dane's eyes were cloudy. "I keep trying to find out, but I still don't know."

Kyle dressed with special care, wanting to look just right for her date with Dane. Laughing at both her adolescent anxiety and euphoric anticipation, she pulled on Levi's only to eventually discard them in favor of her black leather pants. Then she stood naked in front of the closet, unable to decide on a shirt. She dressed, and stripped again. Finally, she settled on a pair of black jeans, a loose white silk shirt, and boots. On the way out the door, she grabbed her leather jacket.

The ride to town was exhilarating. The ocean vistas, always beautiful, seemed to shimmer with hope and promise, much as her heart did at the thought of seeing Dane again. She must have daydreamed half the way to the city, because before she knew it, she was pulling her bike into the familiar line in front of the club. Inside, she was surprised to find the room already wall-to-wall people and the air thick with the expectation of adventure. When she finally maneuvered her way up to the bar, the bartender came over to her immediately and handed her a small snifter of brandy. Kyle stared from the glass to the bartender in surprise, one eyebrow raised in silent question.

"From a friend."

Nodding, Kyle forced herself to sip slowly and turned unhurriedly for her first real survey of the room. She saw Dane at once, her back against the wall by the jukebox. She was standing much as she had been the first time Kyle had seen her, half in shadow. Her slender figure was encased in soft dark leather, and Kyle caught glimpses of the swath of black around her left wrist as her hands moved slowly in the air while she talked. Kyle's heart pounded, but she continued her inspection of the other women in the room, although no one else interested her. No one there stirred her the way Dane did. She doubted anyone ever would again.

The drink had been a signal. *I know you're here. Now you know that I am, too.*

Kyle was uncertain of the next move, but she understood that it would be Dane's. And she knew that she should wait. With every second that passed, her excitement grew.

The suspense of waiting was finally broken by a deep voice whispering softly in her ear.

"You look good tonight."

The tone was cool, the faint wisp of breath on her neck hot. Kyle's stomach tightened as if the words had been a caress.

"I'm glad you like it."

"Oh, I do." Dane moved closer, shifting in the crowd so that her slender legs straddled Kyle's thigh. She pressed her hand against the soft curve of Kyle's back. "You left something of yours behind the other day."

Kyle couldn't read anything in Dane's blue eyes. "I don't know wh—"

Dane held up Kyle's lighter. Before Kyle could speak, Dane slid it into the pocket of her leather vest. "But, since I'm not giving it back..." From her pants pocket she withdrew a gold lighter edged in black, exactly the opposite pattern of the first, and handed it to Kyle.

Smiling, Kyle closed her fingers around the gift. "Thank you."

Nodding, her lips curved in a ghost of a smile, Dane turned to the bar. "Mick!"

The bartender, hurriedly mixing drinks, looked over at her.

"A bottle of brandy—and another glass." When the bottle arrived, Dane filled her glass and poured more into Kyle's. She rocked her hips against Kyle's thigh. The pressure ratcheted up the arousal that had simmered in her depths all day and that had skyrocketed the instant she'd seen Kyle walk in the door. "We should have a fire to go with this."

"We don't need one." Kyle lifted her glass in a small salute.

Dane smiled then, her gaze softening. "Dance?"

Kyle nodded, following Dane's lead through the crowd. The music was fast, the bass heavy and relentless, pulsating with a rhythm that reflected the pounding excitement in her flesh. They danced close, only a hot layer of air between them, as—hips thrusting and eyes hungry—they teased one another with the promise of pleasure. When the next song slowed, Kyle slid into Dane's arms and twined her fingers through the hair above Dane's collar.

"All week, I've thought about your hands."

Dane's heart raced. "Tell me."

"They make my skin burn." Kyle ran her tongue over the sensitive skin just below Dane's ear. "They make me weak." She licked the trickle of sweat that glistened on the edge of Dane's jaw. "And wet."

"Do you like that?" Dane's throat was tight. Kyle had a way of taking the scene from her, but instead of being threatening, that effortless reversal of power was incredibly exciting. She shivered and raked her teeth carefully along the pulsating artery in Kyle's neck. When Kyle jerked, Dane ran her hands possessively down Kyle's back and cupped her hips. "Or should I stop?"

"No," Kyle whispered, rotating her pelvis against Dane's. "Not until I come."

Dane stifled a groan; her head was light and her limbs heavy with lust. She tightened her hold and slid her breasts and stomach and thighs sensuously against Kyle. The music faded, and the crowd receded, and when they finally parted on the far edge of desire, they were both shaking.

"It's time to leave." Dane entwined her fingers with Kyle's and led the way back to the bar. With her free hand, she reached for the bottle that still sat, untouched, where she had left it. "We'll take the brandy."

"Whatev—"

Kyle's reply was interrupted by a chilling voice from behind them.

"Very nice little scene, Dane." Brad stepped into view, her smile unctuous. "Or is Kyle topping now?"

When Dane stiffened, Kyle automatically reached out to touch her arm.

Quickly, Dane pulled away and, her eyes like stone, met Brad's gaze squarely. "Leave it alone."

"I don't think so." Brad ran a finger down the center of Kyle's chest, chuckling when Kyle jerked away. "You seem to have something I want."

"No," Dane said tightly. "There's *nothing* here for you."

"Have you forgotten?" Smiling still, Brad grasped Dane's left wrist in a vise-like grip. She twisted, forcing Dane off balance with the strength of her hold. "Do you want me to show you how it really should be done?"

Dane paled.

"Or do you still remember?" Brad's voice was soothing as she ran her thumb back and forth across the fragile skin, tracing the fine blue veins. "You do, don't you?"

"No," Dane murmured, staring at Brad's fingers, suddenly back in another room, in another time. She shook her head, but the hunger tore at her. "There's nothing you can do to me now."

"Brad," Kyle said tensely, shocked by the lost expression on Dane's face, "let her go."

"I can still do it, Dane," Brad said as if Kyle hadn't spoken. As if she and Dane were alone in the old nightmare. "Because you still want me to."

Dane looked from Kyle to Brad, her eyes clouded with anguish. "No, I—"

"I can, and I will," Brad's tone was lethally gentle, "if you don't leave right now."

"Kyle..." Dane shuddered and pulled her arm from Brad's suddenly loose grasp. "I'm sorry."

"What..." Kyle stared dumbly as Dane pivoted quickly and pushed into the crowd. After a second's hesitation, Kyle bolted after her. When she finally shouldered through the door to the sidewalk, Dane was halfway across the street.

"Dane, wait!"

Without breaking stride, Dane pulled open the door of a gray Camaro and threw herself into the front seat.

"Dane!"

Kyle stared after the fading taillights, stunned. Finally, she unhooked her helmet from her bike and straddled the wide machine. As she rose to kick start the engine, Brad came up beside her.

"You're not leaving, I hope."

"What did you do to her?" Kyle raged, her eyes blazing.

Brad raised surprised brows. "You saw—I didn't do a thing. She always *has* been a little bit too high-strung."

"I don't know what hold you have on her," Kyle said, struggling hard not to swing a fist into Brad's face, "or what you've *done* to her. But you're nothing compared to her."

Kyle roared away, but Brad's laughter haunted her long after the sound of her voice had faded into the void.

Tortured by memories, Dane careened through the streets. The sensation of Brad's hand on her arm seared her flesh. She could still see Kyle's eyes searching her face, confused and questioning. Disappointed.

I was wrong to think I could put any of it behind me, to think that I could change. Wrong to want Kyle—to let her want me. Wrong.

She wanted it to be over; she wanted to bury her pain and expunge her guilt. She slammed the car to a stop, jumped out without even locking the door, and strode across the street in a fury. Breathing hard, she pounded on the door. It opened at once, as if she had been expected.

The woman eyed her appraisingly, her smile cruel. This time she said nothing, but merely stepped aside to allow Dane to rush past.

"Let me have something." Dane shed her jacket on the bench beside the door.

The woman studied her for a long moment, then nodded. "Go upstairs. It's open."

Dane climbed the stairs, her mind carefully blank. She would not think of Brad or Kyle or her own broken dreams. She entered the warm room and methodically began to remove her clothes. When the woman returned, she was naked.

"Give me your arm." The order was brisk, the tone clinical.

Dane hesitated.

"Do it."

Closing her eyes, Dane offered her left arm. The strap was tight where it wrapped around her biceps. She flinched at the sharp point of pain that pierced her skin. It had been a very long time, but immediately she saw another woman, another time.

Brad. Her chest burned before the soothing calm displaced the pain. She began to drift and had to strain to hear the next words.

"Are you ready?"

Mutely Dane nodded and allowed herself to be led again to the scaffold against the wall. She waited calmly in a haze of shifting light, her mind and body rapidly dissociating. When the first blow came, she was aware of the stroke of leather on flesh, but it seemed to be happening to someone else. As the lash cut trails of fire across her bare back, she acknowledged each strike with a slight shudder. Still, the pain blessedly failed to penetrate to her core.

From a distance, she saw Brad's face, heard her voice...

Where is Kyle?

Desperately, she searched the encroaching darkness, but she couldn't find Kyle. There—a vise-like grip on her arm. Brad's hands on her skin, preparing her, owning her. Something hurt, somewhere inside...

It must be Brad. Taking back what is hers. Claiming my soul. Again.

She had tried so hard, and now Brad had won. She hurt.

No! I won't let her do it again.

This time she would not beg; she would not break.

I won't ask her to stop—not this time.

Soundlessly, she absorbed the blows. The snap of the cat sounded far away, and she wondered whom Brad was disciplining now. She felt something tremble inside, but it didn't hurt. It didn't hurt anymore. She was free—no one could touch her anymore. Sighing, she closed her mind to the sound of the lash, grateful at last for the peace.

When the woman finally lowered her aching arm, the room was deathly quiet. As she stared at Dane uncomprehendingly, she realized she had lost herself in the frenzy of her strokes. The red glow of the lights glittered eerily on Dane's naked back while rivulets of crimson streamed to the floor.

"Dane," she whispered fearfully, dropping the lash and rushing forward. Quickly she released the restraints, barely managing to catch Dane's limp body as it slumped to the floor. Her hand came away damp from Dane's back.

Stomach heaving, she pressed unsteady fingers against Dane's neck and found a rapid, thready pulse. Weak with relief, she covered the naked woman with a blanket from behind the bar and began to gather the clothes that had been folded and piled neatly in the corner.

Brad taught you well. Too well.

Caroline reached across Anne in the dark, groping for the phone. Through sleep-clouded eyes, she peered at the bedside clock. It was four o'clock in the morning.

"Hello?" She coughed, trying to clear the sleep from her throat.

"Caroline?"

The voice was a deep, unfamiliar rumble.

"Yes?"

"A friend of yours needs your help—now. The 2000 block of Durango Drive."

"What—who?" Caroline bolted upright in bed and shook her head at Anne, who was awake now, too, and staring at her in alarm. "Who is th—"

"She'll be in a gray Camaro."

Then the line went dead.

"Anne!" Caroline leapt out of bed. "Get dressed. Dane's in trouble."

"What happened?" Anne asked urgently, fumbling for clothes.

"I don't know." Caroline searched on the bureau for her wallet and keys. "Someone called. Said she needed help."

"Are you sure?" Anne pulled on her sweatshirt while racing through the house in her lover's wake. Once in the Jeep, with Caroline driving at breakneck speed, she asked again, "What did she say?"

"That a friend was in trouble." Caroline was sick to her stomach. *Oh, Dane. Please, no.*

"Where are we going?" Anne was frightened. She'd never seen Caroline so panicked.

"Up this block somewhere," Caroline replied frantically. "Do you see Dane's car?"

"Over there—on the left!"

Caroline screeched to a halt beside the familiar car.

"Honey, it's empty." Anne's voice quivered.

Caroline sprang from the Jeep, Anne close behind. She yanked on the driver's door, and it opened to reveal a blanket-covered figure laying motionless on the rear seat, one bare arm dangling over the edge. She would recognize that hand anywhere. So like the rest of Dane—bold, strong, and exquisitely gentle.

"Oh God." Fighting back a sob, Caroline pushed the front seat forward. *"Dane."*

Anne looked over Caroline's shoulder and cried out in shock. "There's blood all over the seat."

"I know." Surrealistically calm now, Caroline leaned into the rear seat and pulled the blanket away from Dane's face. She touched her neck and sighed with relief. The pulse was strong. "You need to follow us home in the Jeep, babe. I'll drive Dane's car."

"Shouldn't we go to a hospital?"

"No," Caroline said with finality, replacing the blanket and straightening up. Her eyes were bleak as she settled into the driver's seat. "She'd never stay. We'll call someone in the community to check her at home. I can't risk her waking up in the ER and just walking out the door."

And she probably would. Wordlessly, Anne squeezed Caroline's arm. "Let's just get her home."

CHAPTER SEVENTEEN

Kyle paced her living room, phone in hand. She had called Dane's number, and the kennel's, all day. No one answered. The tape at the kennel said someone would return her call shortly, but no one ever did. She looked at the clock. 9:00 p.m.

Where the hell is she? Or is she just not answering the phone? God damn her! She's not getting off this easy. She can't just ride away and expect me to let her go. Not anymore.

She tossed the phone on the chair, the same one they'd made love in just a week before, and strode angrily into the kitchen. She snatched her jacket off the hook and slammed the door. Once on the Harley, she gunned the engine and roared down the drive, spewing gravel in her wake. The drive to the city passed in a haze of anger and concern. She wanted to think that Dane was just hiding, nursing a bad temper. But in her heart, she didn't believe it could be that simple. Dane's suffering had been too clear.

She's hurting and she doesn't want anyone—me—to know. But why?

She looked for Dane's car along the crowded street in front of Leathers. Once inside, she searched the room feverishly, but Dane was not there. She hadn't really expected her to be, but she'd hoped.

"Beer," she snapped to the bartender and pulled a cigarette from her jacket pocket. She fumbled her lighter from the pocket of her jeans and smiled grimly at the shiny new gold surface. *Souvenir. Of what, for Christ's sake? What is it we really have if she can disappear like this in a heartbeat?*

She drew in the smoke, coughed, and crushed out the cigarette. Another scan of the room proved as fruitless as the first had been. She recognized no one. After ordering another beer she didn't want and didn't drink, she was ready to leave. Dane was gone, and she was close to convincing herself that she didn't care when a familiar-looking woman approached.

"I'm Chris. We met here a few months ago."

"Hi." Kyle smiled slightly. "Sorry, I didn't recognize you at first. How are you?"

"Okay." Chris shrugged and regarded Kyle uncertainly. "Listen, you're a friend of Dane's, aren't you?"

"I know her."

Chris looked around and then lowered her voice unnecessarily in the noisy room. "Some of us were wondering, well...There are always stories, and most of us never believe them. But, still, you never know...sometimes when you go home with a stranger..." She looked at Kyle expectantly.

Fear burgeoned in Kyle's churning stomach. "I don't know what you're getting at."

"Some people heard...there's been talk." Chris flushed. "We heard there was a bad scene. That Dane got mixed up with a heavy top, that there was...trouble. The rest of us, we worry, you know? No one knows who the top is."

"I don't know either." Kyle tried to quiet her racing thoughts. *What does* trouble *mean? What if she's hurt? God, how will I find her?*

"Okay, well, if you hear anything..." Chris shrugged and started to turn away.

"Wait." Kyle grasped her arm urgently. "Do you know a couple—Anne and Caroline—friends of Dane's?"

Chris frowned. "I've seen them in here."

"Do you know where they live?" Kyle's heart pounded.

"I don't know them that well, but someone here's bound to know. Wait a minute—I'll ask around."

Kyle paced by the door until Chris returned with an address and directions.

"Thanks."

She didn't hear a reply—she was already running toward her bike.

Caroline tried to ignore the persistent ringing of the doorbell. She sat at the kitchen table in a worn sweater and faded jeans, knowing that she looked as if she hadn't slept in days.

"Hon," Anne asked tentatively as she poured more coffee, "shouldn't I answer that?"

"I guess," Caroline answered. She looked over at Anne and realized that her lover was as exhausted as she. "Never mind, babe, I'll get it."

When she opened the door, Kyle quickly stepped inside and then stopped abruptly, instantly aware of Caroline's state. "Sorry. Is Dane here?"

"Yes." Caroline's voice was as colorless as her face. "You can't see her."

"Is she all right?"

"Kyle—"

"I have to see her."

Sighing, Caroline regarded Kyle for a long, weary moment. "Come with me."

Kyle followed through the house, pausing at the kitchen door as Caroline spoke to Anne. Kyle couldn't hear the conversation, but she saw Anne cast a weary, worried glance in her direction.

"It's all right," Caroline said to Kyle, motioning her in. "Sit down."

"Coffee?" Anne asked.

Kyle shook her head, her gaze riveted on Caroline, who leaned heavily against the nearby counter. "Where is she?"

"She's sedated. She won't know you're here."

Kyle shook her head. Fear twisted in her guts. "I don't care, I need to see her."

"Caroline, I don't think—" Anne objected.

"Please," Kyle whispered.

Anne sighed.

Caroline continued to look at Kyle. "It's not pretty. Are you really sure you want to?"

"I'm sure," Kyle said, needing to know.

"I'll come with you."

"I'm all right," Kyle answered tightly. "Just tell me where."

Caroline shook her head. "I'll come with you."

She led Kyle down a hallway to a room in the rear of the house. No light emerged from the partially open door.

"Just a minute," Caroline said, motioning for Kyle to wait at the threshold. She entered and lit a small lamp in the far corner, leaving most of the room, including the bed, in shadow. After calling softly for Kyle, she slipped tiredly into a chair in the darkness along the wall.

Kyle closed her eyes for one brief instant, then resolutely pushed the door all the way open and approached the bed. Hands clenched into fists at her sides, she made no sound and merely stood looking down at Dane for a long time. When her legs began to shake, she sank slowly down to the floor beside the bed and pushed her back up against the wall for support. Staring straight ahead, she reached up and rested her fingers in the golden hair framing Dane's face. Then she closed her eyes and gently let the strands fall through her fingers. Picturing Dane's satin-soft skin in the firelight—how it glowed with perspiration as they made love—she saw the sharply etched muscles in Dane's back as she rose above Kyle in ecstasy. Tracing the fine lines in Dane's face, Kyle remembered how she looked just before orgasm. *Oh Dane. Why?*

She sat still for a long time, listening to Dane's quiet breathing. When she finally felt the strength return to her limbs and anger flooded her heart, adding its own brand of strength, she stood. Then, eyes clear and heart steeled, she stared down again at Dane, burning the image into her soul.

Dane lay on her stomach, her face on the pillow, her arms curved upward around it as if in an embrace. A thin white sheet covered her to just above her buttocks, leaving her back exposed. A raw, open wound extended from the base of her spine to the top of her shoulders. Kyle was able to see the pattern of crosshatches from what must have been a thick whip, even though the individual lash marks had blended into one continuous abrasion. Mercifully, the bleeding had stopped, leaving behind patches of crusted coagulation among islands of swollen flesh. The sinewy planes of Dane's perfect body were obscured by fluid pooled in the layers of injured tissue.

Kyle rested her fingers one last time on Dane's head, then turned abruptly and walked from the room. She found Anne still in the kitchen and regarded her with eyes as cold as a winter sky. "Do you have any scotch?"

"I think so." Anne rose. "I'll look."

"Thanks." Kyle sat back down at the table and lit a cigarette, turning the small gold lighter aimlessly between her fingers.

A moment later, Caroline switched off the hall light behind her and sagged into a chair across from Kyle, pushing her graying hair out of her eyes.

"Are you sure you can take care of her?" Kyle asked tonelessly.

Caroline nodded. "I have before. Never like this, but I can manage."

Kyle took the scotch from Anne and swallowed what was in the glass. She closed her eyes for a second. "Who did this to her?" Her voice was harsh, her pain apparent. *I'm going to find her. I'm going to kill her.*

"Dane did it, Kyle." Caroline's eyes when she regarded Kyle were bright with sympathy. "I don't know whose hand held the whip. She's never told me. But she sought it; she allowed it."

"She's done this before?" Kyle swallowed, unable to resolve the disparate images of Dane laughing and whole with the broken woman lying unconscious in the other room. "I never saw a scar. Her body, it's..." Kyle's voice broke. "Her body is perfect."

"It's never *been* like this before." Caroline raked fingers through her hair. "She's always known when to stop. Something must have happened." She glanced uneasily at Kyle and Anne. "There's a track mark on her arm."

"Drugs?" Kyle wanted to scream or curse or break something, but she forced back the fury and despair. She *had* to understand. "Jesus. Is that what's at the bottom of this?"

"No. She's been clean for close to three years. Before that, with Brad—oh God, if you knew how hard Dane has struggled, how far she has come."

"Don't you think I want to know?" Kyle's voice broke and so did her thin hold on composure. Tears filled her eyes as she clutched the edge of the table with white-knuckled hands. "I have to know. We've made love, and sometimes she's let me close. But then before I know it—she's...gone. I can't even hold her now." She closed her eyes then, the tears she had held back for hours burning hot trails down her cheeks. She saw Dane again in her mind and sobbed. "She's lying in there, her body battered and broken. What must her heart be like? Don't you realize I *have* to know what's happening to her? Oh God, Caroline. Please help me."

"It's okay," Caroline lied, wrapping her arms around Kyle's shoulders and rocking her. "Come on. We'll go into the den and talk."

Caroline spoke softly, her words taking Kyle back in time. "Dane met Brad—oh, I guess seven or eight years ago, because of the dogs. Dane had been around show dogs since she was a kid because her family had been into it. Brad owned a small kennel, and Dane started working there part-time when she was still in school. That was about the time she started exploring power, too. Back then she was pretty much alone in her interests. It seems like the guys have always been more comfortable with sex play and power roles than women have. But that didn't stop Dane—she found the places to go, met like-minded women. She did a lot of experimenting but never got into anything serious until Brad."

"They were lovers," Kyle said dully, thinking how love and hate were such passionate and often interchangeable emotions.

"Mmm, lovers? I guess. Sex partners is more like it, but even that didn't happen until a few years ago," Caroline mused. "I was away finishing up grad school when Dane first met Brad, so I got a lot of it secondhand."

Noting Kyle's questioning look, Caroline shrugged. "English literature. I don't miss it a bit." She held up the scotch bottle she'd brought in with her, but Kyle declined with a shake of her head.

"I want to hear this straight." *I want to feel this, however much it hurts. Is that what Dane wanted? To hurt, to feel that terrible pain. God, why?* Kyle rubbed her aching forehead. "Christ, I want this not to be true. How could she..." She glanced at Caroline ruefully. "Sorry."

Caroline waved the apology away. "Anyhow, once I got back to town, Dane and I would get together every few weeks, and she would talk to me about what she was into—I have to admit I was pretty opposed to it all at first. I felt the way many women did— do, I guess—that one of the best things about being a lesbian is that there *are* no more gender-based role designations, divisions, or limitations. No more dominance and subordination. Any sort of polarization seemed to threaten that freedom. We argued—I always took the intellectual point of view while Dane responded from the gut."

Caroline laughed sadly and looked past Kyle to some place beyond the small, cozy, book-filled room in which they sat side by side on a sofa. "That's always been one of the big differences between Dane and me. I can keep most things at a distance, and I'm pretty good at hiding behind my own rationalizations. Dane just lets everything in and tries to take it all. She said she could feel something inside of her that wanted to get out, some place that could only be touched by a certain kind of physical experience. She thought that BDSM would do that for her. Her ideas weren't very defined in the beginning, but talking with her made me look at my own feelings a little differently, made me acknowledge my own interest in the possibilities inherent in the nexus of sex and power."

Kyle leaned her head back and stared at the ceiling, but she was seeing herself curled up in front of the fire, totally captured from the first instant by that potent image of one woman kneeling before another. "I understand that—what she was trying to find in herself through that kind of interaction. But this..." She turned wounded eyes to Caroline. "This...how did she get to *this?*"

"The first few years, she was into what people typically think of when they imagine S/M—straight dominant and submissive roles, not much beyond limited sexual encounters. Then around five years ago she became involved with Brad." Caroline grimaced. "I hate that woman now, and I didn't like her much then. She was—well, she wasn't much different than she is now.

She uses people. People to her are just playthings for her amusement. I can't figure her out, and I'm not sure I really want to, but I don't think she feels—or cares about—anything. Sadomasochism was a perfect outlet for her. She could play any game she designed, be completely in control. And Dane became her pawn. Do you happen to have a cigarette?" Caroline paused and drew a shaky breath. "This is harder than I realized it would be."

"Thank you for telling me." Kyle reached for the jacket she had tossed over a nearby chair, found her cigarettes, and handed one to Caroline.

"I wouldn't ordinarily discuss Dane's past—even Anne doesn't know it all." Caroline shrugged. "But something's got to be done about Dane, and I can see that you care. And I know that you touched her."

No, you're wrong. She never let me that close.

Caroline drew on the cigarette and coughed. "Just don't tell Anne about this. She'll kill me. I quit two years ago." She took one more drag and absently dropped the butt into a glass on the coffee table. "Well, Dane and Brad got into a very heavy relationship. Brad always topped, of course—it's a matter of pride for her that no one's ever topped her. I think the sex was pretty rough—Dane would never tell me much." She laughed grimly. "As often as I tried to get the details. But this was more than sex play. Brad controlled Dane's life—their whole relationship was very role directed. Brad delighted in having Dane at her total command—her own personal toy. She also had ways of keeping Dane under her thumb. Brad had a side business—selling drugs. She made a big point of being clean herself, but she'd sell anything to anyone. She liked to keep Dane high because it made her even more compliant. And of course the addiction strengthened Brad's hold on her. In their last few months together, Dane was using regularly, and Brad kept her supplied."

"Fuck." Abruptly, Kyle pushed up from the sofa and started to pace. "I'm sorry, Caroline, but I just don't understand it. How could Dane do that to herself? How could she let someone do that *to* her? It's—sick. Maybe we're all sick."

"You don't really believe that, do you? You don't have to be into power to do drugs, and you don't need drugs to like sex play, either." Caroline was too tired to be offended, and she knew that Kyle was hurting. "There are plenty of people who like BDSM in bed, and who conduct their daily lives just like everyone else. Sometimes fucked up, sometimes not. Dane was addicted—to the drugs, yes, but to Brad or what Brad made her feel, too. Why? I don't know. *Who knows* why we use alcohol or drugs or sex or work or some other addiction to feel good, or better, or just to get through the day." She stood, too, and eased her cramped shoulders. Sitting on the floor by Dane's bedside for hours had not been kind to her body. "Certainly Dane has been self-destructive. We all have that capacity—maybe some people more than others. I'd never call Dane weak, but sometimes when she just can't seem to bear her own feelings, she falls back into old patterns. I know she's trying to block some kind of emotional pain when she does this to herself. She's trading emotional pain for a physical pain she can live with, and most of the time she's been careful. Until this time."

Kyle ached just to imagine what Dane must have suffered. Voice hoarse, she said, "Go on."

"After a while, Brad began to get tired of her game with Dane. It had gotten too easy, and Brad was bored." Caroline took a deep breath and studied Kyle carefully. "It's important that you understand that this is not something Dane would ever tell you herself. She wouldn't want you to know this. In order to express our power needs, physically or emotionally, there has to be an understanding between two people. Power is given, not assumed, and it's anything but static. There can be no top without the consent, the belief and trust in her, by the bottom. If the top doesn't feel that the bottom believes in her dominance—in her power—then there can be none. It's a fluctuating balance which is created by the two people who have agreed to participate. That's why the roles aren't rigid. Switching is easy, if consent is mutual. Dane would feel that this knowledge of her would make her weak—powerless—in your eyes. She would feel that you could never believe in her, that you could never grant her the power that she needs to express, if you knew the truth. Does that make sense?"

"Yes," Kyle said slowly. "The very first time with Dane I knew that if I wasn't a part of what was happening, *with* her, that it couldn't happen. But there's more to her than just her sexuality. She's honest and tender and, sometimes," she swallowed around the sudden constriction in her throat, "so vulnerable. I care about her for a hell of a lot more reasons than just sex."

"*I* believe you," Caroline stated. She touched Kyle's arm sympathetically as the two of them sat down again. "But you've got to remember that Dane needs to feel a certain way, especially with a lover. She may not always want to be actively involved in a power role, but she's got to believe she *can* if she needs to. It's part of who she is—and most importantly, it's who she *wants* to be."

"Tell me the rest," Kyle said quietly.

"Brad took Dane to Encounters. It's a place—"

"I've been there."

"Dane was pretty drugged up, and things had been going badly with Brad for a long time. I think Dane was desperate to keep from losing Brad—I don't know if she feared losing her drug connection or her connection to herself. At any rate, Brad decided that Dane needed to be punished. She didn't really need a reason. Encounters was the perfect showplace for Brad. It provided her with all the entertainment she required. It was crowded; people were ready for a scene. Everyone was interested in Brad and Dane. They were such an *intriguing* couple." Caroline's voice was thick with bitterness and old hurts. She shivered.

"So, Brad strung her up naked on the center stage. She did it herself. No assistants. Chains, handcuffs, neck collar, the whole thing. She wanted to display her power, and she did. She used a thin cat on Dane, one that inflicts a lot of pain but leaves very little mark. Dane wanted to please her, and I guess the drugs made it easier for Dane to take a lot of punishment. Brad beat her to her knees, and then she made her crawl. She told Dane she was done with her, that Dane wasn't woman enough for her, that Dane couldn't take it. Dane pleaded with her, humiliated herself in front of everyone. And Brad walked out. I don't know who took Dane home, but someone finally had the sense to call me."

When Caroline faltered, Kyle quietly placed her hand over Caroline's and squeezed.

"Thanks," Caroline said with a shaky smile. "I brought her to my place, but she was so strung out, I didn't know what to do for her. I took her to the hospital, and she ended up in detox. It took her a long time to forgive me for that. She hates not being in control even when she *can't* be."

Caroline searched for the remnants of her drink and drained the glass. Kyle sat staring out the windows, noticing for the first time that the sky was beginning to lighten with a pale red predawn glow. It reminded her of the scene room at Encounters, of standing in the dim red light while Dane caressed her until all she craved was that single instant of mind-shattering oblivion. *Am I all that different from her?*

"And she's been clean since then?" Kyle asked.

"Yes. When she was released, she called me. She was hollow; she practically echoed with emptiness. She wouldn't see anyone; she didn't go out. Luckily, she started working for a local breeder—a small operation, but Dane was bright, she made contacts, and before long, she moved up. I'd started handling at about the same time, and we took the plunge and got our own place." Caroline smiled. "Dane is consumed by the work; it's helped to keep her straight. Anyhow, once we got the kennel off the ground, Dane started to go out again. She never gets involved; she never lets anyone top her. But she has *never* been like Brad. She never abuses anyone or tries to humiliate them."

"I know."

"She and Anne dated when Anne was just starting to come out. Dane was a gentle teacher—everything that Brad had never been to her. But she never let Anne close to her, and I...I fell in love with Anne." Caroline regarded Kyle with troubled eyes. "Dane always says she doesn't mind—that Anne turned to me for the affection Dane couldn't give her. I'll never know for sure. Dane's had other women, but never anyone more than a night or two. She's afraid. Afraid that if she loves someone she'll lose herself again, like with Brad."

"And what about this other thing—this punishment she inflicts on herself?" Kyle asked grimly.

"It doesn't happen very often—usually only when something really gets to her. She's generally so damned controlled, but when she's unable to deal with someone getting too close, or when she wants someone to *be* close, she drives the feelings away with physical pain. I guess it's easier for her that way."

"And you think that's healthy? I can't imagine how anyone could enjoy inflicting pain like that. I might enjoy possessing her, controlling her, even pushing her limits physically—but I could never do that to her."

Caroline held up her hand. "What happens between Dane and this top is *not* the usual thing. There are always extremists in *any* community. Some women enjoy physical punishment—within safe limits. For some, it heightens erotic pleasure, intensifies sexual experiences; there are only a few who really like to get heavy about it. And they're usually involved with someone they trust very much—someone who is experienced enough to know both her own limitations and her partner's needs. What goes on between Dane and this top is *not* ordinary. Whoever she is, she's a true sadist. She obviously takes pleasure in dominating Dane in such a brutal way. Until this time, Dane's been very careful. The punishment has been severe, but she's never been seriously injured. Something went wrong this time. Someone lost control. I suspect it was Dane. *God,* I wish I knew what happened."

"I know what happened." Kyle got up slowly and crossed to the windows. The red had bled away and the sky was a flat gray. "We were at the club two nights ago. Dane had set a scene, and we were both very into it. Brad must have been watching us for a while. I never saw her until she came up to us. Suddenly, it was like I wasn't there anymore. Something was happening, but it was between Brad and Dane. Dane told Brad to leave us alone, and Brad challenged her. She taunted Dane, said that Dane—she said that Dane still wanted Brad to control her. When Brad grabbed her arm, I thought Dane was going to pass out. She turned pale, and suddenly she was just...gone. I didn't know what the hell was going on."

"I do." Caroline shuddered. "And I'm sure Brad knew how much it would affect Dane. Dane hates for Brad to touch her. It's...symbolic, in a way. Dane never shot herself up. Brad always did it for her."

Kyle's stomach roiled. "God, how can anyone be that cruel? How can Brad do that to her?"

"She does it because she knows she still can. Don't you see? It's still the same dynamic. Dane *lets* her do it. And then she hates herself for what she sees as her own weakness. She must have gone to—to whomever it is she goes to—because she wanted to forget her own powerlessness. Having you see it happen must have made it much worse for her."

"But I went after her," Kyle protested, angry and hurt. "She didn't have to run from me."

"But how could she stay?" Caroline's tone was gentle with sympathy. "She must have felt humiliated in your eyes."

"That's crazy! Sex is one thing—love, feelings—that's something else."

"Not for Dane," Caroline said.

"So now what am I supposed to do?" Kyle slumped back, utterly drained. "How do I reach her now?"

"I don't know. I guess you'll have to wait for Dane to realize that she's still worth loving."

"When she's well, tell her I was here." Kyle got up, her face set. "Tell her I saw. Tell her I know. Tell her I know *everything.* And tell her that I want her—that I'm waiting for her. Will you do that?"

"How long will you wait?"

Kyle's jaw tightened, and she blinked away tears. "I don't know."

CHAPTER EIGHTEEN

K yle waited.
Call me. Trust me. Give me a chance.
She phoned the kennel daily to ask Caroline or Anne about Dane's condition, but they had little to tell her, beyond the assurance that she was healing.

Healing? What does that mean—that her body is mending, or that her heart has stopped bleeding?

While she waited, she worked. Day after day, burning with anger and aching with despair, she barricaded herself in her shop from first light until well into the night. Nancy came to the shop sporadically, never questioning Kyle about her silence. If Kyle had been more aware of Nancy's presence, she would have found her friend's unusual desire for distance odd. As it was, she was grateful not to have to lie about the source of her unhappiness.

When she managed to sleep, she dreamed of Dane. Fragmented images of joy and anguish—a relentless mélange of soaring hopes and shattered dreams. In her sleep, she wept. Awake, she raged.

On the too-frequent nights when sleep eluded her altogether, she rode for miles on her Harley. Sometimes she parked on an overlook and stared at the black ocean until the sun came up. It was impossible not to remember her first glimpse of Dane, the first dance, the first kiss—the last.

Still, the call did not come, and she stopped phoning for updates. It was up to Dane now. She watched the days on the calendar turn into a week, two weeks—three, and still no word from Dane. Eventually, even her work could not stand between

her and her loneliness. She did not want to return to the clubs—
she had no desire to be surrounded by women who could still
touch, when she felt only abandoned and alone.

Reluctantly, not knowing what else to do, on a Friday
afternoon a month after the fateful night at the club, she phoned
the kennel again.

"Hello?" Anne sounded both harried and desperately hopeful.

"It's Kyle."

"Oh." Disappointment. "Hey."

"You okay?" Kyle gripped the receiver hard. *Dane? Is she all
right?*

"Not really." Anne sighed. "Caroline and Dane have been at
a friend's cabin in the mountains since last week. It's been raining
non-stop up there, and some of the roads are washed out. There's
no phone in the cabin, the cell reception sucks, and I haven't
heard a word from them in two days. We're due at a show
tomorrow, but if I don't hear something soon, I'll have to cancel
our entries. If they don't make it back in time, I won't be able to
handle everything myself."

"Can I help?"

"What do you know about handling dogs?"

Kyle laughed. "Not a thing. But I suppose I could walk them
around or something."

"Give me until tonight," Anne replied. "If I haven't heard
from them, I'll call you."

"Okay. Sure." Kyle hesitated. "How's Dane?"

Anne was silent for a moment. "She's healed on the outside, I
guess. Who can tell with her what's happening on the inside?"

"Is she—hell...she's not hurting herself still, is she?"

"She's not doing any drugs, if that's what you mean. Or...the
other." Anne sighed. "I've never seen Dane like this before. She
started back to work about a week after...it happened. She spends
all her time with the dogs, and she hardly talks at all...not even to
Caroline. Sometimes she stays at the kennel all night. Caroline
was getting frantic, and she finally got Dane to agree to go to the
mountains for a while. Now you know as much as I do."

"Thanks." Kyle struggled to bury the feelings of helplessness, wishing for the anger, a much more welcome emotion, instead. "I'm sorry to put you on the spot."

"Kyle," Anne's voice was gentle, "if there's any way you can be patient..."

"I'm trying. It would help if she'd just talk to me."

"It's not you, you know."

"Yeah. Well..." Kyle blew out a breath. "Let me know about tomorrow, huh?"

"Will do. And thanks."

Without looking up from the table leg she was carefully fitting with a new connecting dowel, Kyle grunted a greeting when Nancy entered the workshop later that day.

"God, Kyle. How did you get so far ahead of me?" Nancy dropped her handbag onto the counter and surveyed with dismay the furniture piled everywhere, awaiting her appraisal. "There must be a dozen pieces here."

"Been busy." Kyle glanced up absently, then dropped her hammer and gaped. Nancy was stylishly attired as usual, but the expensive clothes didn't hide her worn appearance. She'd lost weight, her color was washed out despite the expertly applied make-up, and her eyes were hollow.

"Jesus, Nance! You look awful. What's wrong?"

"Nothing," Nancy said, looking away uncomfortably. When she reached for her coveralls, Kyle detected a fine tremor in her hands.

"Bullshit." Kyle tossed her tools aside and stalked over to her. "What's going on?"

"I *said* it was nothing. You haven't been looking so great yourself."

Kyle ignored the attempt to deflect her. "Look, I know I've been a bitch to be around. Come on, let's go up to the house and talk."

"I don't want to talk." Nancy stared at Kyle angrily. "I came here to get some work done, all right?"

"No, it's not all right." Kyle caught Nancy's chin gently in her fingers and looked into her eyes. "Have you been seeing Brad?"

Nancy jerked her head away. "Now and then."

"What is she giving you?" Kyle fought back nausea.

"Oh, please. Are you forgetting that you've been known to try a few things now and then?"

"Try, sure—who hasn't?" Kyle shook her head. "But we're not talking about the occasional recreational indulgence, are we? How often have you been seeing her?"

"A few times a week. Look, I don't want to discuss—"

"Nancy," Kyle kept her voice even with effort, "you have no idea what Brad is capable of."

"I'll tell you what I know," Nancy shot back. "That she's a hell of a lot more interesting than any of the men I've met in the last few years. So what if I have a little fun—no one's getting hurt. Roger hardly knows I'm gone. Besides, I still put out for him when the thought crosses his mind—which isn't all that often."

Kyle blinked, stunned by Nancy's vitriol and by her powers of denial. "Will you just listen to me for a minute? Brad doesn't care about anyone—she uses people. If you let her control you, she'll use you until she's tired of you, and then she'll toss you aside."

"You're wrong, Kyle." Nancy tossed her head in defiance. "I'm not your precious Dane. I'm not weak, and I'm not as easy as she was to beat!"

If it had been anyone other than Nancy, Kyle would have struck her. She quivered with fury. "Whatever Brad told you about Dane, she was wrong. She doesn't know her. She never has."

"You don't know Br—"

"Go home, Nance." Some part of Kyle knew that she should try again to reach her old friend, but her anger prevailed. "Go home before we say things we'll never be able to forgive."

Nancy left without another word.

Kyle dragged herself from the chair and groggily answered the phone.

"Yes?"

"Kyle? It's Anne."

Kyle cleared her throat and glanced around the room. It was dark. She must have fallen asleep. "Yeah—hello. Sorry."

"Did you mean it when you offered to help at the show?"

"Yes." She grimaced. *Dogs. What was I thinking? What do I know about dogs?*

"Can you come to the kennel in the morning—around six? I've decided to go to the show without them. We might as well try."

"Where is it? I'll be there."

After Anne gave her directions and rang off, Kyle wandered around the still house. Whereas she had always been content to be alone in the world she had built with her own hands, now it seemed to echo with loneliness. Too weary to think, too saddened by her encounter with Nancy, she fell fully clothed onto her bed and closed her eyes.

Mercifully she did not dream.

When Kyle reached the kennel at a few minutes before six, she found Anne loading large dog crates into the van with the help of another young woman. Both wore jeans, Daneland T-shirts, and backwards ball caps with dogs gracing them.

"Hi."

"Morning," Kyle replied as she grabbed one end of a crate and lifted.

"Kyle, this is Sofia. She's going to watch the shop while we're gone."

Kyle nodded in greeting. "Any word from Caroline?"

"No." Anne was clearly worried. "It's not like her to be out of touch for so long." She forced a smile. "Come on, I'll introduce you to your charges."

With the irrational hope that Dane would appear at any moment, Kyle followed Anne inside. Photos, many of Dane and Caroline, covered the walls in the hallway. Kyle's heart lurched just from seeing Dane's face in a picture, and although she wanted to linger and study each one, she looked away and hurried after Anne.

"This is Troy, and that's Arno, and this is Falon," Anne said, indicating three monstrous-looking animals.

"Do I shake hands?" Kyle wondered just what she had gotten herself into.

"They're really very well behaved." Anne laughed. "Well, except Troy hates all other males, of any size, so you have to be firm with him. The other two won't give you any trouble at all. Come on, I'll tell you all you need to know while we drive."

It sounded simple enough as Anne outlined it. All Kyle had to do was get the correct dog to the correct ring at the correct time so that Anne could show it. Then Kyle would take the one that had finished showing back to the van. But when she saw the morass of people and dogs milling about the show grounds, she felt her confidence disappear.

"Uh—I don't know about this."

"It'll be fine." Anne maneuvered the van into a relatively shady corner, rummaged around between the seats, and came up with a show schedule that she handed to Kyle. "I've outlined exactly where you have to be and when. Don't worry. The dogs are pros—they'll know what to do."

"Right." Kyle was far from convinced despite Anne's reassuring tone. Nevertheless, she was soon seduced by the excitement of the show. The first time she led Troy over to the show ring, she felt as proud as if he were her own.

"Okay, Troy old boy—go get 'em!"

She watched Anne intently and thought Troy looked splendid. She couldn't believe it when the judge, who had spent several minutes carefully comparing Troy with another dog, chose Troy's competitor for first place.

"What the hell is wrong with that guy?" Kyle growled in a low voice when Anne returned with the dog.

"Oh, him?" Anne laughed at Kyle's outrage. "I knew that would happen. He likes them long in the back and Troy's not." She thumped the dog's muscular shoulder. "Troy happens to be a perfect standard, but judges aren't always objective. But we know we won, don't we, boy?"

Still grumbling to herself, Kyle exchanged Troy for Falon, led Troy back to his crate, and made it back to ringside in time to see the final cuts. This time she was not disappointed.

Anne was jubilant when she returned with the first-place cup. "God, will Dane be happy. These are Falon's first points, and it's only her second show!" She stopped when she saw Kyle's face. "I'm sorry, Kyle. I haven't even asked you how you're doing. We have a few minutes. Let's take a break."

After settling the winner away, the two women sprawled in the shade near the van.

"So," Anne asked between gulps of water, "how have you been?"

"Pretty lousy." Kyle shrugged. "I keep hoping Dane will call, but I guess that's stupid." Her voice betrayed her bitterness.

"It's not stupid." Anne touched Kyle's knee briefly in sympathy. "I know it doesn't help, but I think if she were going to call anyone, it would be you."

"But you don't think she will?" Kyle studied the young woman seriously, impressed by the depth of understanding in her clear blue eyes.

"I don't know." She sighed. "I don't know if she's forgiven herself yet."

"For what?"

Anne gave Kyle a curious look. "For failing." She stood abruptly, as if sorry she had said so much. "Come on. It's show time."

With the last animal in tow, they headed back for the final entry. They were almost to the ring when Caroline rushed up to them and caught Anne in a fierce hug.

"Oh, babe, I'm so sorry." Caroline kissed Anne quickly, then nodded to Kyle. "I couldn't reach you by phone to tell you we were on our way, and then the damn Jeep got stuck in a washout on the way down the mountain this morning. What a mess!"

Anne glowed with relief. "It's okay, you're here now. Besides, Kyle really saved the day."

"Thanks so mu..." Caroline fell silent when she realized that Dane had joined them.

Kyle, her eyes riveted on Dane, was pale. Anne tugged Caroline away toward the ring.

"Hello." Kyle studied Dane, trying to judge her condition. She looked thinner. There were fine lines around her eyes that hadn't been there before. There was no trace of warmth in the blue eyes that glanced over Kyle, no hint of tenderness in her smile.

"Hello, Kyle." Dane shifted her gaze, unable to bear the sadness that was etched in every line of Kyle's face. "Thank you for helping Anne. I'm afraid she's had to handle too much alone these past few weeks."

"She's been doing great. She seems really good at all this."

"I know," Dane said quietly. She cleared her throat and forced herself to meet Kyle's eyes. She owed her that much. "About the last time we met. I'm sorry about what happened. I'm afraid I blew our scene."

"My God, Dane," Kyle gasped in amazement, "Do you really think I give a damn about that?" Her voice pleaded for Dane to hear her as she desperately searched the rigid planes of Dane's handsome face for some sign that Dane felt anything for her. "Do I have to tell you how much more you mean to me than that?"

Dane's expression betrayed none of her inner turmoil. From the moment she'd returned to awareness, she'd ached to see Kyle again. Even as she'd dreaded the moment, dreaded seeing the disappointment in Kyle's eyes, she'd longed for the surcease only Kyle seemed able to bring her. But she'd locked herself away and stayed silent, too ashamed to reach out. *I'm so sorry I let you down. So sorry you saw me break.*

"I was hoping you'd call." Kyle spoke quietly, without recrimination. Dane's eyes were dull with pain, and her own heart bled to see it.

"I got your message," Dane said woodenly. It had killed her to learn that Kyle had seen everything, *knew* everything. She hated knowing that Kyle had seen her like that, so pitifully weak. "You must know you deserve better. I'm sorry you had to find it out quite like that."

"You're wrong." Kyle risked raising a hand to stroke Dane's cheek. She was desperate to reach her, and their physical bond had always been so strong.

Dane flinched and pulled her head back. "Don't. Please."

Her hand still in the air between them, Kyle felt their tenuous connection slipping away. "Dane, I lo—"

"It's time to move on, Kyle." Dane's tone was as cold as her eyes. While she still could, she turned her back and walked away.

"Dane!"

Dane did not stop; she did not look back. *Goodbye, baby.*

CHAPTER NINETEEN

K yle resumed her relentless absorption in work, while her pain and frustration transformed into an all-consuming rage. Rage at Brad for her cruelty, rage at Dane for succumbing to it, and—most of all—rage at herself for being unable to stop caring. Her isolation became complete as Nancy turned up at the shop with diminishing frequency. Even when her friend did come to work, they talked little and avoided all mention of their personal lives.

When Caroline reached out to her, calling to ask about her absence from the discussion group, Kyle replied bitterly that she'd heard all there was to hear. Caroline persisted, but Kyle gave her no room to talk. Finally, Caroline stopped calling.

Eventually, when the silent house and the crushing emptiness became unbearable, Kyle went back to Leathers. But the connection she had always felt to the other women there was gone. She approached no one, touched no one. No one caught her attention, nothing stirred her heart. Until she saw Dane.

Late one night Kyle turned from her solitary contemplation of the scarred surface of the bar, her attention drawn to the far side of the room. Dane was ensconced in her old place, looking aloof and distant. And just as with the first time Kyle had seen her, she was instantly captivated. Her heart triple-timed, and her skin misted with the anticipation of a touch she had missed for so long. As if feeling the intensity of Kyle's heated gaze on her skin, Dane turned her head and met Kyle's eyes. Her glance flickered over Kyle's face once, briefly, her expression betraying no recognition. Then she slowly and deliberately looked away.

The rejection was so agonizing that Kyle was forced to turn her back. When she could breathe again, she wanted only to extinguish the pain. She was desperate to erase the lingering image of Dane's cold blue eyes passing over her as if she and Dane had never touched. Steeling herself, she ordered another beer and looked over the possibilities, carefully avoiding Dane's corner of the arena.

Finally, she focused her attention on a woman standing alone, her back against a pillar. She looked young, but not *too* young, dressed in low-slung skin-tight jeans and a scant midriff-baring top beneath a faded denim jacket. The glint of silver flickered at her small tight navel. She wore heavy motorcycle boots and, at first glance, looked tough and insouciant. But when her eyes fell on Kyle, who was staring at her pointedly, she quickly averted her gaze.

Not so sure after all. Kyle smiled to herself and lit a cigarette. She smoked leisurely, finished her beer, and ordered two more. Unhurriedly, she carried them both through the crowd until she was at the young woman's side. Up close she could see that her smooth features were unlined, her blond hair falling in gentle disarray over clear bright eyes. Although color rose to her cheeks, she continued to stare ahead, waiting for Kyle to initiate contact.

Kyle handed her the beer. "Yours is warm," she said in a low voice.

The woman immediately tossed her half-empty bottle into the receptacle behind her and took the cold one Kyle offered. "Thank you."

Smiling slightly, Kyle ran her hand lightly down the young woman's exposed forearm and curled a finger under the thin leather bracelet that circled her right wrist.

"Are you serious about this?"

"Yes."

Wordlessly, Kyle insinuated an arm behind the blond and slipped a hand beneath the edge of her jeans at the hollow of her spine. Circling her fingers, Kyle felt the muscles tense at her touch. For an instant, she considered walking away. But she had nowhere to go, and the game had begun.

"I need to know your name." Kyle continued to knead the firm flesh, drawing the young woman closer. She pressed her hips against a firm thigh, knowing her companion would feel that she had come equipped for anything. The pressure against her own body teased her already swollen flesh, but the arousal was a distant pleasure. What she cared about was exciting the blond. "Any name, it doesn't matter."

At that moment, Kyle realized that it *didn't* matter—that she didn't need or want to know anything about the woman other than what was necessary to complete the scene—and she felt another fleeting surge of sadness. But when she concentrated on the roles they would each soon play, the sadness, along with the pain, disappeared.

"Tell me your name," Kyle breathed against a small delicate ear as she caught the navel piercing in her fingers and tugged.

The blond gasped. "Jena. It's Jena."

"Are you tired of the club yet?" Kyle leaned into Jena, her hips insistent against the smaller woman's thighs. "Jena?"

"I've seen everything I need to." Jena lifted hazy eyes to Kyle's. "Now that you're here."

"I'd like to take your clothes off, somewhere quiet and private. There might be other things I'd like to do." Kyle was going by instinct now, playing out a fantasy that had somehow become real. She was vaguely aware that she was not really physically aroused, but still she was excited. She was excited to be in control, to be creating the events moment to moment. "Do you understand?"

"Yes." Jena turned, fitting her pelvis to Kyle's and parting her thighs to accommodate the firm form nestled beside Kyle's fly. Heavy-lidded, she murmured, "May I make one request?"

Stomach tight, Kyle nodded.

"Please don't mark me."

Kyle hid her shock, but she couldn't keep the image of Dane, her back a river of ruin, from filling her mind. She fought back the nausea and concentrated on the woman who was slowly thrusting against her.

"I agree," Kyle said hoarsely. She took Jena's hand. "Come on."

Kyle did not look in Dane's direction as she led the girl from the club, but their hasty exit did not go unnoticed.

"You could go after her, you know," Caroline said quietly from beside her friend.

"No." Dane stared straight ahead, cradling the bottle of beer, now warm, in lifeless fingers. She'd watched the scene unfold— she hadn't wanted to, but she couldn't seem to help herself. At least the pain of watching Kyle seduce another woman made her feel *something*. Since the incident with Brad and its devastating aftermath, she hadn't felt much of anything. When the physical torment had abated, the emotional anguish had begun. The remorse and recrimination had been exquisitely painful; when combined with the shame of having lost all control in front of Kyle, the agony had become unbearable. All she could do was withdraw. From everyone, everything.

She wouldn't have gone back to Leathers at all if Caroline hadn't insisted. And the first time she'd seen Kyle, her former lover had not seen her. There was a new hardness in Kyle's face and an emptiness in her smile. Even so, Kyle looked so good. And seeing her, Dane couldn't help but remember. The memory of her happiness at being with Kyle had a surreal quality, and she wondered if it *had* all been a dream. Dream or not, the joy was gone, lost on the tide of her own blood.

"It's too late." Dane tossed her beer away. "She's already gone."

"You don't know that." Caroline carefully touched Dane's arm. Dane was very skittish about being touched now. "Dane...you can't just stop living."

"I'm doing all I can." Dane's expression was bleak, but her voice resolute. "I need to get out of here."

Kyle drove quickly but carefully, following directions Jena shouted as she clung to Kyle on the back of the motorcycle. Once inside the apartment, Kyle shed her jacket and lifted Jena's from her shoulders.

"Take me to your bedroom. Do you have a candle?"

"Yes—by the bed." Jena's voice sounded small in the dark.

"Good." Kyle took Jena's hand. "Just turn the lights on out here. Leave the bedroom dark."

"All right."

The small room was neat, the furnishings simple but stylish. There was an oval area rug in the center of the wood floor.

"Stand by the bed." Kyle lit the bedside candle with a flick of her lighter. Then, slowly and carefully, she undressed the young blond woman. She started with her top, catching the lower edge in her fingers and directing Jena to lift her arms as she drew it over her head. When the pert, firm breasts came into view, Kyle ran a fingertip along the outer contour of each one. Jena shivered, her eyes huge and locked on Kyle's face.

Kyle turned her in the flickering light, palming her breasts, studying her reaction as she squeezed gently and fingered the already hard nipples. She could tell the younger woman was excited—she trembled at each light caress of Kyle's exploring hands. Kyle pressed against her back, still working her breasts, and brushed warm lips over Jena's ear. "Shall I stop?"

"Oh no," Jena moaned, covering Kyle's hands and forcing Kyle to grip her breasts harder. "No. Please."

"You'll need a safe word." Kyle trailed her hand down the softly heaving abdomen, toying with the piercing while she caught the skin beneath Jena's ear in her teeth and bit down until Jena whimpered. "Tell me now, while you still can."

Trembling, Jena leaned her head back against Kyle's shoulder, and eyes closed, whispered the word. Doing so, she sealed their contract of trust. She trusted Kyle to respect her limitations, her boundaries, regardless of how Kyle might feel or what Kyle might want. And Kyle, in turn, trusted Jena to be the guardian of her own body. Only Jena could know when her limits had been reached.

"I'm going to tie you down, and then I'm going to make you come until you can't breathe, or think, or feel anything else." Kyle kissed the spot she had just tormented with her teeth. Then she stepped around to face the softly swaying young woman and reached for the button on the low-cut jeans. Moving quickly, she opened the fly and pushed the tight material down, taking the wisps of cotton beneath with it.

"Kick off your boots and step out of these pants."

The instant Jena was nude, Kyle placed her face down on the bed, throwing the pillow aside to prevent it from obstructing the young woman's breathing. Then she unbuckled her wide, wear-softened leather belt and drew it from the waistband of her pants. "If something happens that hurts you in a way you don't like, use your safe word. I'll stop."

Jena turned her head and looked back over her shoulder at Kyle. Her hips circled indolently against the bed. "Hurry."

Laughing, Kyle bound Jena's hands securely to the upper part of the bed frame. "You'll have to pay for that." She leaned down, ran her tongue the length of Jena's neck. Her voice was low, husky. "Maybe I *won't* let you come."

"I'm sorry." Her breath caught when Kyle drew a hand down the center of her back and massaged her slowly clenching buttocks. "May I...oh...may I give you something?"

Surprised, Kyle leaned back from the bed. "Yes."

"On the back of the closet door."

Kyle found a short-handled crop with numerous fine leather strands extending a foot from its end. Her heart plummeted when she closed her hand around it. Even though Jena was asking her to use it, she wasn't sure she could. She found it more and more difficult to look at Jena's naked back without seeing Dane, again and again. The scene was hers; she could refuse. But there was Jena's pleasure to be considered, and as the top, it was ultimately Kyle's responsibility to create a scene that both partners would find satisfying, within acceptable limits for each. She gripped the leather-wrapped handle, its thickness matching that of the candle that burned by the bedside, and stepped up to the prone figure awaiting her pleasure.

Straddling Jena's hips, her crotch tight to the swell of the firm buttocks, Kyle started with the stout handle, the leather strands entwined in her fingers. Slowly, she traced each muscle, every bone, in Jena's back and shoulders with the edge while rhythmically thrusting against Jena's body. She heard Jena gasp at each new contact and felt the increasingly frantic press of writhing muscles between her thighs. The pressure between her spread legs was arousing, but Kyle wasn't interested in her own climax. Jena's pleasure was her goal, the power her aphrodisiac. As Kyle turned the crop in her hand and drew the leather strands along Jena's sweat-misted back, she realized that in this instance it was the *possibility* of pain that was erotic, rather than the actual infliction of punishment.

When Kyle finally did push back on her knees and use the crop for what it was intended, she wielded it gently, taking care that the blows were not hard enough to inflict damage. The effect was instantaneous. Jena responded to each snap of leather on skin with a soft groan, and her hips convulsed, rising and falling with increasing speed.

She's going to come if I keep this up. God, she's almost there.

Without even thinking about it, Kyle reversed the crop once again and slid the handle up the inside of Jena's thigh until it was nestled between her legs—resting between the swollen folds of her sex, but not inside her.

"Oh God," Jena moaned, tightening her thighs, trapping the crop against her screaming flesh. "I'm so close...please."

Kyle rocked the handle along Jena's clitoris until the soft cries and frantic motion indicated that the blond was about to go off, then she tossed the crop away and forced her own leather-encased thigh between Jena's. She slipped one hand beneath Jena's pelvis, seeking the moisture she knew she would find as she entered her from above to complete the circle. Inside, she thrust hard against rapidly spasming muscles, outside she stroked the turgid nerve endings, controlling Jena's body to the very end. When Jena screamed and came, shuddering and sobbing, Kyle felt her own stomach-clenching tension ebb away.

She felt no need to reach orgasm herself; it was enough that Jena had. The excitement and power she had drawn from the encounter was enough. She released Jena's hands, pulled the sheets over her, and kissed the back of the drowsy woman's neck. Then she left her.

The experience with Jena provided temporary relief from the seething unrest Kyle couldn't shake, and she found herself drawn again and again to this easy solution for her despair. She quickly discovered that the rumor she had heard was true: experienced tops were always in demand. Without intending it, she found that she no longer had to seek out partners. Whenever she entered the club, there was always someone more than willing to end the night with her. She developed considerable skill at creating and controlling a scene; she learned to recognize what would excite her partners by the way they responded to her first advances, and came to appreciate the subtle signals that indicated a woman's experience and desires.

To her greater amazement, Kyle became quite accomplished with a variety of crops and whips. Her initial unease at causing physical pain abated as long as she was sure her partner took pleasure in it, and so long as Kyle could trust the woman to know her own limits. To be safe, Kyle never played a scene with anyone young or inexperienced—or high. She even stopped drinking completely when planning on a scene, just to ensure that she would never lose control.

And although she rarely achieved physical release with her partners, she *was* able to lose herself for a few hours in the intensity of a scene. For a while, that was enough. She often remained completely dressed, and she never allowed anyone to top her. Without realizing it, she became the archetypal top—cool, controlled, physically distant. She could create a scene, give pleasure in the way her partner wished, and walk away untouched herself.

But as time passed, an overwhelming sense of loneliness would suffuse her on the long drives home. Once home, she couldn't sleep. She recalled images of the woman she had just pleasured, and felt nothing. There was no one who moved her, no one able to penetrate her self-constructed barriers. She sat with a brandy watching the intricate patterns of flame dance in the fireplace, wondering what was happening to her.

As her sense of detachment grew, her encounters became less frequent. The brief intimacy reminded her all too painfully of how much she longed truly to touch someone, and to be touched in return.

CHAPTER TWENTY

The evening was cool, and Kyle was on her way in with an armful of wood when the phone rang. She dumped the logs and grabbed the phone.

"Hello."

"Kyle, this is Roger." His anxiety rippled across the invisible connection. Before Kyle could respond, he went on hurriedly. "Is Nancy there?"

"Uh, Roger..." Kyle cursed under her breath. She hated to lie. "She—"

"Never mind. I know she isn't." He sighed, a sound like surrender. "I guess I've known for a long time that she wasn't with you or any of the other friends she said she was visiting."

"Hell, I'm sorry, Roger." Kyle empathized with him, but she really didn't know what to say that wouldn't sound false. "Maybe she just got held up somewhere."

"You don't understand. She didn't come home last night at all, and there's no sign that she's been back to the house today. I wouldn't have called you if I knew what else to do."

"Roger, why don't you come over here." Kyle squeezed the bridge of her nose, silently berating Nancy for her thoughtlessness. "You sound like you could use some company. She'll show up sooner or later."

"Kyle, do you think you could find her?" Roger hesitated. "Maybe...just ask her to call me or something. I need to know she's all right. The rest—well, that's something else."

"But I don't *know* where she is." Kyle's frustration quickly gave way to guilt when she realized that she had very nearly excluded Nancy from her life completely. Suddenly she felt very selfish. She'd been so absorbed by her own pain that she hadn't even tried to reach Nancy. "I'm sorry."

"I know she's your friend, Kyle, but I love her, too," Roger continued. "You must have some idea where she goes at night."

"Why should I?" Kyle asked warily, hating not knowing just how much of Nancy's secret life Roger understood.

"She's seeing a woman, isn't she?" Roger asked quietly. "It's different this time—it's not like her little flings with men used to be. She's been so preoccupied that she doesn't even pretend to hide what she's doing. I always felt before that she just wanted a little diversion, but this time something's changed." He stopped, obviously distraught. "I should have confronted her before this, but I was afraid if I questioned her, she would just leave for good."

Fuck. Kyle didn't see that she had any choice. "Look, Rog— Nancy has been going out to some clubs—women's bars. I thought she was just curious, looking for something new. I don't know if she's actually involved with anyone. We haven't really been talking much lately."

"But you know the places, right?"

"Yeah." She sighed. "I'll try to find her. I can't promise she'll listen to me. But I'll look for her, and if I find her, I'll call you if she won't. Okay?"

"Thank you," Roger said in relief. "I'll be at home."

Right. Thank me. It's my fault she ever met Brad. Jesus, I hope that's not who she's with. Kyle walked into the bedroom, stripped off her work clothes, and resolutely reached into the closet for her leathers. She pulled on pants, a black T-shirt, the leather vest. It was time, she thought, to do something for someone else. She couldn't help Dane. It had been much too late. Maybe it wasn't too late for Nancy.

Kyle scanned the street outside Leathers for Nancy's Ferrari. It wasn't there, but Brad's Mercedes was. Kyle still hoped that Nancy wasn't with her, but in her heart she knew that she was deluding herself. As soon as she entered the club, she saw them—

sitting at a table in the rear, in the shadow of one of the large square columns that dotted the room. Even from a distance it was apparent that Nancy was drunk or high on something. She listed heavily against Brad's side, one arm slung around Brad's waist.

Kyle walked directly to them and pulled up an empty chair from a nearby table. She turned it around and straddled it, her arms folded across the back.

Brad looked at her in surprise, a slow smile playing across her lips. "Why, Kyle. Do sit down. What are you drinking?"

"Beer," Kyle said, noting the glazed look in Nancy's eyes. She had never seen her so disheveled. Kyle's anger, simmering for so long, flared anew.

"Nance," she said, touching Nancy's arm gently, "are you all right?"

Nancy stared at Kyle, blinking in confusion. "Kyle?"

"Of course she's okay." Brad pushed an untouched bottle of beer in Kyle's direction and nuzzled Nancy's neck. She twined an arm around Nancy's waist and cupped her breast, obviously fondling her nipple through the sheer material of the rumpled silk blouse. "She's just a little tired out. We've been busy, right, honey?"

When Nancy closed her eyes and moaned, her head lolling on Brad's shoulder, Brad laughed. Never stopping the teasing movements of her long fingers, she eyed Kyle with interest. "She's not *yours*, is she, Kyle? Because I've been training her to come just for me."

"Isn't this a little beneath you, Brad?" Kyle's voice was arctic but her stomach burned with acid. She wanted to leap across the table and squeeze her hands around Brad's throat. "*She* can't be much of a challenge for you, can she? A novice, and straight at that."

Kyle tipped her bottle to her lips and watched Brad carefully. She could detect no reaction behind Brad's impenetrable facade. Kyle pushed. "I suppose after a while you lose your edge. You can't really get it up to top someone who's really a challenge."

"There's never been anyone who could compete with me," Brad said smugly, although a flash of anger sparked in her dark eyes. "Ask Dane. She'll tell you just how good I am."

"There's someone now, Brad." Kyle's hands clenched around her bottle at the mention of Dane's name, but she was determined to maintain her self-control. Everything depended upon it. She offered the challenge that she knew Brad couldn't refuse. "*I'm* the one woman left who can top you."

"What makes you think I'd let you try?" Brad was clearly intrigued. No one had ever even dared to suggest it.

"Because you know I can," Kyle said flatly. "And if I can't," she continued, making the final gamble, "you can have *me*—any way you want."

At last Brad's icy demeanor cracked. She leaned across the table, eager hunger on her face. "And how is it decided. If you succeed or fail?"

"I want you on your knees to me, Brad." Kyle edged forward until her face was very close to Brad's. "I want to hear you beg." *Just like you had Dane.*

"You're a fool." Brad laughed. "But even a fool can be interesting. When?"

"Right now." Kyle shook her head when she saw Brad look around the room. "Not here. Encounters."

Brad stared at Kyle in amazement. *What an advantage she's giving me. Everyone at Encounters will see her fail. And then I'll have her, right there in front of everyone. It's too good to turn down.*

"Let's go." Brad stood, then coldly regarded Nancy, who had slumped back in her chair like a broken, abandoned doll. "I'm sure the *lady* will find someone to look after her."

"Go tell the bartender to call her a cab." Kyle's voice was harsh and firm.

Stunned, Brad stood still, searching Kyle's stony countenance. Then she grinned. "All right."

The two women were silent as they threaded their way through the crowd to the door, but their departure did not go unnoticed. More than a few people stood to follow them out.

The excitement of a heavy scene was in the air.

"I'll drive," Kyle said when they reached the street.

Brad, curious and uncharacteristically off balance, watched Kyle walk to her motorcycle and remove a black saddlebag. When

Kyle returned to the Mercedes, she held out her hand, her eyes never wavering from Brad's.

Brad hesitated, dangling the keys in her fingers as she considered the angles. *What is she trying to do? Psych me out? Not possible.* Laughing, Brad tossed the keys in Kyle's direction and sauntered around to the passenger side. *But the more rope I give her, the more I'll have to hang her with.*

As Caroline pulled the Jeep to the curb, she noticed Dane staring down the street with a grim expression. She followed her friend's gaze and saw a car just rounding the corner out of sight.

"Who was that?"

"No one." Dane shut her eyes briefly, but it made no difference. Kyle's figure was unmistakable. As was Brad's.

I shouldn't have come back. She'd avoided the club for weeks. She'd watched Kyle change even as rumors had spread about the "new top," recognizing the coldness that slowly smothered all feeling, all tenderness, until only emptiness remained. It had happened to her. She'd wanted to warn Kyle, to tell her to keep searching, not to give up. Someone would come to love her—as Kyle had come to her. But too paralyzed by her sense of failure, she couldn't. And so she had stopped going out to avoid witnessing the inevitable ending to the age-old drama—the destruction of hope, the death of the innocence of the heart.

"Come on." Caroline stood by the side of the car, holding Dane's door open. "I finally got you here. Let's go get a drink."

Dane looked up, surprised to realize she had been drifting again. She seemed to lose track of things so easily these days. "Right," she said, easing her long legs out of the cramped space under the dash. "I'm with you."

They hadn't made it the length of the bar before Mick approached them.

"Look, you two, I'm sorry to bother you, but I've got a problem."

Both Caroline and Dane regarded the bartender in surprised confusion.

"What's the matter?" Dane asked.

"It's that woman over there—Brad's, uh, friend. Brad left her here and told me to get her a cab. But I can't get anyone to drive her home. She lives way up the coast." The burly bartender shrugged sheepishly. "Do you know somewhere she can stay? I hate to lay this on you, but I'm here until three, and she's already wasted."

Dane recognized Nancy. "I'll go talk to her. See what I can do."

"Wait a minute," Caroline said, grabbing the beers Mick offered. "I'm coming with you."

Nancy, bleary-eyed, regarded Caroline and Dane blankly when they joined her. "Hi there." Her voice was slurred. "Come to rescue the damsel in distress?"

Caroline smiled at her compassionately. "Are you all right, hon?"

"Oh, sure. Just fine." Nancy searched in her purse for a cigarette. "I've been deserted—and insulted too, I think."

Swearing, she extracted a crumpled cigarette and then pushed the clutter on the table around. "Matches. I know I saw matches."

"Here," Dane said. "I've got a light."

When Dane reached over to light her cigarette, Nancy grasped her wrist and stared at the small black and gold lighter.

"Where did you get that?"

Dane stiffened, but she lit the cigarette and gently withdrew her arm. She cradled the object in her palm and smiled sadly. "From a friend."

"Some friend," Nancy snorted. "That *friend* just left here with my girlfriend...or whatever the hell she is." She swallowed the rest of her drink and raised an eyebrow at Dane. "Buy a lady a drink?"

"I'll go find some coffee," Caroline murmured.

"Tell me what happened," Dane said quietly, watching Nancy intently while nodding her thanks to Caroline.

"Damned if I know." Nancy sagged back and pushed one trembling hand through her disheveled hair. "God, I'm a mess."

"Try to remember what happened." Dane dragged her chair around and rested her hand on Nancy's knee. "It's important, Nancy." She swallowed. "Kyle could be in trouble."

"I doubt that." Nancy grimaced and tried to focus on Dane's face. "They were making some sort of bargain or something. 'I'll do this if you do that'—it didn't make any sense. Kyle—" her voice broke suddenly. "Kyle was acting like some damn avenging angel. Out to save my honor." She looked at Dane astutely, her eyes clearing for a moment. "Or *someone's* honor."

Caroline placed a Styrofoam cup of steaming coffee on the table. "Try to drink some of this. I think it's safe."

Dane shifted tensely. "Tell me what Kyle said to Brad."

"Dane," Caroline said, afraid for her, "let it go."

"No." Dane clenched her fists where they lay on her thighs. "No. Kyle doesn't know Brad. She doesn't know what she's capable of." She turned back to Nancy, her eyes hard. "Think. What did Kyle say?"

"She said something about being the only left top—" Giggling softly, Nancy shook her clouded head. "No, that's not right. The only top left? I *know*—the only one left who could top Brad." Her eyes, suddenly clear, bore into Dane's. "That's a bitch, isn't it? Top the perfect top."

"What else?" Dane's stomach was queasy.

"Something about if Kyle couldn't, Brad could do whatever she liked."

"Oh, Christ," Dane groaned. She turned to Caroline, her face set. "Can you take Nancy home with you?"

"I'll take care of her." Caroline's expression grew tight with alarm. "But where are you going?"

"I'm going after Kyle."

"Where?"

"I know where," Dane said grimly.

"Don't get into it, Dane." Caroline grabbed Dane's arm, forgetting Dane's aversion to being touched. "It's not your problem!"

"Oh, but it is, Caroline." Dane carefully removed her friend's hand. "It always has been."

CHAPTER TWENTY-ONE

Kyle maneuvered Brad's Mercedes quickly through the familiar streets. She didn't spare Brad even a glance. When first Dane's, then Nancy's, face flickered through her mind, she pushed the images away but allowed the fury to remain. Her hands tightened on the wheel.

Beside her, Brad feigned a relaxed pose while she studied the granite-like planes of Kyle's face. She didn't want to break the silence, to give in first, but Kyle's utter disregard of her presence was disquieting. She wasn't used to being ignored; she was used to being desired—or feared. Inwardly uncertain, she slid her hand under the passenger seat and detached a small, slim container.

When Brad removed a small plastic bag from the box, Kyle glanced over and shook her head. "No drugs. I want to be sure you remember every single time I touch you."

The command and certainty in her voice caught Brad off-guard. There wasn't anything quite as sexy as a top in total control, even to another top. Brad hesitated for a moment and then replaced the contents of the container and slipped it back under the seat. She ignored the flutter of excitement in the pit of her stomach. *It doesn't mean anything.*

By the time they reached Encounters, it was already crowded. The tables ringing the center stage were full. Women slipped in and out of the shadows near the scene rooms, while others jostled for a place at the bar.

"Nice crowd," Kyle remarked nonchalantly. She was relaxed, sure of herself. She even began to enjoy the anticipation of what was to come. She ordered a drink and turned to Brad. "I left my saddlebag on the back seat of your car. Go get it for me."

Brad's head snapped up, and she started to protest. Then she smiled. *All right, if that's the way you want to play it. You can have your chance. It will make my victory all the sweeter.* She took her time finishing her drink, although she wanted to down it fast and order another, just to settle her nerves. Then she went to retrieve the bag.

Kyle sipped her drink, keeping her eye on the center stage. When several women approached it, evidently preparing to start a scene, Kyle strode over to them. Quietly, she said, "I'd like you to wait. I have something planned for Brad up here."

The top, a woman half Kyle's size, struck a pose—legs slightly spread, arms crossed over her chest—and studied Kyle through narrowed eyes. Kyle let her look, standing easy. She had no need to flaunt her dominance or to challenge another top's status. This wasn't about *her,* it was about Brad.

"I'll owe you," Kyle added.

The top nodded curtly. "All right, but it had better be good."

"Oh, it will be." Kyle knew that word of a heavy scene to come would circulate quickly through the bar. She stepped onto the stage, feeling many eyes upon her, and carefully checked all of the restraints hidden in the shadows. Someone dimmed the lights, leaving only a diffuse spot centered on the scaffold at mid-stage and a single strobe that swept the area at intervals.

When she turned around, the room was unnaturally quiet. The hush of many heartbeats and the tremor of shared anticipation rode thick on the air. Kyle's heartbeat, though, was slow and steady, her mind totally focused on one face. Brad stood alone at the edge of the raised platform, the heavy leather satchel in her hand.

When heads turned to stare at her, Brad felt perspiration break out on her back and under her arms. Now there was no turning back. Kyle awaited her on the steps of the stage. Brad stepped up, her head high, careful not to lower her gaze. As it was, Kyle held the advantage over her, being taller, but now she appeared even more commanding. The tight black leather encasing her chest and thighs gleamed in the intermittent flash of the strobe.

"Last chance, Brad," Kyle murmured as she took the bag from Brad's hand. She let her fingers graze Brad's arm, felt her flinch. She smiled, a thin, knowing smile. She understood Brad, because she understood herself. Power was their true drug of choice, the one thing they had in common—the one thing they both craved, no matter who wielded it. She could smell Brad's need. "One more step, and there's no turning back."

Brad knew how badly she would lose face if she turned away. Kyle was the only one who had ever come close to usurping her position in this dark shadow world—not even Dane had ever garnered such a reputation as a top. *All I have to do to beat Kyle at this game,* my *game, is refuse to acknowledge her dominance. I can take whatever Kyle offers, absorb the punishment* and *the power, and then I'll win. No one will ever dare to challenge me again.*

"I'm not going anywhere." Brad squared her shoulders. "I still don't think you can do it."

"Take your jacket off. Fold it neatly, and put it down."

Brad complied, her movements showing no diffidence, and then regarded Kyle belligerently.

"I won't wipe that arrogant look off your face," Kyle said too quietly for anyone else to hear, "because I'm going to enjoy watching it crumble so much."

Turning slightly to one side, she motioned for Brad to precede her toward the scaffold. In the silence, the hiss of matches flaring sounded like a living beast stealthily approaching.

"That's far enough."

Catching Brad's arm, Kyle positioned her midway between the side posts of the scaffold so that she faced the room. Her next words came in a lethal whisper. "I want you to see them watching you."

Quickly, Kyle stepped off to the side, placed her bag on a small ledge in the shadows, and slid the long zipper open. The sound was magnified in the dark, quiet room. She removed wide, well-padded leather shackles attached to short chains. She hooked the chains to the rings set into the wooden arches, returned to

Brad, and slowly drew her fingers down the center of Brad's body until they dipped fleetingly between Brad's thighs. She smiled when Brad tensed.

"Time to play."

Slowly, purposefully, she slipped a long, slim object from the inner pocket of her vest. When the switchblade snapped open, it caught the reflection of the lights and glittered in her hand. A murmur passed through the crowd. Brad's eyes fixed on the six-inch blade in astonishment.

"You haven't got the guts." Brad's voice belied her certainty.

"Oh, but I do."

Eyes locked on Brad's, Kyle deliberately cut each button off the front of Brad's shirt with a practiced flick of her wrist. When the shirt fell open, exposing Brad's small firm breasts, Kyle quickly reached down and pushed her hand into the leather waistband of Brad's pants. She jerked the material away from the taut flesh beneath, creating a narrow space between Brad's abdomen and the pants. While Brad gaped in surprise, Kyle turned the knife sideways and slid the flat of the blade straight down along the underside of the zipper. Then she abruptly released her hold on the material and left the gleaming black handle nestled against Brad's pale abdomen.

"Stand very still, now," Kyle warned mockingly as she stepped back. "It's sharp."

Fuck, are you crazy? Brad's stomach muscles danced against the cold steel, and sweat trickled down her sides. The point nudged against the swell of her sex. She twitched and felt a tiny point of pain. *Jesus.*

Methodically, Kyle stripped off the remains of Brad's shirt. While Brad stood naked from the waist up, the knife protruding from the top of her pants like a misplaced phallus, Kyle carefully applied the restraints to Brad's ankles and wrists. She drew the chains tight until Brad stood with her arms straight out and her legs slightly spread. When done, Kyle pressed against Brad's back, one hand around Brad's middle teasingly stroking the knife handle, her mouth close to Brad's ear.

"Funny how something so deadly can make you hard, isn't it?" Kyle pressed the shaft against Brad's belly. "You are, aren't you?"

"Fuck you," Brad gritted. Fear, usually someone else's, always aroused her. But her body didn't know the difference. She was throbbing. If she hadn't been terrified of driving the point of the blade into her clitoris, she would have thrust back against the elusive pressure. It was all she could do to stay stiff-legged and still.

"Oh—I forgot. No safe word." Kyle jiggled a chain with one hand and flicked the knife handle with a fingertip. Brad moaned quietly. "You can get out of the restraints anytime you like." She waited a heartbeat. "But if you do—I win."

"Fuck. You." The words were barely a whisper; all Brad's senses were centered on the blade with the razor-sharp edge lying against her skin. Nothing had happened. She hadn't been hurt. But her blood ran hot, and her body sang with arousal. The slightest movement, even a breath, sent shivers of excitement down the blade and into her center. *It won't work.* But still she felt the restraints on her arms like bands of iron. *Can I get out? Christ, what if she uses that blade on me?*

Kyle shifted to Brad's side so quickly, Brad barely registered her movement. Eyes wide, Brad looked down to see Kyle's hand wrapped around the knife handle, her fingers pressed into Brad's belly.

"In," Kyle moved the knife a millimeter, knowing just where the tip lay, "or out? Makes you want to come, doesn't it?"

Brad stopped breathing. She lost all awareness of an audience. There was only Kyle and the knife and her own need.

"Not yet," Kyle growled as she pulled the knife free of Brad's body with a wrenching motion, as if pulling it from her depths. She heard someone gasp and realized with satisfaction that it was Brad. Sweat beaded on Brad's breasts and began to trickle in uneven streams down her sculpted torso. Under the red lights it looked like blood.

Kyle smiled grimly, the room having receded from her view; she saw only Brad, helpless within her power. For an instant, she saw Dane and the raw, oozing wounds. Rage threatened to usurp her reason. She shook her head; she needed all her concentration now. "You have such a beautiful body. No one has ever marked you, have they?"

Heart pounding, Brad stared straight ahead.

"No," Kyle mused. With the tip of the blade, all of which was visible to the crowd in the blackness of the room, she outlined Brad's breasts with intricate movements. She lightly scratched the skin with the point, not deep enough to draw blood. "Guess that will be my pleasure."

The blade was everywhere—now nearly piercing the nipple, now close to the soft, vulnerable underside.

Brad panted, her eyes slightly unfocused. At any moment, she expected to feel the sharp lancet spear her flesh. The steel flashed as Kyle moved it rapidly from hand to hand, finally bringing the point to rest in the hollow at the base of Brad's throat. When Kyle pushed hard enough to dimple the skin, Brad arched her neck away to relieve the jagged pressure. Adrenaline, the product of fear and thwarted excitement, poured through her. Her heart pounded, her loins pounded, her flesh cried out to run—or to surrender.

"I could end this now," Kyle whispered, her mouth against Brad's neck next to the blade. She pressed, and Brad pulled against the restraints. "It would be quick," she bit hard enough to leave teeth marks, "and you'd only feel the smallest point of pain. Like a needle driven into your arm."

Kyle knows! Brad's senses reeled. *She knows about Dane...and Nancy?*

"But I don't need drugs to control you. That would be too good for you, Brad. Too simple." Kyle held the knife to the straining woman's throat with one hand, and with the other she smoothed a hand down the rigid abdomen to cup the leather-bound crotch. Smiling with grim satisfaction as the muscles quivered under her touch, she squeezed until Brad whimpered. "I want much more from you than your life. I want your soul."

The ice in Kyle's voice settled like a cold hand around Brad's heart. In the center of her being, fear burgeoned like a living beast. She finally understood that the game they played was not a game and the stakes not reputation, or even life—but sanity.

She moaned as Kyle sliced the blade along the sides of her legs and slashed the leather open to her knees in several rapid, powerful thrusts. Her skin was untouched, but her flesh felt flayed open nonetheless.

"Now," Kyle grated as she released Brad's wrists, turned her so that her back was exposed to view, and quickly refastened the shackles, "we play by *my* rules."

Kyle stepped back from the naked woman, lit a cigarette off the gold lighter in her pocket, and walked to the shadows. She selected a long-stranded cat from her bag. She knew that Brad could hear her movements but that she could not see her. *Good.*

Satisfied with her choice, Kyle moved from the shadows to the cone of light at the front edge of the stage and gauged the distance to her unwilling submissive. She grinned humorlessly at the irony. With a quick flip of her wrist, she tested the whip. The snap of the leather sliced through the thick air, and when Brad flinched at the sound, Kyle smiled for real.

She flexed her arm, cracked the whip. Brad jerked again, silent as the first blow landed.

Kyle knew how to work a body. She knew how to coax out the subtle differences between pleasure and pain, to ignite just the right nerve endings until sensory overload made it impossible to distinguish between the two. At first her strokes were teasing, glancing off the contour of Brad's back and buttocks, stinging for an instant and then gone.

And at first, Brad fought the pain, determined to withstand any punishment Kyle could deliver. She would not be subdued; she would never give in. As the force and rhythm of Kyle's delivery increased, Brad twisted in her restraints, seeking to escape the next blow. But Kyle had primed her well. Despite her rising panic, the arousal that had been fired by the long, torturous preparation escalated. The tension of the knife ritual, the powerlessness of being restrained, and the tantalizing pinpoints of flickering stimulation created by the lashes blurred the edges of pain into lust. Even as she tried to resist, her body betrayed her, her flesh swelling and pulsating to the rhythm of the cat. She bit back her moans—of pleasure, not fear—as she struggled to contain the tantalizing pressure building in her thighs and pelvis.

Her hips thrust in time to the strokes, each short-lived blow a caress. *I want to come. Oh God, I want to come.*

Dane shouldered her way through the crowd of people on the stairs waiting to pay their cover and tossed a bill to the bouncer. As she started to brush past her, the heavyset woman grabbed her arm.

"Just a minute," the woman said. "There's a heavy scene going on in there. Take it easy."

"Sorry." Dane slowed her headlong rush, but still pushed insistently through the crowd until she could get a view of the stage. When she did she stopped short, her stomach clenching. Kyle, awesome in full leathers, stood in front of Brad's suspended body hefting a heavy braided whip. Even in the subdued lighting, Dane could make out the flush on the skin of Brad's back, and she knew that Kyle had been working on her for a while. As she watched, Kyle's arm arced, and the cat landed with a sharp crack across Brad's lower back. Barely able to stifle a moan, Dane watched as Brad's body instinctively jerked away.

Another blow landed with a crack, the flesh recoiled, and Dane closed her eyes. She was back in another dimly lit room, the echo of leather breaking skin resounding through her body. Flinching at the sound of each strike, pain suffused her mind. Trembling, she relived the moments of her own destruction.

Brad cried out, every blow carrying her closer to release. Her mind still rebelled, but her body had made the inevitable transition from rejection of pain to the acceptance of pleasure. She abandoned her need to resist Kyle's power—she welcomed it. The lash on her back became a soothing caress, the swelling of her injured flesh the blossoming of desire. There was no thought, only sensation, as the first exquisite ripples of orgasm trickled along her spine. Her hips thrust to the rhythm of the contractions; her neck arched back in rapturous agony. Her moans penetrated the darkest corners of the room. *I'm coming. Oh...soon...soon.*

Kyle's mind was numb; her eyes blind. She no longer felt the people pressing close to her; she couldn't hear Brad's cries. Her arm had become the vehicle for her anger, the whip the embodiment of her own pain. The rhythm of the blows echoed the fury in her heart. Redemption was near. At last, she would drive the demons from her soul with the power of the cat.

"Kyle, stop!" Dane grabbed Kyle's arm, twisting her off balance. The blow fell wide, striking the floor impotently.

Eyes glazed, Kyle stared at Dane uncomprehendingly and tried to wrench her arm away. "Let go."

"No." Dane brought her other hand down hard on the shaft of the whip. "Kyle! Look at me, Kyle."

"Dane?" Kyle blinked, still confused. *Why are you here?*

"Then look at her," Dane whispered, still holding Kyle's whip arm tightly. "That was *me*, don't you see? It could *still* be me. Don't do what they did to me. Oh God, Kyle, don't become like them."

Kyle's vision cleared. She saw Dane's face, wounded but fiercely strong. She turned, saw the woman collapsing against her restraints, dangling at the end of her own desire. Heard the broken woman plead.

"Someone else can finish her off." Kyle tossed the heavy instrument of torture at Brad's feet, sick of herself. As she turned away, her husky voice echoed throughout the room. "I'm done with her."

As the crowd parted to let them through, Kyle closed her mind to the sound of Brad still calling her name.

CHAPTER TWENTY-TWO

K yle sank into the passenger seat, mentally and physically exhausted. She didn't know where they were going— she didn't care; all she knew was that she had become what she most hated—a user of people, an abuser of power. She was no different than Brad—a sadist unaffected by another's suffering, a hand that held the whip without tenderness, without feeling. In those last moments with Brad at her mercy, she had wished only to inflict punishment, no longer seeking the delicate balance between pleasure and the physical boundaries of pain. She had been tested, and she had failed. Drowning in remorse, she surrendered to despair.

*Jesus. Just like Brad. Just like...*She glanced at Dane, the sharp planes of her face ethereal in the moonlight. *She's so beautiful. And I'm just like the ones who hurt her. God. I'm just like them now.*

"Let me out," Kyle said suddenly, pulling on the door handle. It was locked; they were traveling well over thirty miles an hour. She didn't care. She needed to be alone with her anguish. "Dane, let m—"

"No." Dane watched the emotions play across Kyle's face, feeling her agony and her guilt. "Where would you go?"

"Anywhere. What does it matter?"

Dane longed to reassure her, to tell her that the sorrow and the shame would pass. Kyle had not lost herself, not yet, because if she *had*, she would not be suffering. And if she had truly passed beyond redemption, nothing Dane could have said or done would have made her drop that whip, not until Brad had broken under the lash.

"It matters to me." Dane parked her car in front of her apartment and went around to open Kyle's door. "Please come inside."

"Why?" Kyle struggled in an agony of uncertainty—afraid to hope for salvation, desperate to banish the terrible loneliness. "Didn't you see what I just did?"

"I saw. It will be all right." Dane knew only one way to convince Kyle that deliverance was possible—the only way she herself would understand. If she could convince Kyle now that she was worthy of Dane's trust, she could free her. She held out her hand. "Kyle, please."

The sound of her name, spoken so gently, gave birth to a sliver of hope. Trembling, Kyle reached out. She shivered at the first touch of Dane's warm skin against her cold palm. It had been so long, and the road had been so lonely. Unprotesting, she followed Dane into the bedroom where her journey had begun a lifetime ago. Head bowed, a dark figure shadowed in the muted light, Kyle stood in the center of the room wondering where along the way she had lost herself.

Dane approached Kyle slowly and framed her face with both hands, lifting the dark head until their eyes met. *You already have my heart. Let me give you my body. Let me heal you.*

Kyle searched the depths of Dane's eyes, wanting to lose herself in their tender mercy. *What if it's too late?*

Without a word, Dane sank to her knees, her hands lightly grasping Kyle's thighs, her head down, supplicant. Reverently, she pressed her face into the soft leather between Kyle's legs. There was no one else in the world she would do this for. There was no one she had ever wanted so much. This was not sex; this was salvation. Hers, and she hoped, Kyle's.

When Dane grasped the zipper and tugged it down, her mouth slightly open to embrace the flesh her hands exposed, Kyle grabbed her wrists. "No."

Dane looked up, her face beseeching. "Please."

"No," Kyle repeated breathlessly, pulling Dane to her feet. "That's not what I need."

"Then tell me." Dane swallowed, remembering the image of Brad's humiliation, remembering the sound and the feel of the leather rending her back. "Anything."

The ultimate trust.

"*You* top me," Kyle implored. *Take me back, Dane. Make me yours.*

"I can't." Dane turned her face away, fear and uncertainty twisting through her soul. *How can you trust me when you've seen my weakness? How can you put your life in my hands?*

"You *can*." Kyle remained unmoving, scarcely breathing, afraid that Dane would leave her again. Afraid she would be abandoned to the demons that would surely claim her this time. Dane was the only point of light in the dark landscape of her soul. Only she could lead her out of the night.

"Dane," Kyle whispered in desperation, "please. I need you to..." *Free me.*

"By your leave," Dane whispered, turning to meet Kyle's eyes. *Give me permission. Give me the courage.*

"Yes." Kyle let her hands fall open at her sides, releasing Dane's arms. Head back, eyes closed, she opened herself to the promise of peace. "Anything." *I trust you.*

Dane undressed her gently, reverently caressing each inch of flesh she exposed. The restraints she passed around Kyle's wrists were as soft as satin. When Kyle was bound face up on the bed, Dane whispered, "Watch me now."

As Kyle bore silent witness, Dane slowly stripped herself bare and stood boldly above her captive lover. She smiled as Kyle's eyes widened with desire, and life burst within her like the sweet kiss of daybreak awakening the darkest night. Kyle had given her this joy, returning her power, restoring her soul.

When Dane lay down upon her, Kyle arched upward, desperate to hold her. Instead, she melded with her lover along the length of her body, drawing Dane in with every cell. With her body restrained, Kyle's spirit soared, welcoming Dane into every corner of her being.

"Please take me," Kyle whispered. *Take me deep, take me back, take me home.*

Eyes open but hazy with need, Kyle knew only the feather-light caresses of warm lips against her skin and gentle hands stroking her face, her hair, her breasts. Relentless fingers played her nipples until currents of pleasure streaked through her straining muscles and pounded into her swollen, aching clitoris. A warm tongue and taunting teeth blazed a burning trail down the center of her quivering body.

When Dane kissed the soft skin high on the inside of Kyle's thighs, never touching the pulsating center of Kyle's raging desire, Kyle writhed in search of release. She whimpered, struggling for the first time against the leather that bound her. "Please, oh please. Dane...touch me now."

Let me go. Set me free. Keep me safe.

Dane lingered for a moment longer, holding Kyle's passion like a fragile bird in her hand. When the power of their common desire rose within her, filling her, she lowered her mouth to Kyle's waiting flesh. She brought her slowly to climax, teasingly, tormentingly, until Kyle's orgasm could no longer be contained. At the moment the wild fluttering beneath her lips turned to pounding spasms, Dane pressed her fingers into her, claiming Kyle completely. Dane's fulfillment at that moment surpassed any she had ever known, and her tears mingled with the essence of Kyle's pleasure.

As soon as Kyle quieted, Dane removed the restraints and stretched out beside her, cradling Kyle in her arms. She kissed Kyle's softly fluttering lids and drew her still-shuddering body even closer. Fulfilled, having consummated her need in Kyle's satisfaction, she rested her cheek against the top of Kyle's head, feeling her lover's rapid heartbeat against her breast.

"Thank you," Dane whispered. Kyle had entrusted her with this moment, and she had not failed. Drifting in the first true peace she had known in years, she was surprised into wakefulness by Kyle's lips moving on hers.

"I've missed you so much." Kyle slid her tongue into Dane's mouth, gently exploring and caressing. When she felt Dane's hips begin to move restlessly beneath her own, Kyle eased away. She met Dane's eyes, saw the questions in them. "I've been so lost."

"So have I." Dane fisted her hand in Kyle's hair, her eyes wounded and unsure. "There are scars, Kyle. Inside...and other places."

"Let me touch you."

Kyle waited until Dane nodded and relaxed her hold, then she slowly but firmly turned Dane onto her stomach. She knew what she would see, but she hadn't truly been prepared. Heart bleeding, Kyle stared at Dane's back, forcing herself to memorize every inch of tortured flesh. Hands trembling, she rested her fingers against the testament of Dane's pain and traced each ridge of scar. Tears falling on the reminder of Dane's torment, Kyle kissed the unscarred places on her lover's sides and shoulders, then tenderly moved her lips over the ravages of Dane's once-flawless skin. When she had finished caressing each hurt, wishing to heal each wound, she turned Dane over to face her once more. She gently stroked Dane's face and brushed the tears from her cheeks.

"I love you," Kyle whispered.

Dane sighed, her soul free at last.

"I love you."

Dane opened her eyes and immediately reached for Kyle. The bed was empty. She threw the covers aside, panic making her heart race.

"Kyle!"

Before Dane reached the bedroom door, Kyle, dressed only in her unbuttoned leather pants, appeared in the doorway.

"What?" Kyle, her expression taut with concern, took Dane's shoulders in her hands. She saw the fear swimming in Dane's eyes, and her throat tightened. "Baby, what's wrong?"

"Sorry," Dane whispered. She rested her forehead against Kyle's and closed her eyes. "I...I thought you'd left."

Kyle tightened her hold, unable to bear the uncertainty in Dane's voice. "No. I'm not leaving." *Not until you tell me to.* "I was making coffee. I seem to remember you prefer yours in bed in the morning."

Grinning, her anxiety subsiding, Dane leaned back in Kyle's arms. "There's a lot of things I like in the morning."

"Yeah, well," Kyle murmured, her eyes traveling down Dane's nude form, "you should probably get back in bed before you freeze, and we'll see about those other things."

When Kyle returned a few moments later with two mugs of coffee, Dane was propped up on the pillows looking much more settled. Kyle held out the coffee and sat on the side of bed. "Here you go."

"Thanks." Dane regarded Kyle steadily. "How are you feeling?"

Kyle sipped the hot brew, barely aware of the taste. She'd awakened to the sound of Brad calling her name, and her stomach had nearly revolted at the memory. If it hadn't been for Dane pressed to her back, one arm around her waist, she thought she might have been sick. She shuddered. "Not so good."

Dane's heart thudded painfully. "Something I did? Last night?"

"Jesus, no," Kyle remonstrated. She set the mug aside and put her hand on Dane's forearm, gripping it tightly. "I don't know what I would have done if you hadn't come for me...if you hadn't been with me here, last night." She struggled for words. "I think you might have saved my life."

"And you, mine. I haven't felt anything for a long time," Dane whispered, staring at the fingers wrapped around her arm. The last person who had touched her that way had been Brad.

Kyle followed her gaze. *She never likes anyone to touch her there.* She jerked her hand away. "I'm sorry."

"No," Dane said quickly, catching Kyle's hand and lacing her fingers through Kyle's. "It's okay." She smiled into Kyle's worried eyes. "It's good...when you touch me. Anywhere." She pushed the covers aside. "Come back to bed."

"I keep seeing her," Kyle confessed as she stood and pushed down her pants. As she slid into bed and curled into Dane's arms, she sighed. "I've never been like that when I've topped. I didn't care what she felt; I didn't care how much she hurt."

"Brad will survive." Dane smoothed a hand over Kyle's hair and stroked her neck. "She'll talk herself into believing it was all her idea and that you really quit because she outlasted you." She lifted Kyle's chin and kissed her softly. "I know that wasn't you up there last night. A small part of you...maybe. But not the whole of you, and that's what matters."

"How can you be so sure?" Kyle drew her head away and pressed her lips to Dane's breast, above her heart. *How can you trust me with your body? With your soul?*

"You cried for me last night," Dane whispered. She circled Kyle's shoulders and drew Kyle over her, opening her legs to enclose Kyle's thigh. She found Kyle's mouth with hers and let her kiss speak of love. Slow and gentle and certain at first, building inexorably to a passionate tryst. She moaned into Kyle's mouth and lifted her hips, urging Kyle to reach for her, into her.

"I love you," Kyle choked, slipping her hand between their bodies to find Dane wet and open and ready. When she felt the smooth, strong muscles close around her fingers, she groaned. Watching Dane's pupils flicker and darken to deep pools of desire with each thrust, her heart filled with wonder and thanks.

"Stay with me," Kyle murmured, meaning so much more than the moment. She felt Dane's thighs clench and the first rush of her climax ripple through her depths. "Say yes, Dane."

Dane's hips lifted, and she clutched Kyle's shoulders hard. The far side of ecstasy beckoned, sweet and terrible in its beauty. "I...love you."

"Say you'll stay." Kyle pushed harder, deeper—saw Dane's eyes grow cloudy with the need to surrender. "Say yes."

"Yes," Dane cried, giving Kyle all she had. "Oh God, yes."

Caroline looked up from her third cup of coffee of the day at the two familiar figures behind Anne. Kyle wore her leathers still; Dane was in denim and boots. Caroline's sigh of relief was audible. "Thank God you're here. Don't you believe in answering the telephone, Dane?"

"Sorry...I turned it off." Dane straddled a chair at the table and pulled one over next to her for Kyle.

"Well, then tell me everything. You owe me *that* much for scaring me half to death."

"We're both all right." Dane's tone suggested understatement.

Caroline regarded her friends through narrowed eyes, instantly noting the glow in Dane's expression that had been absent for years. Kyle looked tired, but peaceful. And from the way Kyle's gaze was fixed on Dane's face, Caroline was certain that Kyle looked tired for a very good reason. "Yeah. You *do* look all right. Both of you."

"How's Nancy?" Kyle asked. "Dane said you took her home?"

"No, I ended up bringing her here. I called her husband last night to tell him she was okay and convinced him to wait until this morning to pick her up." Caroline grimaced. "She was so strung out, I thought it would be better if she slept some of it off. You just missed them." Caroline looked carefully at Dane, knowing how sensitive she was about certain subjects. "She's been into some pretty heavy drugs. She'll have a hard time for a while."

"Nancy's tough. She'll make it, as long as she stays away from Brad." Kyle's voice was laced with sorrow and regret. "Christ, I got her into that situation, and then I let her down when she needed a friend. I could have prevented this."

Dane shook her head. "I don't think so, Kyle. Brad..." She stopped and drew a long breath. "Brad can be very enchanting when she chooses to be. And she reads people's needs very well. She knows how to find their weaknesses, and she uses them. Then, with the drugs...she owns you."

Kyle's hand strayed to Dane's back, stroking her gently, knowing her flesh as her own. She didn't try to stop Dane from remembering, knowing it was the only way for Dane to heal. "She might have had part of you once, but no more. No more."

"She doesn't have either of us anymore." Dane met Kyle's gaze and leaned into the caress, accepting the love and respect in Kyle's touch. Kyle had gifted her with that the previous night, by entrusting Dane with her body and her heart.

Caroline blinked, astounded. *Dane is sitting there, obviously reliving the dark times with Brad, and Kyle is right there with her. Loving her, supporting her. Now Dane finally has a chance to heal.*

"You know," Anne said quietly from where she stood leaning against the counter, "when someone has a need, a need she can't even define, and another person not only calls it by name but answers it—that's pretty tough to resist. I don't think anyone could have stopped Nancy from getting involved with Brad." Anne pulled out the remaining chair and sat, briefly touching Dane's shoulder in passing. "Or you either, Dane—back at the beginning. What counts is that you made it through, right?"

Dane smiled at Anne as Caroline watched, open-mouthed. Even *she* rarely confronted Dane about her past quite so openly.

"How come you never said that years ago, Chicken?" Dane asked kindly.

Anne shrugged. "I was just a kid then—what did I know?"

As they all laughed, the tension of the last tumultuous hours began to fade.

"Dane?" Kyle's voice was gentle.

"Hmm?"

"The woman you went to for...discipline. Who is she?"

"Her name doesn't matter." Eyes sad, Dane shook her head and reached for her lover's hand. Lacing her fingers through Kyle's, she drew their joined hands to her thigh, connecting them. "She's what remains when love dies, when we no longer believe in the possibility of its return. All that's left is anger and then, not even that—just the need to define ourselves, our existence, by the power we can wield over someone else. She's the person either of us might have become if we hadn't risked loving one more time."

They kissed softly, two women united at last by a single unbreakable bond. Love.

The End

About The Author

Radclyffe lives with her partner, Lee, in the Northeastern United States and divides her time between writing and the practice of surgery. She states, "As long as I can remember, I have loved books—the look and feel and magic of them. When I discovered my first volume of lesbian fiction at a time when there were very few to be found, I knew I had discovered a treasure. I still feel that way every time I open a new book celebrating our lives and our love."

Her works include the Honor series *(Above All, Honor* revised edition, *Honor Bound,* and *Love and Honor)*, the Justice series *(Shield of Justice,* the prequel *A Matter of Trust, In Pursuit of Justice,* and the upcoming *Justice in the Shadows* to be released March 2004), as well as the romances: *Safe Harbor* and its sequel *Beyond the Breakwater, Innocent Hearts, Love's Melody Lost, Love's Tender Warriors, Tomorrow's Promise, Passion's Bright Fury,* and *Love's Masquerade.*

In addition to writing, she spends her time collecting classic lesbian pulp fiction, enjoying the many facets of the life she shares with her partner, Lee, and planning the next book.

Look for information about forthcoming works at www.starcrossedproductions.com.

Coming from SCP in March

Justice In The Shadows
By Radclyffe

CHAPTER ONE

Dr. Catherine Rawlings awoke, naked, her cheek against her lover's shoulder. They'd slept with the window open in the bedroom of her first-floor apartment, and a faint breeze ruffled the curtains at the window. It was dark. *Five a.m.?*

Soon the alarm would go off and another day would begin. She loved awakening to the still-new pleasure of Rebecca's body, but even so, she was uneasy, haunted by all that remained unfinished. The last few weeks had been so intense, both personally and professionally, that she'd hardly had time to absorb it all. Despite her police detective lover's reservations, she'd agreed to consult with a joint police and federal task force formed to expose a local child pornography ring. In the process of profiling the perpetrators, she'd become friends with some of the investigators and had also become deeply invested in stopping the abuse of helpless young girls. And in the last twenty-four hours, things had gone terribly wrong. Now one woman lay in a coma, the team had been shattered by jurisdictional rivalries, and the criminals were no closer to being apprehended.

Her last conversation with Rebecca just before they'd fallen into bed, both physically exhausted and emotionally numb, came back to her.

"What's going to happen now?"

"I'll be back on regular duty in a day or so, and I'll have new cases to worry about." Rebecca rested her cheek against Catherine's hair and closed her eyes. *"It happens like this in police work. You work your ass off and then you can't make the case because of a technicality, or you do make the case, but the perp plea-bargains it down to nothing."*

"So you're letting this go?" Catherine asked, surprised.

Faintly, Rebecca shook her head. "Clark will pull the plug on this task force—he's probably already made the call. But I'll keep doing what I'm trained to do until we make this right—for Jeff, for Michael, for those young kids."

Jeff Cruz had been Rebecca's partner in the Special Crimes Unit of the Philadelphia Police Department until he and an undercover detective, Jimmy Hogan, had been murdered three months before. Their killer was still at large, their murders unsolved. Michael Lassiter had been struck down only hours before by a hit-and-run driver in a thwarted attempt to kill J.T. Sloan, her lover and the civilian computer consultant on the task force. She lay in the intensive care unit at University Hospital in critical condition. Jeff, Michael, those nameless teenagers—victims all.

"I'll keep doing what I'm trained to do until we make this right..."

Make it right. That's what Catherine's lover did. Stood for right, sometimes at peril to herself. Catherine's right hand rested on Rebecca's left breast, her fingers motionless against the ridges of scar tissue. Some of the scars were only days old. She didn't need to trace the outlines to feel each one intimately. She saw them with her eyes open or closed. She saw them in her dreams.

Catherine shivered and pressed closer.

"Catherine?" Detective Sergeant Rebecca Frye kissed the top of Catherine's head, one hand drifting up and down her arm in a slow caress. She was still a bit stunned to find herself in Catherine's bed—in her life. They'd been together four months, and for a large chunk of that time, she'd been in the hospital recovering from a near-fatal gunshot wound. *Hardly the best way to start a love affair.* "Are you cold?"

"No." Catherine turned her head to press her lips to the skin beneath Rebecca's collarbone. "I love you."

Rebecca caught her breath. "I can't get used to hearing that. It's so...damn good." She held Catherine tighter.

"We'll practice," Catherine murmured. "But I don't want you to get too used to it."

"No chance." Rebecca felt Catherine shiver again. "Is it last night?"

"What?"

"Whatever it is that's bothering you." Rebecca laced her fingers softly into the thick auburn hair at the base of Catherine's neck, stroking her slowly.

And you wonder why I love you? You, with your cop's instincts and your gentle hands. Catherine took a deep breath and made a conscious effort to shake off the melancholy. "I keep thinking how unfair it all is. You and the others—you worked so hard, put yourselves at risk, and to have it all taken away—God, aren't you angry?"

"You worked just as hard helping us nail down the perp's identity," Rebecca pointed out. "Aren't *you* angry?"

"*Yes.*" Catherine startled herself with the vehemence of the reply. "God, yes. I am *so* angry about Michael being hurt, and Sloan suffering, and Jason putting his life on the line. And you— working around the clock when you're barely out of the hospital. It's just so...unjust."

Rebecca laughed quietly, and the sound was harsh with frustration. "I can't think about it that way. Because if I do, I'll turn in my badge...or pick up a bottle again."

"I'm sorry," Catherine said swiftly, realizing that she was just getting a taste of what was Rebecca's daily fare. As a psychiatric consultant to the police force, she'd seen the alcoholism, the broken marriages, and the gradual loss of humanity resulting from the stress and frustration of the never-ending violence and senseless brutality that police officers faced regularly. She'd witnessed it clinically and thought she'd understood it, but now that she'd experienced the disillusionment and helplessness personally, she felt it like an ache in her bones.

Catherine rose up on one elbow to study her lover's face in the rapidly breaking dawn light. Rebecca looked drawn, and with good reason. She wasn't yet completely recovered physically from the gunshot wounds, and she couldn't be emotionally healed from the loss of her partner or her own near-death, either. Her state of mind, however, was difficult to ascertain. Like many cops, Rebecca kept her pain and uncertainties to herself. "You have to deal with this all the time, and I'm not helping, am I?"

"You're wrong." Rebecca drew Catherine down and kissed her mouth, then murmured, "You are the one sane thing in my life."

"You don't know how glad I am that's true." Catherine framed Rebecca's face with her hands, lightly tracing the strong jaw with her fingers, then skimming through the thick blond hair. She thought about the bottle of scotch that Rebecca had purchased only the week before and then poured down the sink without drinking. Searching the deep blue eyes, Catherine tried to see what Rebecca could not share. "Do you still want to drink?"

"Every day." Rebecca's full mouth lifted into a shadow of a grin. "But I'm okay. I promised I'd tell you if I got into trouble, and I meant it."

"Thank you." The words were barely a whisper as Catherine's lips brushed Rebecca's.

"I love you. You don't ever have to thank me." Rebecca kissed her again, then shifted upright, drawing Catherine with her. Encircling her with an arm and softly cupping her breast, Rebecca rested her chin atop Catherine's head and mused out loud. "I *know* Avery Clark and his whole Justice task force ties in somehow with Jeff Cruz and Jimmy Hogan being assassinated. That can't be a coincidence. Clark might think he can just pull the plug on this operation and we'll take it lying down, but he's wrong."

Catherine's heart thudded painfully. "What are you going to do?"

"Just dig around a bit." Rebecca was evasive, both out of habit and out of a desire not to alarm Catherine. She'd lost more than one lover who couldn't stand the constant worry of being involved with a cop. She didn't intend to let that happen with this woman. What she felt for Catherine went far beyond anything she had ever known, and the thought of losing her made her stomach churn. "I know Sloan won't walk away from what happened to Michael, and I'd rather keep her busy doing computer checks for me than worry that she's running around grabbing people by the throat."

Remembering the fury in Sloan's face when she had accosted Avery Clark in the hospital, accusing him of being responsible for her lover's injury, Catherine could only agree. "She's in agony, Rebecca. She feels guilty for what happened, helpless to change it, and she's terrified of losing her lover. Until Michael recovers, she's going to be very volatile."

"I'll keep an eye on her," Rebecca promised. *As if anyone could control Sloan.*

"Who's going to keep an eye on you?" Catherine asked, only half-teasing. "Watts?"

Rebecca snorted, thinking of the overweight, perpetually rumpled, and generally believed to be washed-up cop she'd been saddled with after Jeff's death. The same cop whom she'd gone through a door with the night before without a second's hesitation and whom she'd entrusted with Catherine's life when she'd thought herself about to die. "Yeah, right."

Catherine merely smiled.

"What are you doing today?" Rebecca asked lazily, turning to stretch against Catherine's body, running both hands up and down her lover's back. When she circled her palm in the small hollow at the base of Catherine's spine, she felt her tense. She pressed harder, insinuating a leg between Catherine's thighs. "Hmm?"

"Back to routine." Catherine's voice was husky and slow. She rested a hand against Rebecca's chest, rubbed her thumb across a nipple. She smiled when Rebecca gasped. "Rounds in the morning, then clinic...ahh, yes, right there...in the afternoon. I thought...that's nice...I'd stop to see...Mmm..." Catherine tilted her head back, her eyes hazy. "Unless you intend to make good on what you've started, Detective—"

Rebecca grinned and slid one hand between them, cradling Catherine's breast as she rocked her leg a little higher. "I do."

"Oh, thank God." Catherine felt Rebecca's mouth on her neck, felt teeth against her skin, and felt herself grow heavy and wet. "When you touch me..." She lost her thought as fingers closed around her nipple, sending streams of pleasure streaking along her nerve fibers. Her stomach clenched with excitement.

"What?" Rebecca squeezed the hard nub, twisting very gently, her head suddenly light at the sound of a quiet whimper. "When I touch you...what?"

Catherine found Rebecca's eyes, tried to focus on them through the blur of desire, needing something to keep her from surrendering to passion too soon. "You make me...forget...everything. Oh God...stop for a...second."

"Too much?" Rebecca murmured, easing her grip on the tense nipple.

"Too good. You'll make me come."

"Didn't you just say…" Rebecca's eyes widened as fingers stole between her thighs, sliding unerringly around the hard ache of her own desire. She felt a tug along her length, and her whole body twitched. "Ohh…Jesus, don't do that unless you want me to go off right away."

"Not right away." Catherine stroked her lightly. "But soon."

Rebecca's brain was already swimming. She drew her fingers down Catherine's abdomen, laced them through the silken hair between her legs, glanced gently over her clitoris. "You're so beautiful."

"Kiss me while you make me come," Catherine breathed against Rebecca's mouth.

Their lips brushed tenderly, as lightly as a breeze through summer leaves, their fingers echoing the kiss over flesh ripe with promise. A sigh, a quiet moan the only sounds. A lip sucked gently between careful teeth, the touch of a tongue soothing the tiny bite. A lift of hips, a flood of arousal, a cry cut short by the quick rush of pleasure.

"Catherine," Rebecca whispered. "I love you."

"Please," Catherine moaned. "Don't stop…" *touching me, loving me, needing me…*

When their tongues slid inside warm welcoming hollows, hands followed, until they filled one another, body and soul. They pressed ever closer, muscles straining, hearts thundering, blood racing, climbing for the heavens.

Rebecca groaned, shuddering in Catherine's embrace. "You're making me come."

"Yes, oh yes." Catherine pressed her face hard to Rebecca's chest as she clenched around the fingers curled inside her being, holding her very life with certainty and strength. "I'm coming…with you. Always…you."

Coming Soon From StarCrossed Productions

Justice in the Shadows
Radclyffe

In a shadow world of secrets, lies, and hidden agendas, Detective Sergeant Rebecca Frye and her lover, Dr. Catherine Rawlings, join forces once again in the elusive search for justice.

Rebecca is aided in her struggle to uncover a pornography ring and expose its connections to a traitor within the police department by a rag-tag team of dedicated cops and civilians: JT Sloan, a cybersleuth who is committed to avenging her lover's devastating injury and walks the fine line between justice and revenge; Dellon Mitchell, a young police officer who discovers an unforeseen talent for undercover work; and Sandy, a prostitute who develops an unexpected passion for cops. Ultimately, this secret investigation may risk not just their careers, but may cost one of them their life.

These Dreams
Verda Foster

Haunted from childhood by visions of a mysterious woman she calls Blue Eyes, artist Samantha McBride is thrilled when a friend informs her that she's seen a woman who bears the beautiful face she has immortalized on canvas and dreamed about for so long. Thrilled by the possibility that Blue Eyes might be a flesh and blood person, Samantha sets out to find her, certain the woman must be her destiny.

When Tess Richmond becomes aware that a private investigator has been hired to investigate her, she plans to teach the woman a lesson she won't soon forget, never even suspecting the terrible mistake she's about to make and the fragile heart she'll decimate in the process.

Samantha's first meeting with Tess ends in an act of heartbreaking cruelty that leaves her shattered, her faith in a beautiful destiny destroyed by Tess' misplaced revenge and hatred of the father who abandoned her. When Tess realizes her mistake, she wants to make amends, but can she ever rebuild the trust that was lost, or the love that was denied?

New Releases From StarCrossed Productions

Love's Masquerade
Radclyffe

Plunged into the often indistinguishable realms of fiction, fantasy, and hidden desires, Auden Frost discovers a shifting landscape that will force her to question everything she has believed to be true about herself and the nature of love.

It began one winter morning when Auden set out to interview for a much-needed position as an editor in the nonfiction division of Palmer Publishing. Haydon Palmer, however, the powerful young head of the company, offers Auden something far different—something that ultimately forces them both to confront their deepest fears and utmost desires. Unable to resist Hays's challenge and unaware of the charismatic woman's closely guarded secrets, Auden soon finds herself on a journey that will transform both their lives.

The Price of Fame
Lynn Ames

When local television news anchor Katherine Kyle is thrust into the national spotlight, it sets in motion a chain of events that will change her life forever. Jamison "Jay" Parker is an intensely career-driven *Time* magazine reporter; she has experienced love once, from afar, and given up on finding it again...That is, until circumstance and an assignment bring her into contact with her past.

Kate and Jay's lives intertwine, leading them on a journey to love and happiness, until fate and fame threaten to tear them apart. What is the price of fame? For Kate the cost just might be everything. For Jay, the price could be the other half of her soul.

To find more great books by these authors and many more, visit our website at

www.starcrossedproductions.com

SCP will be attending the following events in 2004. Make plans to join us and meet your favorite authors in person!

**BardCon 2004
Orlando, Florida
May 28-30**

**DC BardFest
Washington, DC
October 2-3**